MURDER ON THE CLASS TRIP

They stepped off the elevator and dashed down the hall to the corner unit. Sandra inserted her key and cautiously opened the door. There was an eerie foreboding stillness as they entered.

Sandra spotted a half-eaten sandwich on the kitchen table. "Someone was here last night. Stephen's too anal retentive to not wash the plate when he's done eating."

"Sandra, look," Maya said, directing her attention to a manila envelope sitting on top of the built-in bar adjacent to the living room.

Sandra walked over, picked up the envelope, and unsealed it. She pulled out some papers and quickly perused them. "It looks like the reading material Suzanne said Tess was going to bring over here for Stephen."

"Then she *was* here," Maya said.

Sandra had a sinking feeling. Without saying another word, she marched past Maya to the master bedroom, stopping suddenly in the doorway, gasping in shock, throwing a hand to her mouth. Maya rushed to her and stopped short as well in the doorway.

The two women gaped, horrified, at Tess's body lying on top of the king-size bed.

Books by Lee Hollis

Hayley Powell Mysteries
DEATH OF A KITCHEN DIVA
DEATH OF A COUNTRY FRIED REDNECK
DEATH OF A COUPON CLIPPER
DEATH OF A CHOCOHOLIC
DEATH OF A CHRISTMAS CATERER
DEATH OF A CUPCAKE QUEEN
DEATH OF A BACON HEIRESS
DEATH OF A PUMPKIN CARVER
DEATH OF A LOBSTER LOVER
DEATH OF A COOKBOOK AUTHOR
DEATH OF A WEDDING CAKE BAKER
DEATH OF A BLUEBERRY TART
DEATH OF A WICKED WITCH
DEATH OF AN ITALIAN CHEF
DEATH OF AN ICE CREAM SCOOPER

Collections
EGGNOG MURDER
(with Leslie Meier and Barbara Ross)
YULE LOG MURDER
(with Leslie Meier and Barbara Ross)
HAUNTED HOUSE MURDER
(with Leslie Meier and Barbara Ross)
CHRISTMAS CARD MURDER
(with Leslie Meier and Peggy Ehrhart)
HALLOWEEN PARTY MURDER
(with Leslie Meier and Barbara Ross)

Poppy Harmon Mysteries
POPPY HARMON INVESTIGATES
POPPY HARMON AND THE HUNG JURY
POPPY HARMON AND THE PILLOW TALK KILLER
POPPY HARMON AND THE BACKSTABBING BACHELOR

Maya and Sandra Mysteries
MURDER AT THE PTA
MURDER AT THE BAKE SALE
MURDER ON THE CLASS TRIP

Published by Kensington Publishing Corp.

Murder on the Class Trip

LEE HOLLIS

Kensington Publishing Corp.
www.kensingtonbooks.com

KENSINGTON BOOKS are published by

Kensington Publishing Corp.
119 West 40th Street
New York, NY 10018

All Kensington titles, imprints, and distributed lines are available at special quantity discounts for bulk purchases for sales promotion, premiums, fund-raising, educational, or institutional use.

Special book excerpts or customized printings can also be created to fit specific needs. For details, write or phone the office of the Kensington Sales Manager: Attn.: Sales Department. Kensington Publishing Corp., 119 West 40th Street, New York, NY 10018. Phone: 1-800-221-2647.

The K and Teapot logo is a trademark of Kensington Publishing Corp.

First Printing: December 2022
ISBN: 978-1-4967-3653-6

ISBN: 978-1-4967-3654-3 (ebook)

10 9 8 7 6 5 4 3 2 1

Printed in the United States of America

Murder
on the
Class
Trip

Chapter 1

Max Kendrick walked out the gates of the Maine State Prison in Warren with exactly what he had entered with a few years earlier. The same plaid-checkered, musty shirt on his back. A scuffed leather wallet that was empty except for an expired driver's license in the back pocket of his faded jeans. And a crushing, overwhelming feeling of shame. He hadn't had an easy time of it. Former cops were always prime targets for abuse by other inmates in the prison system. And Max had suffered greatly on that score while incarcerated. He had been threatened and beaten up more than once. He had been moved to different cell blocks several times to avoid the more violent convicts with their own personal axes to grind. But Max was nothing if not resilient. He had endured, kept his head down, and pushed his way through his sentence. And now, he was a free man, having served his time after his conviction on a slew of corruption charges.

As his wife, Maya, watched him emerge, his eyes squinting from the harsh midday sun, she noticed how much he had aged in those few short years. And yet, she still recognized the impossibly handsome patrolman she had fallen in love with almost twenty years ago, that day when she had first started as a rookie at the South Portland Police Department and he had been assigned as her training officer. When they were both young and filled with wide-eyed optimism and hopelessly in love, before it all went so spectacularly wrong.

Their daughter, seventeen-year-old Vanessa, who physically took after her mother's dark Latin features but had inherited her Scottish father's sharp sense of humor and boundless charm, broke into a run toward her dad the moment she spotted him ambling past the gates and into the parking lot where they had prearranged to meet.

Max, still blinded by the sun, stopped in his tracks, somewhat startled by the sense of someone suddenly charging toward him, but he quickly realized who it was, and threw his arms wide open to embrace her. Father and daughter hugged for the longest time, and Maya could see the tears welling up in Max's eyes as he held on tightly to Vanessa, the best thing to come out of their long-fractured marriage.

Welcoming her father home was all Vanessa could talk about these last few months. She had just assumed he would move back home and live with them again, but Maya knew in her gut that that was hardly a sure thing.

Not by a long shot.

Maya had struggled in the beginning, both financially and emotionally, following Max's arrest and trial. There were divorce papers, decisions to make, but in the end, she couldn't deny the fact that she still loved the man, and she finally told him that she would be there for him when he got paroled.

But she was understandably reticent. There was so much to still work out. So much had changed. The big rambling colonial house the family had lived in when Vanessa was growing up had long been sold to pay down Max's exorbitant legal costs. Maya and Vanessa were forced to downsize after Max went to prison, settling on a far more modest two-bedroom one-bath home they were renting as Maya tried to get her fledgling private investigation firm up and running.

Since his incarceration, Maya had established a whole new life without Max. Vanessa, on the other hand, was ready to pick right up right where they had left off. She wanted nothing more than to just be a normal family again, but Maya knew all the challenges that lay ahead.

Max's sudden presence was going to upend everything.

There would be a lot of trial and error.

She wasn't even sure if she was ready for any of this.

But she did know one thing.

She was happy he was finally out from behind bars.

His debt to society had been paid and he was now free to make a fresh start. And she would do whatever she could to make this transition easier for him. She just didn't know if she could be a good wife again. Or if he was ready to be a husband. They were both way out of practice.

Max raised his eyes to meet Maya, and she mustered a warm smile.

Max, with a muscled arm around Vanessa's shoulders, led his daughter back over to her mother. There was a slight hesitancy on Max's part when they reached her. He was clearly debating whether he should go in for a passionate kiss, or just a hug, or, most awkwardly, a forced handshake. Max chose a quick, friendly peck on the cheek, nothing too loaded.

"Nice to see you, babe," he said. "Thanks for . . . showing up."

Maya nodded, taking him in. "Of course."

She studied his apprehensive face.

Yes, he had aged.

There were some crinkles around the eyes that she hadn't seen before, not even at their monthly visits at the prison.

She wanted to keep a comfortable distance.

But she now found it incredibly hard.

Not with him standing so close to her, looking so nervous and vulnerable.

Waiting for her to make the first move.

Maya couldn't take it anymore. She finally reached out and grabbed him by the shoulders, pulling both him and Vanessa toward her and into a tight family group hug.

That's when the waterworks started.

Maya found herself crying.

Sobbing.

Overcome with relief and, yes, happiness.

"I love you," Max whispered softly in her ear.

She nodded, tensing up a bit.

He could feel it. She could almost hear him berating himself in his mind for going too far too soon.

But the more he held her, the more she relaxed in his warm embrace, until she was finally able to say it back to him. "I love you too."

She had made a promise to him to try to be a family again. And she was going to work hard at keeping that promise, praying it would all work out the way it was supposed to in the end.

Vanessa squeezed Max one more time before breaking the hug. "Come on, Dad, let's go home."

Chapter 2

A pleasant, polite assistant who had introduced himself as Chad ushered Maya and her partner, Sandra Wallage, into the spacious office of South Portland High School principal Caroline Williams, who sat behind a large oak desk adorned with family photos and stacks of papers.

"Can I get you ladies coffee?" Chad asked sweetly.

"Yes, please, black, thank you," Maya, the caffeine junkie, quickly answered.

Sandra shook her head. "I'm fine, thank you, Chad."

He nodded slightly and scooted out as Principal Williams stood up and extended her hand. "I appreciate you coming in on such short notice, ladies."

"No problem at all," Maya said, shaking the principal's hand before taking a seat.

Sandra followed suit.

They were both excited.

They hadn't had a paying client in weeks.

Bills were due.

They needed work.

Of course, Sandra was fine financially. She never had to worry about bills. This was more Maya's constant concern.

The ominous message from Principal Williams on the office voice mail that morning suggested she needed their expertise in solving a serious problem. They were reasonably certain that there was no issue with their own kids, who were both students at the school, since the principal had not contacted them at home, choosing to phone the office instead.

"How can we help you?" Maya asked, striking a professional tone.

Principal Williams sat back down in her chair and sighed. "Well, I'm in a bit of a bind. One of my teachers, Dory Baumgarten, is having hip surgery next week, and Stan Lennox, he's the father of Kevin Lennox, a senior, had to go out of town unexpectedly for work, leaving me high and dry."

Maya and Sandra exchanged confused looks.

Realizing the two women had no clue what she was talking about, Principal Williams plowed ahead. "They had both agreed to chaperone the senior class trip to Washington, DC, next week, and now they have both pulled out at the last minute," Williams calmly explained.

"Wait, what?" Maya asked, pivoting back to the principal.

"I was hoping you two might be open to taking their places."

"As chaperones?" Sandra gasped.

"Yes. It's a four-day excursion, led by our history teacher Fern Wiggins. You know Fern, she's such a lovely lady, and she's been planning this trip for months. She had a devil of a time raising the necessary funds, but in the end, against all odds, she managed to do it, God bless her." Williams noticed the blank looks on Sandra's and Maya's faces. "You both look somewhat perplexed."

"We thought you wanted to hire us," Sandra said.

"As *detectives*?" Williams chuckled. "Goodness no. What would I need detectives for? I can assure you my husband Amir is aggressively faithful. He would never stray, not in a million years."

"People hire detectives for a whole host of reasons," Maya said quietly. "It's not always to tail cheating spouses."

"Well, I'm sorry for the confusion, but I need you as parents, not private detectives," Williams said. "I thought since both Vanessa and Ryan are going on the trip, you might be willing to fill in, since it is such an essential part of their educational experience."

Maya could sense Sandra wavering, and knew she needed to nip this in the bud immediately. "I'm sorry, but we're very busy; we're presently working on a number of cases."

It was a bald-faced lie.

And by the look on Principal Williams's face, she instinctively knew it.

Williams sighed. "Well, I can't say I'm not disappointed. I just hope we don't have to cancel the whole trip."

She said this almost as if issuing a warning.

Chad returned with Maya's coffee and handed it to her. Maya gulped it down, frantically working up a response as Chad scurried back out of the office. Sandra watched her, amused. Finally, Maya carefully set the cup down on the edge of Principal Williams's desk, took a deep breath, and exhaled.

"I'm sure you can find a couple of replacements for Dory and Stan," Maya said offhandedly, eager to get out of there as fast as possible. She knew what a handful their own kids could be, let alone twenty-five of them on a long bus trip and four days of touring the nation's capital. She shot up to her feet and spun around, heading for the door. "Good luck. Let's go, Sandra."

Principal Williams called after her, "Would you do me a favor, and just think about it?"

Maya was halfway out of the office when Sandra's voice stopped her in her tracks.

"Yes, absolutely. We will think about it."

That was Sandra.

Supermom.

And a major pushover.

Never wanting to disappoint anyone.

"I promise to keep looking, but if you could give me an answer by Friday, that would be terrific. If I haven't found anyone by then, I'm afraid I'm just going to have to pull the plug on the whole thing."

Maya knew how much Vanessa had been looking forward to this trip. Ryan, too, according to Sandra. But this was too much of an ask. There was no way she was going to put herself through something as stressful and chaotic as a class field trip out of state.

Outside the office in the hallway, far away from

the prying eyes and ears of the principal and her staff, Maya huddled with Sandra.

"You're not serious about going, are you?"

"No, of course not, but I didn't want to just turn her down flat, without at least offering to think about it. It makes us look like bad parents."

"We're not bad parents to worry about our own emotional well-being, and believe me, chasing after a band of out-of-control teenagers in a strange city would not be good for our overall mental health."

"I just said we'd consider it; I didn't commit us in any concrete way," Sandra assured her.

"Fine, so we just pretend to give it some thought, and then first thing Friday morning we call Williams and tell her we can't do it, a big case needs all of our focus and attention, something like that."

"Right. I'm sure she can find two other parents; I mean there's over twenty kids going. Why ask us?"

"Because you're a Senator's wife and you were the PTA president at one point, you're like the perfect guardian to look after kids; you ooze responsibility. Why she would ask me is the bigger mystery! I'm always late for the parent-teacher conferences and my husband just got out of prison."

"You're a good mother, Maya," Sandra insisted.

"I would definitely agree with that," someone said from behind Maya.

They both turned to see a handsome young man in his late twenties, wearing an aqua-colored Polo shirt that brought out the ocean blue in his intense eyes. He had shaggy blond hair and a friendly smile. From the whistle he wore around his neck, it was obvious he was some kind of sports coach.

"Lucas, it's been forever," Maya said, giving him a hug before turning back around to Sandra. "Sandra, this is Lucas; he's the new athletic director."

He brightened at the sight of Sandra.

As he took Sandra's hand to shake it, you could almost see an electric charge shoot through him.

"Lucas Cavill," he said in a deep, melodious voice.

"Sandra Wallage," she said modestly, although it was debatably a false modesty since everyone in the state of Maine knew who Sandra was, given her husband served as one of its United States Senators.

"Lucas was one of Vinnie's protégés," Maya said.

Coach Vinnie Cooper had worked for decades at SoPo High. He was a legend and a close personal friend of Maya's. He was now heading up a college program in Illinois.

"Vinnie taught me everything I know," Lucas said. "He also put in a good word for me when his replacement didn't work out last year. I owe him everything. Give him my best when you talk to him."

"I will," Maya promised.

"What brings you here? Is Vanessa in hot water?" Lucas cracked.

Maya chuckled. "No, she's much better behaved than I ever was in high school. Principal Williams is trying to wrangle us into chaperoning the senior trip to DC."

"That would be awesome. I'm already signed up. As the new guy, Williams basically told me, I was in no position to say no. Please tell me you're going, so I'll have some fun people to hang with. No offense to Fern Wiggins, but let's face it, she's a little too high-strung to be considered anywhere near fun."

"We're thinking about it," Sandra said.

"No, we're not," Maya argued. "It's a hard pass."

"Well, I'm a cockeyed optimist, so I'll keep thinking good thoughts," Lucas said.

A couple of female students wandered past them, giggling and whispering amongst themselves, clearly covertly discussing the hunky new coach.

Lucas checked his watch. "I'm late for a phys ed class. Maya, good seeing you . . ." He stopped and stared at Sandra. "Sandra, a real pleasure."

"Same here," Sandra answered, slightly flustered.

Lucas bounded off, ignoring the gazes of those smitten female students huddled together next to a locker.

"He is so into you," Maya remarked.

"Oh, please, he is not," Sandra said dismissively. "He's like a whole decade younger than me."

"Barely a decade, and trust me, I know the guy, and I can tell he likes you . . . *a lot.*"

"Maya, no."

"What?"

"Don't start."

"Start what?"

"This whole matchmaker thing. That's the last thing I need right now. Especially after what happened last year."

A whirlwind romance with a billionaire tech guy that ultimately crashed and burned. Perhaps it was too soon after her separation from her husband, Stephen, but it had certainly soured her on any relationships, at least in the short term.

"Fine, I will stay out of it," Maya said.

Sandra gave her a skeptical look.

She didn't believe her.

And for Maya's part, she didn't exactly believe herself either.

Chapter 3

Sandra's son Ryan slammed his fork down, his eyes fixed on his mother, who was seated at the head of the dining room table. "Please tell me you did not say yes!"

Sandra took a small bite of her Chicken Milanese and chewed thoughtfully before answering. "I said we'd think about it."

"But you can't; you just can't," Ryan protested, swiveling his head around to his girlfriend, Vanessa, who sat next to him. "Tell them they can't."

Vanessa glanced at her mother, Maya, who was sipping a glass of Chardonnay on the other end of the table, and casually said, "You can't."

Her father, Max, who was next to Maya, stabbed at a few of the roasted curried carrots left on his plate. He chuckled softly to himself, seemingly enjoying all of this.

Maya set her wineglass down. "Listen, I'm with

you two. The last thing I want to do is go on a trip with a bunch of rowdy teenagers."

"Then why are we even having this discussion?" Ryan huffed.

"Because your mother wouldn't let me dismiss the idea out of hand. She's forcing us to drag out our decision and pretend that there is a possibility we might agree to go."

Ryan picked up his fork and a knife and began to nervously cut a piece of meat, brutally sawing it and then popping a hunk in his mouth. "But why? What's the point? You're not really going to go, right? I mean, the whole idea of this trip is for us to get *away* from our parents for a few days!"

Sandra leveled her eyes at Ryan. "No, the idea is for you to learn a little about history and politics in our nation's capital. And please stop talking with your mouth full."

Max gave an involuntary snort, then quickly snatched up his napkin and wiped his mouth. "Excuse me. This chicken is amazing, Sandra."

"Thank you, Max."

"I haven't had a meal this good in . . . I don't know when."

Sandra smiled, not sure how to respond. She wasn't sure if she should acknowledge his last few years spent in prison.

Maya cackled, sensing her discomfort. "He's not referring to the prison slop he's been ea___ for the last four years. I'm just a really lous___ ___ home."

Max gently put a hand over Maya's ___ "You do your best, babe."

"Dad's actually the chef in the family, we used to watch all those Food Network shows together on Sundays when I was a little kid, and then we'd go experiment in the kitchen all afternoon, and then Mom would come home and she'd get so mad because it looked like a bomb went off in the kitchen," Vanessa said, laughing at the memory.

"Can we get back to the more important topic?" Ryan whined. "If you two go, the whole trip will be ruined! It'll be so humiliating having our mothers hovering around us the whole time!"

"I had no idea I was such a supreme embarrassment to you," Sandra said, winking at Vanessa, who grinned.

"Vanessa, why aren't you more upset about this? I thought you'd be more helpful lobbying against this."

"Because I'm not worried. I know the last thing my mom wants to do is tag along on this trip. She would hate every minute of it. Trust me, it's never going to happen. They're not going to end up coming with us."

"She's right," Maya said. "Google the most painful torture methods, I guarantee you that chaperoning a senior class trip is in the top five."

"How about dessert?" Sandra offered, standing up. "I made a Peach Cobbler."

Max's eyes lit up. "That's my favorite."

"I know; I did my research."

When she had decided to host the Kendrick family for dinner, Sandra knew she had to make it ⸱⸱al. Max had only been out of prison for a few ¹ was still adjusting, and she wanted to make his first dinner out memorable, which meant grilling Maya for all his favorite foods.

"I'll help clear," Maya said, about to stand up.

Max stopped her. "No, I'll do it. You sit and enjoy the rest of your Chardonnay."

Max picked up some empty plates and followed Sandra into the kitchen, where she was stacking some in the sink to rinse off and transfer to the dishwasher later. She reached into the cupboard and pulled out a stack of small dessert plates and then grabbed a knife from the drawer to cut the cobber cooling on top of the stove in a baking pan.

"I appreciate you doing this tonight, Sandra. Everything has been so delicious. Maya told me you were a master chef."

"Years of practice trying to be the perfect wife," Sandra sighed. "Thank God those days are over."

"I actually didn't vote for him," Max mumbled, instantly regretting it. "Sorry, I don't know why I said that. I had nothing against your husband, but I was a hard-nosed conservative cop and he was a liberal politician and my knee-jerk reaction was always to vote against his party."

Sandra smiled. "Don't worry, Max, if he runs again, I probably won't vote for him either."

"I don't know; he's done some good things on prison reform. I actually got to see some of that up close. So maybe, who knows? Luckily, the state of Maine allows convicted felons to still vote . . ."

Max gave her a wry smile.

Sandra could see the pain in his eyes.

The man was fully aware of the destruction he had brought upon his family when he was arrested.

Max shifted uncomfortably, not wanting to show too much emotion. He cleared his throat and set the dirty dishes down on top of the ones Sandra had already placed in the sink. "I was a little worried about meeting the boy Vanessa hasn't stopped talking about for the last year and a half. I wasn't sure what to expect. But Ryan strikes me as a really good kid."

"He is, except for his apparent repulsion for having his mother accompany his class to Washington, DC, but nobody's perfect."

"Maya says you have two sons?"

"Jack's away at college in Boston. Doing very well, so he tells me. But he's a born politician like his father, so he's always about optics. I have the sneaky suspicion there might be some hanky-panky going on with one of his housemates, which he's hiding from me because I gave him a lecture on how he should focus on his studies the first year, not dating. But he's an adult now, so I really don't have much of a say."

Sandra cut five pieces of cobbler, sliding them on the plates with a spatula and then adding a scoop of vanilla bean ice cream on top of each one.

Max took a beat, watching Sandra prepare dessert. He then leaned against the counter, hands clasped awkwardly in front of him. "I was worried about Maya after I got sent to prison. She has a tendency to close off, emotionally I mean. She never had a lot of friends outside the department, and when she quit to start her own private detective business with her old partner Frances, and then Frances left, I was afraid she'd be all on her own and I was concerned how all that would play out. But then I heard you stepped in, and Vanessa told me how much Maya liked you, and well, I just want to say thank you. It's nice to see Maya with such a loyal best friend . . ."

For a moment, Sandra thought Max might cry.

But he didn't.

He seemed to catch himself and remain stoic.

No tears for this tough guy.

"Maya means the world to me," Sandra said. "I've grown very fond of her, very protective."

Max seemed to pick up on the subtext. "I promise you, Sandra, I'm going to work very hard, very hard, to earn back her trust. Hers and Vanessa's."

"That's good to hear," Sandra replied.

Maya suddenly appeared in the kitchen. "I was going to help, maybe put some coffee on. What are you two secretly gossiping about?"

"You, of course," Sandra answered matter-of-factly, handing two dessert plates to Maya. "Here, take these out; I'll put the coffee on. I was just about to ask your husband what he planned to do now that he has a fresh start?"

"I have been thinking about that," Max mused. "I was a cop for over twenty years; I have tons of experience investigating crimes. Maybe I could help you two out at your office."

Maya froze in the doorway to the kitchen, tightly gripping the dessert plates.

Max instantly noticed. "Not as a third partner or anything like that; just an extra hand. It might be fun."

Maya still didn't move.

"Or maybe not," he muttered, disappointed.

She slowly turned around. "I'm just not sure it would be such a good idea living *and* working together, Max, at least right away. Maybe down the road when things are less chaotic and unsettled . . ."

"I guess I didn't see things right now as chaotic."

"Max, I didn't mean . . ."

"Or unsettled."

Sandra wasn't sure if she should interject anything at this juncture.

She had instantly liked Max from the moment she first met him.

And there was no question how much he loved Maya and Vanessa.

But she and Maya had a good thing going.

They weren't exactly flushed with success from this recent joint endeavor, but they were getting clients, paying the overhead, making a small profit each month. If anyone had told her two years ago she would be a partner in a private investigation firm, she would have thought they were stark raving mad. Up to that point, most of her adult life had been spent hosting society luncheons and giving innocuous speeches at political fundraisers, honing her skills at buttering up bloviating Senators and Congressmen and even a couple of Presidents. But a licensed PI? Never.

The idea of Max horning his way in on all of that concerned her.

But she also knew Maya was going to work hard to pick up the pieces of her marriage, and if that meant giving him some kind of renewed purpose, inviting him into the world she and Sandra had built together, she knew she had to at least be open to it.

"I don't think there's any harm in at least considering it."

There it was again.

That word.

Consider.

Just by uttering that one word that morning, she had already caused a firestorm of trouble with the kids for telling Principal Williams that she and Maya would consider chaperoning the class trip to DC, and now she had just gone and done it again.

Maya's face said it all.

Why hadn't she just kept her mouth shut?

Chapter 4

Fern Wiggins entered Maya and Sandra's office on unsteady feet. She had called earlier in the day to make a last-minute appointment, insisting she had something of utmost importance to discuss with the two private detectives, a professional matter. Fern was a scrawny thing, very fragile looking, with oversized thick black horn-rimmed glasses that seemed too big for her face. Her teased-out hair was designed to make her tiny head appear larger than it was but failed in its overall objective. She was also drowning in a tan wool sweater that hung low, making it look more like a dress.

She pushed her heavy glasses back up the bridge of her nose when they threatened to fall right off, and said in a shaky, shy voice, "Thank you for seeing me on such short notice."

"Not at all, Fern, can I get you some coffee?" Sandra offered.

Fern nodded. "Yes, that would be nice. Do you

have decaf? If I have regular this late in the day, I will be more jittery than usual and probably never get to sleep tonight."

"Yes, we have decaf," Sandra said with a smile before crossing over to the small coffee station they had set up in the corner of the office.

Maya, who sat behind her desk, waved toward an empty chair in front of them. "Have a seat, Fern; tell us what's on your mind."

"It's about my husband," she said flatly.

Sandra cocked an eyebrow. "Ed?"

"Yes," Fern sighed.

Maya knew what was coming.

Ed Wiggins was a local part-time contractor who rarely worked and had an uncontrollable roving eye for the ladies.

She had seen him sneaking around on the down low with a number of local women, most of them still young and stupid enough not to see Ed for the opportunistic user he was. He'd wine and dine them, usually on his wife Fern's dime, until he got what he wanted; then he would go running back to Fern, whom he typically counted on to pay the bills.

Maya had always assumed Fern turned a blind eye to her husband's infidelities, but maybe she had been wrong about that. Maybe Fern was genuinely in the dark, clueless, and was only now starting to get suspicious.

Sandra crossed the room and handed Fern her cup of decaf. "What about him?"

"We had a terrible fight last night," Fern muttered.

Maya leaned forward. "About what?"

Fern tremulously raised the cup to her lips and took a small sip. "I think you know. It's so embarrassing to talk about."

Sandra looked confused.

But Maya nodded knowingly. It was an age-old story she had heard from countless married clients. "That's okay, Fern. I have a good idea. This is more common than you might think. We can tail him, get some photographic evidence, everything you might need in the event of divorce proceedings."

Fern's mouth dropped open in shock. *"Divorce?"*

Wait.

Did it honestly just happen again?

Did Maya totally misread the situation just as they had in Principal Williams's office?

By the horrified expression on Sandra's face, it sure did look that way.

Fern glanced around, utterly stupefied. "I'm sorry, what are we talking about? Do you think Ed is cheating on me? How do you know that? Have you seen or heard something?"

It was time for an emergency course correction before things got exponentially worse. Maya pretended to shuffle some papers around on her desk. "No, of course not. I'm so sorry, Fern, I wrote down some notes about a client we are meeting at six this evening. She wants to hire us to look into allegations that her husband is cheating. I totally confused her with you for a second. Isn't that funny?"

Fern did not find it the least bit funny. She shakily set her cup down on the edge of the small coffee table in front of her and clutched her heart.

"You gave me quite a good scare there for a moment. I can't imagine Ed *ever* cheating on me. He's just not the type." She chuckled at the absurdity of the thought.

"Right," Maya said quickly. "Let's backtrack a bit, shall we? What was the fight with Ed about?"

"You," Fern said matter-of-factly.

"*Me?*" Maya said, surprised.

"Yes, you and Sandra."

Sandra folded her arms and moved in front of the chair so she was facing Fern. "Wait, is this about the class trip to DC?"

Fern nodded. "Yes. Ed said he'd help out and fill in for Stan Lennox as a chaperone, which was a huge relief, even though we're still one short because of Dory Baumgarten's hip surgery. But then, out of the blue, last night he changed his mind. He said he suddenly got a contracting job, which I swear is a lie because he hasn't had a contracting job in over two years."

"Why do you think he changed his mind?" Sandra asked.

"He just doesn't want to go. Maybe there's a baseball game on TV he doesn't want to miss? Who knows? It doesn't matter!" Fern huffed.

She might have thought it mattered if she knew it might be that buxom blond barely legal waitress from Applebee's Maya had seen Ed driving around with in his car late at night when she was on a stakeout recently.

"We had a huge row about it," Fern explained. "I told him how important this trip is to me, how I have spent months organizing it, how excited the kids are about going, but he just didn't seem to care. To be honest, Ed's never been very passionate about his work. I simply cannot understand what it is about this job that has him so excited."

"Is he getting paid a lot of money?" Sandra asked.

Fern shrugged. "I don't know. He's being very tight-lipped about the whole thing."

Maya leaned forward again. "Do you want us to find out what the job is?"

Another perplexed look from Fern. "What? No. I don't care about that."

"Then what do you want from us, Fern?"

"I want you to come on the class trip as chaperones! Please, I'm no longer asking; I'm *begging*!"

Maya sighed. "We already met with Principal Williams about this, Fern. I'm sorry, we're simply not available."

"I know you met with her, and you both said no, and so I strong-armed Ed into going, and then I only needed one more, just one more teacher or parent to agree to go. But now Ed has pulled out and I am back to square one. The school has some silly rule about how we need four chaperones and a bus driver, and now the whole trip is in jeopardy, and so I thought I would come to your office and try to appeal to you one last time . . ."

"I'm sorry, the answer is still no," Maya said firmly.

"Well, I guess that's it then." Fern sniffed, on the verge of tears.

"I'm sure you can find a couple more parents willing to go," Sandra assured her.

Fern shook her head. "No, I have gone down

the list multiple times. I've called every parent of every student signed up. No one is available. And believe me, they all have very good excuses." Fern shot a judgmental look toward Maya.

"And you think we don't?"

Fern played dumb. "What?"

"You don't think we have a good excuse?"

"I didn't say that; I just haven't heard one."

"We have clients!" Maya barked.

"Yes, the poor woman you're meeting with at six with the cheating husband. I feel so bad for her. Can you imagine being in the dark like that for so long?"

"Yes," Sandra said absent-mindedly, staring off into space.

"Well, thank you anyway for hearing me out," Fern said, resigned.

"I'm sure it will all work out," Maya said, peppering her words with a healthy dose of optimism.

Fern grimaced. "You were my last hope. I guess we're going to have to finally cancel the whole thing. I had a feeling it would come to this."

Sandra snapped out of her reverie. "But you still have a little more time."

"What choice do I have? This was my last stop. The kids are going to be so disappointed. But maybe we'll try again next year. I feel sorry for the seniors, though; this was their last chance to go before graduation."

Fern stood up to leave.

"Wait," Sandra said.

Maya flashed her a stern look.

"I'll do it," Sandra whispered.

Fern gasped. "Really?"

"Yes, it's only four days; the world's not going to crumble if I'm gone for four days," Sandra said.

Maya couldn't believe Sandra was relenting out of guilt.

But then again, Sandra had always been the more responsible one.

She had been class president in high school.

Maya was more Queen of Detention.

"Thank you, Sandra, thank you. You have no idea how much this means to me. Now I only have to find one more adult before we go."

Sandra and Fern turned expectantly toward Maya.

"I guess I will be holding down the fort here while you're gone," Maya said with a tight smile.

She could see the disappointment in Sandra's face.

But she was not going to change her mind.

No way.

Nohow.

Famous last words.

Chapter 5

When Maya arrived home from the office, she was surprised not to find something cooking in the oven or simmering on the stove. She had come to expect that Max would work his wonders in the kitchen as he had the night before with a tasty shrimp risotto, or the night before that with a perfectly moist roast chicken. She couldn't expect the man to prepare a gourmet dinner for the family every night, but he had been spoiling them. She could hear an Olivia Rodrigo pop song playing in Vanessa's room, and assumed she was in there doing her homework, or, more likely, chatting on the phone with Ryan. The door to the office Maya had converted into a bedroom for Max was open and there was no light on inside. He wasn't watching the local news in the living room, so she assumed he wasn't home yet. She padded into her bedroom and stopped in her tracks. Ambling out of the master bathroom was Max, stark naked. He jumped, just as startled as she was.

"Sorry, I was just using your shower!" he exclaimed, rushing back in to grab a towel.

Once the shock wore off, Maya laughed. "It's okay. It's nothing I haven't seen before."

Max gave her a wry smile as he wrapped a towel around his waist. "I'm not sure how to take that."

She sized him up.

He had not gone soft in prison at all.

He was still incredibly well toned.

He scratched the mat of hair on his chest. "I was hitting the pavement hard today looking for work, and came home feeling a bit grubby. Thought I'd clean myself up a bit before you got home, make myself presentable."

"Any luck?"

He opened his arms wide, showing off his physique. "I think I clean up pretty good, but I will let you be the judge."

"I'm talking about the job hunt," Maya said, chuckling.

Max frowned slightly. He looked as if he was hoping she wouldn't ask.

He slowly shook his head. "Nobody's too eager to hire someone with a criminal record, that's for sure. And even when they are willing, once they get a look at the name on my résumé and put two and two together, they're less inclined to open any doors for a disgraced cop."

He didn't seem to be feeling sorry for himself. He was just stating the facts.

"I'm sure the right thing will come along," Maya said encouragingly.

"Yeah," he said. "I just have to keep looking. Someone's bound to take pity on me."

She could see how much the search was weighing on his self-esteem.

It would be so easy to give in and invite him to work, even if just part-time, with her and Sandra. It wasn't even about the money they'd have to pay him. Max was so desperate to have a sense of purpose again, he would probably volunteer to do some investigative work for free. But she just could not bring herself to say anything, at least not yet. She was still struggling with just having him home again, living together as a family. She could not imagine working with him too. No, it was too soon. She had to believe he would find something, anything to keep busy.

"Don't feel bad about it," Max whispered.

It was as if he had been reading her mind.

"What? Oh, you mean about inviting you to work for the firm?"

Maya wanted to kick herself. She was such a bad actress. Of course that's what she had been thinking about and he knew it.

"If it doesn't feel right to you, then go with your instinct. It's your business, and I respect whatever you believe is best."

He was being so magnanimous.

Was it all designed to make her feel guilty?

"Seriously, babe, I am not trying to make you feel guilty . . ."

Okay, this was spooky now.

"It's how I feel. I'm going to find something, it just may take a little more time than I was hoping, but I'll make it happen, because the last thing I intend to do is become a burden to you and Vanessa."

Maya sighed. "You're not a burden, Max."

He nodded, then tightened the towel around his waist and started out of the bedroom to the converted office with the pullout couch Maya had set up for him upon his return home.

"How's the pullout? Not too lumpy, I hope," she said.

Max stopped and turned around. "Compared to the cot I've been crashing on the last few years, it's like sleeping in a suite at the Ritz-Carlton. You should come try it out with me one of these nights." He winked at her.

"I'll think about it."

This was yet another thing she felt bad about.

She knew Max had expected to come home and pick things right up where they had left off before he was convicted and sent off to prison. She could see how crestfallen he was when they arrived at the house and she had immediately escorted him to the office to drop off his belongings. She had explained well before his release that things would be different, that she needed time, that although she wanted to try to repair their relationship, she still had doubts, and couldn't just jump right back in the deep end of the pool. He promised her he was fine with whatever she needed, and so far he had been true to his word. But the disappointment every night they went to bed in separate rooms was so clearly drawn on his face.

"I'm going to get dressed, then get dinner started," he said as he headed for the door.

"It's already past seven. Why don't we go out somewhere? I have been craving some clam chowder at Gilbert's. Sound good?"

Max hesitated. "Uh, sure . . ."

She knew what the problem was and quickly added, "My treat."

He was broke and in debt and it was torturing him that he had to rely on the financial support of his wife.

"Max, you can't keep beating yourself up just because you don't have a job yet. You're going to get something great and then you can treat us. And I won't settle for just clam chowder at Gilbert's. I want five star, Michelin rated. Oysters, foie gras, the priciest fish, and a really good, and I mean really good, insanely expensive Sauvignon Blanc."

"Deal," Max said, relieved but still bothered. "In the meantime, I want to find some way to contribute."

"You cook for us almost every night."

"No, that's fun for me. I want to do more. Any odd job you can think of. There's got to be something I can do."

Maya looked around. "No, I can't really think of anything off the top of my head . . ." Her eyes settled on some scuff marks on her white bedroom wall. "Wait."

"What? Anything!"

"Well, I have been putting away a little money every month, saving up to hire someone to paint the walls in the whole house. I have been wanting to give this place a fresh look forever."

"I can do that. I used to spend my summers painting the whole inside of my grandparents' house in Dover-Foxcroft."

"Then it's settled. I already have the paint ordered; all you have to do is pick it up. You can get started tomorrow."

"It's kind of a messy job; it'll be disruptive, especially with all of us here in this small house, tripping over each other. Maybe I'll wait until you and Vanessa leave for a few days."

"You mean her class trip? That's just Vanessa. I'm not going anywhere."

"It's kind of perfect, though. I need an empty house to get the job done as quickly as possible, I can work day and night, and well, let's face it, they really need you in DC, otherwise the whole trip will be canceled, and that wouldn't be a good thing for anybody. Babe, it's a win-win."

"Max, no, no way."

He smirked knowingly.

"No!" she said, more emphatically.

The more she said no, the more she could feel her hard stance finally crumbling. How had she allowed the table to turn so suddenly? An hour later, after breaking the news to Vanessa, who surprisingly took it in remarkable stride, Maya was on the phone with a disconcertingly excited Fern Wiggins, who was whooping with joy and thanking her profusely for coming to the rescue at the very last second.

Maybe it wouldn't be so awful.

After all, Sandra would be there with her.

It might actually be fun.

She had no idea in that moment just how wrong she could be.

Chapter 6

Maya knew lots of people in their mid- to late seventies who were still active and spry, youthful, full of vim and vigor. Unfortunately, Clancy Rodick was *not* one of them. Clancy had been a bus driver for the South Portland school district for decades. Maya's earliest memory of him was when she was in the fourth grade and he yelled at her for talking too loud in the back of the school bus. She had shrunk down in her seat, embarrassed, and had never dared to speak again for the remainder of the school year on the two-mile ride from home to school and back. Most of Maya's memories of Clancy after that terrifying first day involved him yelling and screaming, losing his cool, demanding the kids remain in their seats and keep their mouths shut, every morning like clockwork. She didn't blame him. The kids on her bus route to school were a rowdy bunch, and as they all got older, Clancy was no longer so scary to

them, until finally, by the time she was a sopho-
more, when Clancy was transferred from driving
the middle school students and assigned to drive
the high school students, they stopped taking his
roaring orders and threats seriously. He'd still pop
a gasket every morning when the kids got a little
out of control, but by then her peers mostly ignored him. In fact, his shouting had just become
background noise like music on the car radio as
she flirted with the new transfer student, a senior
with his own motorcycle.

Now, watching Clancy behind the wheel of the
school bus, driving them from Portland, Maine, to
Washington, DC, Maya barely recognized him. He
was hunched over in his seat, a tiny man, a fraction
of the size that she had remembered. He had
seemed so towering and formidable when she was
a little girl. Now he looked almost fragile. His
bony, cracked hands gripped the wheel, and his
glazed-over eyes remained squarely fixed on the
traffic in front of him. Fern had been disappointed
to find out Clancy was the only driver available,
mostly because he had already been put out to pas-
ture, only called in when another driver was sick or
on vacation. But after the Herculean struggle to
secure the necessary number of adult chaperones,
Fern was not about to question Principal Williams's decision to recruit old Clancy.

Clancy had obviously mellowed over the years.
After two messy divorces, a bout with prostate cancer, and a lingering estrangement from his only
daughter, who had fled Maine for the warmer
climes of Florida's panhandle, life's blows had finally taken their toll. Clancy lived alone in a small

apartment behind a funeral home, venturing out to buy groceries once a week or to grab a beer at his local watering hole. He had slowed down considerably. And so had his driving.

Maya had noticed when they piled onto the bus early that morning at five for the eight-and-a-half-hour drive to DC that Clancy's faculties were not what they used to be. He nearly sideswiped a parked car as they pulled out of the SoPo High parking lot and as they crawled up the on ramp to Interstate 95 south toward Boston, he kept a steady tortoise-like pace, never tipping over fifty miles an hour as the surrounding cars around the yellow bus zipped past faster, some at seventy-five, eighty miles an hour.

Fern also noticed Clancy's cautious driving and nervously checked her watch. The idea of falling behind schedule before they even arrived at their destination was vexing her, to say the least. She turned to Maya. "Should I say something?"

"Like what?"

"I don't know, 'Can you pick up the pace a little, at least go the speed limit?' "

Clancy turned on the blinker to change lanes when a car behind them honked loudly, annoyed they were going so slow. Clancy glanced in his mirror and then violently swerved the bus, nearly colliding with a tractor trailer that was in the other lane, which caused that driver to angrily lay on his horn. The irate drivers didn't seem to rattle Clancy at all, or maybe, more worrying, he just didn't hear them.

"Look, Clancy's advanced age may be an issue, his eyesight and reflexes aren't what they used to be, but I'm afraid if you ask him to speed up, you might take him out of his comfort zone and he could take some risks that would jeopardize the safety of the kids . . . not to mention *us*."

Fern seemed to buy Maya's logic. "Okay. I guess we'll get there when we get there."

Maya looked around. The kids were all totally oblivious, excitedly chattering away. Way in the back, Maya spotted Ryan and Vanessa sitting together, mashed up against each other, probably holding hands, although Maya couldn't see for sure. She certainly liked Ryan, but they were so young, and she was concerned they were getting way too serious too soon. She wondered if Sandra felt the same way.

Sandra sat in the seat behind her, but they had barely spoken since leaving SoPo High because their fellow chaperone Coach Lucas Cavill, who was seated directly across from her, had been singularly focused on keeping Sandra engaged in a conversation. Sandra pleasantly answered his barrage of questions, politely laughed at his wisecracks, and seemed genuinely appreciative of the attention, but Maya knew her friend and partner well, and Sandra was trying very hard not to give the amorous young man the wrong impression. She would turn away when there was a lull in the conversation, staring out the window at the passing scenery, only to be drawn back by Lucas's efforts to get to know her better. When one of the boys wanted to pump the coach about the upcoming baseball away game schedule, Sandra seized the opportunity to get up from her seat and slide into the one in front of her next to Maya.

"How are you holding up?" Sandra asked.

"I'm wishing I went to church more often when I was a kid. That way I'd be more in touch with God and I could pray to him that He get us to DC in one piece."

Right on cue, the bus jerked to the left and everybody fell forward as Clancy tried to switch lanes again and didn't see a Lincoln Town Car, which had to veer into the emergency lane to avoid colliding with the bus. Another long blaring of a car horn followed.

"My life just flashed before my eyes," Maya said. "Should one of us take over and drive the rest of the way?"

"We're stuck. He's the only one here licensed to operate a school bus," Sandra said. "At least he's not speeding."

"That's an understatement. By the time we get there, it'll be time to turn around and go home," Maya cracked.

"He's doing his best. I have always had such a soft spot for Clancy; I remember him being so sweet. He was always so nice to me when I was a little girl."

"This proves we had two totally different childhoods. I do not have those happy memories of old grouch Clancy at all. My God, you really were the golden child, weren't you?"

Sandra playfully nudged Maya.

Fern whipped around. "I was hoping to tour a few of the big-ticket items today before we checked into the hotel. I have the Lincoln, Washington, and Jefferson monuments on my list that I want to check off today, but at this rate it's already going to be dark by the time we get there."

"I'm sure they look lovely at night," Sandra said, always the optimist.

Coach Cavill leaned forward. "Want to start taking bets on how long it's going to take us to get there?"

"No," Fern said emphatically.

He ignored her. "We all put in twenty bucks. Winner takes all, whoever guesses the closest time."

"Ten hours," Maya said.

"Ten hours and forty-five minutes," Coach Cavill challenged her.

"I believe in Clancy," Sandra said. "I'll say nine and a half."

That was still an hour longer than the time Google Maps said it would take to drive that distance with light traffic.

"Eleven!" Fern sighed, finally giving up.

Fern would go on to win the pot.

By the time they exited the Baltimore-Washington Parkway to New York Avenue, they had been on the road for eleven hours and nineteen minutes. It was almost four thirty in the afternoon. Fern, a stickler about her schedule, insisted they make a beeline for the monuments, dismissing Coach Cavill's suggestion that they go straight to the hotel and tack on the monuments to the following day's schedule.

The stops were more abbreviated than planned. In fact, they decided to just drive by the Washington Monument with everybody cramming up against the windows to get photos with their phones. Then Clancy deposited them off at the Lincoln Memorial, and Fern herded everybody up the steps to see the grand, majestic, giant sculpture of our nation's sixteenth President. Fern prattled on about his consequential presidency, peppering in a few personal details, promising to discuss more when they went to Ford's Theatre, where he was assassinated. Unable to find parking, Clancy just circled around the area until Fern called him on his phone and he pulled up, cranking open the door, watching listlessly as the kids piled on the bus while Fern did a quick head count.

This was Fern's number one priority.

Keeping an accurate head count.

She was meticulous and militant about it because her greatest fear was one of the kids wandering off. And so she counted and recounted and repeated the roll call on the bus to ensure everyone was present and accounted for.

Luckily, every kid, hyped up on sugary candy bars and caffeinated sodas, was present, and they moved on to the Jefferson Memorial, where Fern, visibly exhausted, sidled up to Maya.

"I'm losing my voice; would you mind taking over?"

Maya gave her a perplexed look. "What do you want me to do?"

"Talk about Jefferson, the significance of the memorial, how it was intended to represent the Age of Enlightenment."

"Fern, I got a C Minus in history," Maya said flatly.

Sandra mercifully intervened. "Don't worry, I got an A."

"Of course you did," Maya scoffed.

Maya had to admit, Sandra was a born teacher. She gathered the kids around, reading the words inscribed in a frieze below the dome: "I have sworn upon the altar of God eternal hostility against every form of tyranny over the mind of man." Then she launched into a compelling story about Jefferson and the Declaration of Independence. At least the kids seemed interested. Coach Cavill certainly was laser focused on Sandra, although Maya couldn't be sure whether it was her impromptu history lesson or the top button of her blouse that had come undone. Maya mostly tuned out, calculating how many more hours were left on the trip before the journey home.

Chapter 7

Sandra hadn't bothered unpacking before kicking off her shoes and flopping down on her bed in the room she was sharing with Maya at the Hilton Garden Inn in Downtown Washington, DC. She was utterly exhausted from the long and grueling day. Maya dropped her bag on the small desk underneath the flat-screen television on the wall and fished out her phone to text Max. The room was hardly luxurious but serviceable, and it was still busting Fern's budget for the trip even after a whole year of fundraising and donations from the wealthier parents.

Sandra closed her eyes and was about to drift off to sleep when the pings from Maya's phone announcing incoming texts forced her eyes back open. "Is Max missing you already?"

"No, he's freaking out because the paint on the living room walls looks way darker than it did in the can, so he's sending me photos to see if I still approve." Maya paused, scrolling through all the photos. "Looks fine to me." She texted him back with a thumbs-up emoji.

Sandra sat up on the edge of the bed. "How have things been with him finally home?"

Maya shrugged. "Good, I guess. It'll be much better when he finally finds a job."

"I didn't mean to stick my nose into your business the other night; I just kind of blurted that bit out about how we should consider having him come work with us."

Maya cracked a smile. "I know. It caught me by surprise. Poor Max could see the sheer panic in my eyes. I'm not opposed to him helping us out; it's just that everything is still so new. When he was in prison, Vanessa and I got into a whole new rhythm. I always assumed Max and I were finished. I was *this* close to signing the divorce papers last fall, but then we decided to give the marriage another chance, and I'm still adjusting. In some ways he's the same old Max; in other ways, I look at him and I see a complete stranger."

"He's mostly been out of your life for a while now, Maya; that's to be expected."

"I'm trying to take a wait-and-see attitude, but I keep looking ahead. Vanessa has been the one permanent common denominator that's kept the two of us together, but in the fall she'll be off to college, and then it's just going to be the two of us, and I have no idea what it will be like then."

"You'll figure it out; you're the smartest person I know. Just take one day at a time," Sandra said.

Maya sat down on her own bed. "What about you?"

"Me? I'm fine."

"Being back here in DC, does it remind you of your days as a high-powered Senator's wife?"

"Um, every waking moment." Sandra laughed. "Stephen's already called three times. He wants me to bring Ryan by his office while we're here. I will probably have to get a permission slip from Fern if we plan on breaking off from the group even just for an hour."

There was a knock at the door.

Maya and Sandra exchanged looks.

"Probably one of the kids wanting cash for the vending machines. I swear, teenagers have bottomless pits for stomachs," Sandra said. "Ryan ate two cheeseburgers at dinner."

"I was too tired to eat anything," Maya moaned.

"Me too," Sandra agreed. "But of course now I'm starving."

She crossed to the door and opened it, surprised not to find her son Ryan but Coach Cavill.

"Good evening," he said with a flirtatious grin.

"Oh, hi," Sandra muttered, instantly regretting her unenthusiastic response.

He didn't seem at all deterred. "I'm going stir-crazy in my room. I don't know if you know this, but I'm sharing with Clancy, and he talks to himself. I think he's saying something to me, and when I say, 'What?' he looks at me like I'm some kind of blithering idiot, and yells, 'Nothing!' "

Sandra laughed.

"I had to escape. I'm going down to the hotel bar, and wanted to know if you would like to join me."

Sandra hesitated and glanced back at Maya.

Lucas quickly added, "If you'd *both* like to join

me. I think we all could use a stiff cocktail after the day we've had."

Maya gave him a friendly wave. "You two go ahead. I'm going to stay here and check out the room service menu."

Sandra, her back to Coach Cavill, shot Maya an admonishing look for putting her on the spot like this. She paused, then spun back around.

"Not tonight, Lucas, I'm too tuckered out. I think I'll just pamper my weary bones with a bubble bath and go to bed."

Again, she was regretting the words that had just effortlessly tumbled out of her mouth. Mostly because she could see the coach conjuring up a visual image in his mind of what she had just described.

"Well, if you change your mind, you know where to find me," Coach Cavill said, failing to hide his disappointment. "Have a good night, ladies."

"You too," Sandra chirped.

He slinked off and Sandra shut the door.

"You're torturing that poor boy," Maya joked.

"I don't want to give him the wrong impression."

"Why are you so determined not to give him a chance?"

"You already said it. He's a *boy*."

"He's in his twenties."

"And in my opinion, to a woman pushing forty, a man in his early twenties is still a boy."

"He's in his mid- to *late* twenties, and he's adorable, and he likes you, and I see no harm in a sweet May-December romance."

"Then *you* should date him."

"I have got enough relationship drama at home, thank you very much." Maya flipped through the leather-bound book containing the room service menu. "They have a Maryland Crab Cake that looks pretty good."

Sandra suddenly perked up. "Put that down."

"Why? I'm hungry."

"We're going out."

"But you just said—"

"The kids are safely tucked away in their rooms until morning. We worked hard today. Lucas is right. We deserve a nice evening out."

"So you changed your mind about joining him in the bar?"

"No. I am taking you out to dinner. Stephen and I always loved dining at Dauphine's. It's near the *Washington Post* building, a short cab ride away from here. There's a Duck Jambalaya for two that you will die for!" She noticed Maya vacillating. "My treat."

"The magic words," Maya said, popping up from her bed.

"Should we let Fern know we're going out?" Sandra asked.

"We're not students. What's she going to do? Give us detention? Call our parents? Forget Fern! Let's hit the town!"

Chapter 8

"Sandra! How lovely to see you," the rail-thin maître d' with a shaved head and red goatee gushed as Maya and Sandra swept through the front door at Dauphine's.

"Hello, Charles, love the new goatee," Sandra remarked.

He rubbed it playfully. "I'm single again so I'm going for a new look as I get back out into that awful, unforgiving DC dating world."

"Well, it suits you," Sandra said, giving him a warm hug. "This is my friend Maya."

"Nice to meet you," Charles gushed before turning back to Sandra and whispering, "She's so gorgeous."

"Yes, you can imagine how frustrating it is to be out with her with all the men gazing in our direction but solely focused on her."

"How could they not with those cheekbones?" Charles observed.

"Just a reminder, I'm standing right here and can hear every word you're saying," Maya said, embarrassed.

Sandra giggled, then put a hand on Charles's arm. "I'm sorry, I didn't make a reservation."

"Darling, since when have you ever needed a reservation? Come, I have the perfect table."

He led them across the room. Maya's head swiveled around as she took in all the familiar famous faces. She tugged on Sandra's sleeve. "Hey, isn't that . . ."

Sandra nodded. "Senator Lindsay Graham. I would say hello, but he doesn't like me ever since I had too much Chardonnay at a cocktail party once and mocked his southern accent."

A young attractive man eating with several people at a large table waved at them.

Sandra waved back, smiling. "That's Jake Sherman. He co-founded *Punchbowl News*; it's the hottest daily newsletter about what's happening on Capitol Hill."

Maya gasped as she pointed out another man engaged in a conversation at another table but nodding at Sandra as they passed by. "I recognize him for sure from the news, but I'm blanking on his name."

"Tony Blinken, Secretary of State," Sandra said, nodding back.

"You certainly know all the power players," Maya said, impressed.

Charles stopped at a table for two in the middle of the restaurant. "Here you go. I know you usually like more privacy, but I figured your beautiful friend would prefer to be right in the center of all the action."

"Perfect. You're a prince, Charles."

"If only," he sighed.

"Do you need a dinner menu?" Charles asked.

"Of course not, we're doing my usual."

"Duck Jambalaya for two."

"You remember."

"You're my role model; I have completely memorized you," he joked.

She gave him a peck on the cheek and the women sat down as Charles unfolded two cloth napkins shaped like swans and placed one in each of their laps.

"Enjoy, ladies," he said before scurrying off.

Maya craned her neck around, scanning the room in search of even more famous faces. "I'm disappointed. Why aren't the President and First Lady here?"

"Someone has to work." Sandra laughed as she picked up the wine list and perused it. "They have an excellent French blend from Burgundy if you're in the mood for wine." She glanced up and saw Maya staring at something in the far corner of the restaurant. "See someone else you recognize?"

"Yes," Maya said flatly. "Your husband."

"What?" Sandra swiveled around. Sure enough, in a quiet table in the corner sat her husband, Senator Stephen Wallage, devouring his favorite dish, a grilled pork neck steak and collard greens, while his dining companion, Deborah Crowley, his girlfriend of the moment, picked at a shrimp remoulade. Sandra sighed. "I should probably go over and say hello."

"You don't have to; they haven't spotted us yet," Maya said, snatching the wine list. Her eyes widened. "My God, they have a bottle of red that costs a thousand dollars!"

Sandra grabbed the list away from her and swatted it toward Maya playfully. "I don't want you worrying about prices. I told you, this is my treat."

"If you order a bottle that costs more than fifty dollars I will never speak to you again."

Sandra glanced back at Stephen and Deborah, who now appeared to be in the middle of a very intense conversation. She sighed again. "If I don't go over, someone's going to notice and make a big thing of it. I don't want to end up in Jake's newsletter tomorrow. 'Senator Wallage's soon-to-be ex-wife disses him at Dauphine's.'" She pushed back her chair and was about to stand up when Maya stopped her.

"Wait . . ." Maya whispered.

Sandra turned in time to see Deborah, her whole body shaking with anger, pick up her glass of red wine and hurl it at Stephen, soaking his face and shirt.

"God, I hope that wasn't the wine that costs a grand," Maya said.

The dining room fell silent as the patrons tried to pretend they weren't witnessing the excruciatingly uncomfortable scene.

Deborah shot out of her seat as Stephen reached out to take her hand and pull her back down, but she wrenched free from his grip and shouted, "No!"

And then she stormed across the room, her heels clicking loudly on the hardwood floor, and fled out the door past Charles, who stared at her, mouth agape. Stephen sat sullenly alone at the table and dunked his napkin in a glass of ice water and then dabbed at his stained shirt.

"I bought him that shirt two Christmases ago," Sandra said.

"You're probably going to need to get him another one. That stain's never going to come out," Maya said.

Sandra shook her head in wonderment. "Oh, Stephen, what have you gone and done now?"

Chapter 9

A little color had finally returned to Fern Wiggins's face when she spotted a husky African-American Capitol Police officer marching toward her with Tammy Carter and Amy Blackburn in tow. The two students had wandered off more than half an hour ago just before Fern conducted her twice-hourly head count and came up two short. She sent Coach Cavill off in one direction in the US Capitol Building while she searched the other, her stomach no doubt twisting in knots with each passing moment the two girls remained missing. But now, after an agonizing thirty-six minutes, her wayward students had been returned safe and sound.

"Girls, what did I say about wandering off from the group? I specifically told everyone to stay close together!" Fern snapped, nerves frayed and still on edge.

Tammy and Amy, lifelong friends since the first grade, did not appear at all shaken or chastised.

"We wanted to say hi to our State Representative. We're his constituents, so we figured it would be okay," Tammy said.

"Well, it's *not* okay!" Fern shouted. "You do not go anywhere without my permission!"

Congressman Dan Hamlin was an Air Force veteran in his early thirties who ran for one of Maine's Congressional seats. He had a macho swagger and movie star looks and was incapable of taking a bad photo, so every time he uttered a statement or opinion his handsome mug was splashed on the front page of the *Portland Press Herald*. He had a lot of fans, mostly of the female persuasion, and apparently Tammy Carter and Amy Blackburn were more than willing to break Fern's strict rules in order to have their own personal encounter with him.

"We were so close to meeting him too. I caught a glimpse of him in his office; he's *so* cute," Amy trilled before frowning. "But then Officer Steadman here found us before we had a chance to talk to him."

"Thank you, Officer," Fern sighed to the officer.

He nodded politely and turned to the girls, adopting an admonishing tone. "I don't want to have to round you up again, so no more exploring on your own." He softened a bit. "If you listen to your teacher and behave yourselves, maybe I'll get him to come by and say hello before you leave today."

"Really?" Tammy gasped.

"If he's not on the House floor, I'll see what I can do."

Fern shook Officer Steadman's hand gratefully. "I appreciate you bringing them back. I am so sorry for the inconvenience."

"It's my job. You'd be surprised at the number of kids I have to chase after every day who somehow manage to bypass security." Officer Steadman chuckled.

Sandra and Maya were in charge of a smaller group, including their own kids Ryan and Vanessa and Ryan's buddy Anton, a Russian exchange student, ushering them in Fern's direction near the Rotunda. Officer Steadman beamed happily when he saw Sandra approaching. "Always nice to see you, Mrs. Wallage!"

"You're looking well, Ernie; you've lost weight."

Officer Steadman patted his ample belly. "A little, but the wife says I could stand to drop a few more pounds. I better get back to my rounds."

"Bye, Ernie; say hello to Lissa!"

"Will do," he said, hustling off.

Fern waved her arms in the air. "This way, everybody; we're going to go see the National Statuary Hall now!"

Coach Cavill circled around his own charges, herding them like a cowboy rounding up his head of cattle.

Ryan tugged at his mother's shirt sleeve. "Mom, are we going to have a chance to go see Dad?"

"We'll see, Ryan; we have a pretty full schedule."

"But I told him we'd stop by. It would be rude not to," Ryan huffed.

Sandra just didn't have the strength to argue. "I'll talk to Ms. Wiggins."

"Sandra Wallage, what an unexpected surprise."

Sandra's body tensed.

She had no trouble recognizing the voice.

Taking a deep breath, she pirouetted around and found herself face-to-face with Senator Charles Grisby of the great state of Virginia, who was surrounded by a gaggle of his aides. Although he worked hard at playing up his carefully cultivated persona of a principled southern gentleman, at least on the surface, underneath the lilting accent and hint of face powder to take away the sweaty shine Grisby was a slimy opportunist. A soulless calculating politician and a constant thorn in Stephen's side, a political rival who liked to play dirty. It was more than just an impression; Sandra had seen him operate up close during her time with Stephen in DC. Grisby lied with abandon, espoused strict moral values, and yet put forth bills that would decimate the lives of the poor and undervalued. She despised him. His only redeeming feature had been his choice of a spouse, his wife Clementine, who was polite and sweet and decent and possessed a good heart. She knitted sweaters one Christmas for Jack and Ryan when they were about ten years old. Sadly, she died a few years ago and with her she took what little kindness and compassion Grisby had left.

"What brings you all the way down here from the wilds of Maine?" Grisby asked with a fake smile.

"Senior class trip," Sandra said, drumming up as much friendliness as she could possibly muster under the circumstances.

"Oh, I was hoping you and your husband might be trying to reconcile. I always thought you and Stephen were the perfect couple. I always said if he decided to run for President one day, you'd make an excellent First Lady. Of course Clementine would always remind me that you would make a great President and Stephen would be an excellent First Gentleman."

It was a backhanded compliment to be sure.

No one could have been more thrilled to hear about Sandra and Stephen's marital problems than Senator Grisby. His own approval ratings skyrocketed after Clementine died. A widower was held in much higher regard than a man divorcing his wife, who also happened to be much more popular than him.

"Such a shame," Grisby whispered to himself, slowly shaking his head. "Clementine adored you two together."

"Is that your girlfriend?" Maya piped in.

Sandra turned to see Maya protectively by her side.

"My late wife," Grisby corrected her, smile still pinned in place.

"Oh, right. I must be thinking of the girlfriend; her name began with a *C* too, Chrissy, Christine, the one you were secretly dating on the side after your poor wife's terminal diagnosis."

"I-I'm sorry, who are you—?" he sputtered.

"Maya, Maya Kendrick, a friend of Sandra's, I'm kind of a political junkie; I read all the blogs. She was a masseuse when you first met her, right? And now she's practically your Chief of Staff. She must be *so* smart!"

Grisby visibly flinched. He opened his mouth to speak, but no words came out.

His aides stood frozen, eyes wide, in shock.

"Sorry, Charles, we really have to go. Lovely to see you again," Sandra chirped, steering Maya away, whispering under her breath, "That's the first time I think I have ever seen him at a loss for words."

"Sorry to get so snarky, but I didn't like the way he was talking to you. Are you mad?"

"Mad?" Sandra scoffed. "I could kiss you right now!"

Chapter 10

"Senator Wallage has a very packed schedule today, so I must apologize in advance if we have to cut your visit a bit short," Preston Lambert, Stephen's priggish, possessive Chief of Staff, snipped as he led Maya and Sandra, along with Ryan, Vanessa, and Anton, down the hallowed hallway of the Russell Senate Office Building, the oldest of the three structures that housed the one hundred United States Senators.

"We promise to just pop in and say hi," Sandra replied with a tight smile. She had never been a fan of Preston, and quite frankly, it was obvious to her that he was hardly a fan of hers either. Preston had started out as an assistant, worked his way up to appointment secretary, and was now Chief of Staff. Stephen was well aware of Preston's grating personality and, in the words of his son Jack, "his creepy obsession with the boss," but Preston was a doer, he made things happen, kept Stephen focused, and so that had to be rewarded. Despite his off-putting manner, Preston was too good to lose. Sandra had always felt like an interloper around her own husband when Preston was around keeping a watchful eye on the clock, determined to steer Stephen to his next meeting or floor vote. But she also understood Preston's value and just stayed out of his way. Now that she and Stephen were in the midst of a divorce, Preston had this even more pronounced air of superiority, like he had won the war, vanquished the enemy, namely the one person Stephen trusted as much as him. It didn't bother Sandra in the slightest because she loathed the politics of Washington, and if Stephen needed that kind of energy around him to be an effective voice for his constituents back in Maine, then she was happy to step back and allow Preston to run the show.

Preston eagerly acknowledged any power players of either party who happened to pass by on their way to Stephen's office. Mitt Romney of Utah and Patty Murray of Washington were both on the receiving end of his snakish smile. Sandra knew them both personally, but Preston was on a mission to get them to the office so quickly, neither Senator had time to spot her zipping along behind him.

"How did Fern take the news that we were peeling off from the group for a few minutes?" Maya asked Sandra as they moved down the marbled halls at a clip.

"Oh, she ranted and raved for about ten minutes straight and then lectured me about how rude I was for blowing up her carefully constructed schedule, so I would say, for Fern, not bad," Sandra joked.

Maya laughed as they rounded a corner and arrived at the office of Senator Stephen Wallage. Preston stopped at the door, crossly waving them inside, like an annoyed cast member at Disneyland trying to corral a gang of unruly children lined up for Peter Pan's Flight.

"I was afraid you'd forget to come by and say hello to your old man!" Stephen bellowed as he charged out of his office, sleeves rolled up, tie askew, but still looking handsome and refreshed. He had perfected his typical Washington, DC, look over the years, slightly rumpled and harried but in a sexy, accessible kind of way. It was very on brand with his own carefully cultivated image.

"I know you're busy, so we won't stay long," Sandra said pointedly in Preston's direction.

"No, you're fine, come in; I've been excited to see you all day," Stephen said, wrapping Ryan in a bear hug. He turned to a stunningly beautiful young woman seated at a tiny desk in the corner. She had long wavy brown hair that accentuated her perfectly shaped oval face and deep, glistening emerald eyes. "Tess, would you mind getting everybody some drinks? We have coffee, soda, sparkling or still water . . ."

The girl stood up and forced a smile.

She did not strike Sandra as particularly friendly.

Her movements were stiff and uncomfortable.

Stephen hardly noticed as he made his way around the room, hugging Vanessa, joking about how his son was lucky to be dating someone so above his station, introducing himself to Anton, then finally stopping at Maya. Sandra could see him debating with himself, whether he should just shake her hand or go in for a hug. They had met a couple of times before. Stephen wisely opted for a handshake after assessing Maya's chilly body language.

"You're new," Sandra said sweetly to the girl after she took everyone's drink order.

"Yes," she said shyly, forcing another smile.

"And you are . . ." Sandra asked, prodding her a little more.

"Tess," she said flatly. "Tess Rankin."

"Hi, Tess, I'm Sandra."

She offered a rigid nod.

Not even a "Nice to meet you."

Okay, so they wouldn't be going out for a gossipy girls' lunch anytime soon.

"Sandra!"

She spun around to see Stephen's longtime legislative assistant.

"Suzanne!" Sandra said, rushing over to hug her.

Finally, a friendly face in Stephen's office.

Suzanne was the opposite of Preston, warm and affable, helpful and hospitable. A big mop of dirty blond hair. Thick black glasses too big for her round baby face. Less put together than the new intern, Tess, but certainly attractive.

"I've missed you! You look fabulous as always," Suzanne gushed. She then bounced around the room introducing herself to everyone as Tess handed out bottled waters and then shrank into the background.

Sandra noticed Anton quietly standing by the

door, his eyes laser focused on Tess, who plopped down at her rickety wooden desk and returned her attention to her small desktop computer.

The phone buzzed, and Preston, annoyed that Suzanne was too busy chatting, sighed loudly and answered it sulkily. "Senator Wallage's office, how may I help you?"

Stephen was prattling on about the latest infra-structure bill he was working on, the challenges of getting ten votes from the opposing party to pass it, the option of forgoing bipartisanship and push-ing it through as a reconciliation package so they would only need fifty votes plus the Vice President to break the tie. Ryan and Vanessa listened po-litely, but Sandra could tell they really weren't in-terested in the intricacies of Senate legislation. Finally, Stephen asked about school, allowing Ryan to catch his dad up on how his senior year was going, the spring musical, *Hamilton*, where he had just landed the part of King George with Va-nessa in the key role of Angelica Schuyler. Stephen promised, even crossing his heart, that he would be there for opening night.

Preston slammed down the phone. "We need to get you to the Senate floor for the roll call."

"In a minute," Stephen hissed dismissively.

Preston never flinched.

He was used to being snarled at.

But it was his job to ignore it.

Sandra noticed Maya sidle over to Anton and whisper something in his ear. Anton frowned, then averted his eyes away from Tess and down to the floor. Sandra assumed she had just told him to stop staring at the poor girl and making her uncomfortable.

Preston gathered up some papers. "Okay, I will wait for you outside. I need to make a call. Please don't keep the Senate majority leader waiting too long."

And then he flew out the door.

Tess sat numbly at her desk, not moving.

"Dad, we should take off so you can get back to work," Ryan said, patting him on the back.

"Nonsense, my son is here; the US Senate can wait," Stephen said. "Why don't you show Vanessa the paperweight in my office that once belonged to John F. Kennedy?"

Vanessa's eyes widened. "Really?"

Ryan took Vanessa's hand and led her inside the inner office. Anton, embarrassed by Maya's comment, wandered out into the hallway. Maya followed him to make sure he didn't run off somewhere.

Sandra pulled Stephen aside, out of earshot from Tess, who stared listlessly at her computer screen.

"I took Maya to Dauphine's last night."

"You were there? So was I," Stephen said, surprised.

"I know; we saw you."

"Why didn't you say hello?"

"We didn't want to interrupt. Things looked a little . . . tense between you and Deborah."

"Oh, that, it was nothing," he said, brushing it off.

"It looked like something. She threw wine in your face."

"Sometimes Deborah is, shall we say, a little melodramatic. Believe me, it was nothing serious, just a spat over something silly; I'm actually having trouble remembering what even started it."

Sandra did not believe him.

She had become an expert on reading his face over the years and the glassy-eyed look in his eyes was always a telltale sign that he was not being totally honest, that there was plenty more simmering underneath the surface.

But she was not going to call him out.

Not today.

Probably not ever.

Because in a very short period of time, they would be officially divorced and whatever secrets he was hiding would no longer be any of her business.

But she knew something was going on between him and his new girlfriend and, despite his protestations, it was most definitely dead serious.

Chapter 11

Preston came flying back into the office. He nervously tapped his foot and glanced at his watch. "Stephen, we really need to get going."

"Right, sorry, it was great seeing you all," Stephen said, grabbing the back of Ryan's head and pulling him in for another hug. "Vanessa, if Romeo here gives you any guff, you know where to find me to set him straight."

Vanessa giggled. "Oh, don't worry, I will keep him in line."

Stephen gave her a playful wink and then shot a hand out toward Maya. "Nice to see you again, Maya. I have to say, I've never seen Sandra so happy since she started working with you."

"That's sweet of you to say," Maya said, although her tight smile revealed a distinct guardedness.

He then spun around to Sandra. "We're out of session next week; I was thinking of flying up to

Maine, spending time with you all, if you're not too busy."

"We'll talk," Sandra said, not quite ready to commit.

He moved in for an awkward hug and another chaste peck on Sandra's cheek.

Preston hovered in the doorway, panic now rising in his voice. "Stephen . . ."

"Yes, Mr. Taskmaster, let's go; do you have my speech?" Stephen sighed, rushing out the door.

Preston snapped his eyes toward Tess.

"I emailed it to him, it's on his iPad, and I'm printing out a hard copy now," Tess grumbled. "I'm coming right behind you."

"Okay, well, hurry up," Preston growled as he shot down the hall after Stephen.

Maya held up her phone. "Fern's been texting. She wants to do a head count and she wants everyone by the bus in ten minutes."

"You go on ahead," Sandra said. "I will meet you there."

"Fine, let's move out," Maya said, ushering Ryan and Vanessa out the door. Anton hung back, trying to work up the nerve to say goodbye to Tess, who was busy collating the printed pages of Stephen's speech and didn't even notice him.

"Now, Anton," Maya warned.

Anton glared at her, embarrassed to be bossed around within earshot of his obvious new object of desire, then stalked out of the office.

Completely oblivious, Tess stuffed the pages into a manila folder and scurried out to catch up with Stephen and Preston, leaving Suzanne and Sandra alone.

"And once again I'm left behind to answer the phones," Suzanne lamented. "I somehow thought at this point I'd be a lot closer to my goal of becoming a Pulitzer Prize–winning *Washington Post* reporter."

"I didn't know you wanted to be a journalist. I pictured you running for office. I have been counting on voting for you to be President."

Suzanne laughed derisively. "Maybe when I first moved here I had these grandiose notions of getting into politics, but up close, seeing how the sausage is really made, it kind of turned me off. I'd rather be the one holding the dirty and corrupt politicians accountable."

"Well, if anyone can do it, you can. I would bet on it."

"Thanks for the vote of confidence, Sandra. I wish my parents believed in me as much as you do."

"I always knew you'd make something of yourself from the day Stephen hired you; I could tell right away you were smart, focused, full of energy and spirit."

"I wouldn't even recognize that girl now," Suzanne said solemnly. "Washington has a way of beating every ounce of idealism out of you. I look at Tess, and I see how much she's changed since she got here just a few months ago."

"She strikes me as a not very happy girl."

"She's not. I mean, she was. In the beginning. It's kind of all my fault."

Sandra furrowed her eyebrows. "How do you mean?"

"I knew Tess in college. We weren't close or anything, but we took some of the same poli-sci classes and she seemed really bright and ambitious, and so when Stephen mentioned he wanted to add another intern, I emailed her through the alumni directory, and suggested she apply. When she got the job, I was thrilled. I thought we'd become best buds, that we could embark on this exciting path to power and prestige together, both have huge political careers, but it didn't work out that way. She hates it here. I get the feeling she just wants to leave. I let her crash in my spare room until she found a more permanent place, but she's still there, like she's trying to avoid signing a year lease on her own apartment. Any day I expect her to pack up and just go home."

"What do you suppose is wrong? Does Stephen give her a hard time?"

"No, he's actually really nice to her. Preston treats her like a peon sometimes, but he's not abusive. He knows I will call him out."

"Is it the work itself?"

Suzanne shook her head. "No, it's more personal than that. Early on I invited her out for drinks because I noticed her attitude had started to change. I wanted to know if she was having trouble adjusting, if there was something I could do to help her acclimate better. She clammed up at first, but after a few cosmos she loosened her lips enough to tell me that she was having guy trouble."

"Was she going through a breakup?"

"No, nothing like that. Apparently a man asked her out on a date, and she accepted, but there was no chemistry and she didn't want to encourage him, so she told him she wasn't interested in pursuing anything with him. Well, I guess that set him off and he started calling and emailing her all the time. He wouldn't leave her alone."

"Who was it? Someone who works here in the building?"

Suzanne shrugged. "I pressed her, but she wouldn't say. She didn't want to cause any waves, somehow make it worse. So I'm sure it's someone we all know, a Congressman or a Senator, who knows?"

"That poor girl. If someone is harassing her, she needs to report it. Behavior like that cannot be tolerated," Sandra said, trying hard to keep her fury in check.

"I tried bringing it up again a few weeks ago, but she brushed off, and now she barely speaks to me. I just sit across from her day after day feeling awful because I invited her here and she just looks so miserable. And when we're home she just goes to her room and shuts the door."

"How would you feel if I mentioned this to Stephen when he comes home to Maine next week? I'm sure he would want to find a way to help her."

Suzanne's face tensed. "Yes, but please, promise me you won't say you heard all this from me."

"I promise."

"Thank you, Sandra."

They hugged and said their goodbyes and Sandra hurried back down the hall, heels clicking on the marble floors, where she ran into Maya hanging outside the Senate Chamber.

"Where are the kids?" Sandra asked.

"Back at the bus. Fern refused to do a full head

count until everyone was there, including chaperones! So I said I'd personally escort you back myself."

"Are you kidding me? We are adults; we don't need to be part of a head count."

"She's dead serious about not losing track of *anyone*." Maya snickered.

"I was just chatting with Suzanne. She told me something disturbing about that pretty intern Tess. Apparently she has a stalker and I am guessing it's someone in close proximity to her."

"In the office? That creepy guy Preston?"

"Oh, I doubt it. Preston's gay. Have you seen the googly-eyed way he pines after Stephen? No, I would bet it's someone higher up. The more power they have, the more willing they seem to be to indulge in bad behavior."

Maya nodded in agreement. "By the way, I overheard Stephen practicing his speech. I have to admit, the man is quite an impressive orator."

"Stephen's public speaking skills were never the problem in our marriage. He has a way with words that can make you believe anything," Sandra said wistfully before her face hardened slightly. "No, the problem was never his moving mouth; it was his wandering eye."

Chapter 12

Maya was crushed alongside Fern Wiggins and several students outside the Presidential Box of Ford's Theatre, just inches from the exact location where President Abraham Lincoln was shot by John Wilkes Booth with a single-shot Derringer on April 14, 1865. Fern explained to the students that Wilkes had jumped down to the stage after assassinating Lincoln and took off into the night before he was killed twelve days later while on the run. A couple of students were giggling and shoving each other in the back and got a sharp rebuke from Fern, who then haughtily cleared her throat and continued her well-rehearsed spiel. "Once we are finished here, we will be going across the street to the Peterson House where they carried Lincoln and there we will see the back bedroom where he died and the front parlor where Mary Todd Lincoln waited anxiously for news of her husband's condition." Sandra had already escorted a group of students down to the museum where they could see Lincoln's bloodstained overcoat and the pistol that Booth used to shoot the President.

As Fern pushed her way through the small crowd of students and back down the stairs to look at the stage where the theatre company was performing the comedy *Our American Cousin* when the assassination occurred, the kids' chattering as they pounded down the steps grew exponentially in volume, and Maya could see Fern's face start to flush with anger.

"Keep it down! This is a historic landmark! Show some respect!" Fern snapped.

Maya could tell Fern was at her wit's end.

The kids were not even being that loud.

"They're just excited to be here," Maya quietly remarked, then gently added, "You know, you're allowed to have fun too, Fern."

Fern stared icily at Maya. "I am the one responsible for all these kids. If anything goes wrong, it's on me, and quite frankly, I did not expect them all to be so unruly."

Maya glanced around at her charges. Other than a few on their phones texting and some others gossiping with one another, the majority were docilely following behind their chaperones, actually looking interested in the history they were learning about. "I don't think they're misbehaving that badly, so come on, relax a little."

"I will relax after the last head count and I know that everyone is safely back in their rooms at the hotel."

Maya gave up trying because Fern had no intention of calming down.

When they arrived at the museum, Maya spotted Coach Cavill talking to Sandra as her assigned group wandered around examining all the artifacts in glass cases. Ryan and Vanessa were flipping through a hardcover Lincoln biography. Fern turned to the kids she was herding into the room. "Okay, five minutes to look around, and then it's straight back to the bus, do you hear me?"

Nobody bothered answering her.

Maya approached Sandra and Coach Cavill in time to overhear Sandra speaking firmly. "No, I'm sorry, no."

Coach Cavill looked wounded, then shrugged, muttered an apology, and scooted off.

Maya walked up to Sandra. "What was all that about?"

"I am just getting a little tired of him constantly trying to coerce me into going out on a date with him."

Maya observed Coach Cavill chatting with a couple of boys staring at the Derringer behind glass. "Well, he's so cute and adorable, he's probably not used to having women completely shut him down."

"I regret bruising his fragile ego, but how many times do I have to say no before it becomes harassment?"

Coach Cavill glanced over with a frown, then quickly averted his eyes when he noticed Maya watching him.

"Don't worry, I think he's finally gotten the message. Although I must say, Sandra, I'm not sure why you're being so stringent. He's a nice guy; maybe he deserves to be given a chance. I mean, you have to admit, he's quite the looker, don't you agree?"

"Yes, he's definitely handsome."

"And charming."

"I suppose."

"And funny, I mean he's quick with a quip, he had us laughing on the bus all the way down here, and the kids love him."

Sandra nodded in agreement.

"So what's the problem?"

"There is no problem. I'm just not interested. Okay?"

Maya nodded. "Okay."

There was certainly more to it than that.

Maya suspected after Sandra's budding relationship with the tech billionaire that went south last year only months after her separation from Stephen, Sandra had put a moratorium on dating anyone. But surely after a year she was ready. Perhaps she was just waiting for her divorce from the Senator to be officially final. Maya never liked playing matchmaker, but in her mind Sandra and Lucas Cavill seemed to go really well together.

Fern Wiggins's grating voice, like fingernails down a chalkboard, snapped her out of her own thoughts. "Line up, let's go, back to the bus, this way, everyone!"

Maya followed behind Sandra as they brought up the rear, making sure all the kids were out of the museum and heading outside where Clancy had parked the bus. After one last check for any stragglers and thanking the museum staff for a fun and informative visit, Maya and Sandra headed outside where Fern clutched her clipboard and was presently halfway through her head count. Ryan and Vanessa were the last two left who had not already boarded the bus. Maya noticed Fern's brow furrowing. She was clearly disturbed by something.

"What's wrong, Fern?"

Fern shot her index finger up for silence so she could concentrate, her beady eyes fixed on the paper attached to the clipboard. She counted once, twice, three times. Then, she looked up, horrified. "I'm one short!"

"What? That's impossible," Maya said. "Maybe you miscounted."

"I did *not* miscount! One of the students is not here!" Fern cried, her face now pale and distraught, on the verge of a category five meltdown.

"Well, who is it? Who's missing?"

Ryan and Vanessa looked at each other nervously; then Ryan ran up the steps into the yellow school bus where Clancy was casually reading a Stephen King novel behind the wheel. A moment later, Ryan returned. "It's Anton. He's not on the bus."

Anton.

The Russian exchange student was MIA.

Maya groaned. "When did you last see him?"

Ryan concentrated. "He was with us at lunch, but I don't remember seeing him after that."

Fern gasped, then ran onto the bus, falling on the first step and scraping her knee, but that didn't slow her down. They could hear her yelling inside the bus, "Has anyone seen Anton while we've been here at the Ford Theatre?" There was some unintelligible murmuring before Fern stumbled back out. "Nobody has seen him; he's been AWOL for hours!"

Maya put a firm hand on Fern's shaky elbow to steady her and be close by if she suddenly collapsed from the stress.

Chapter 13

Fern stood outside Ford's Theatre, trembling, but firm in her belief that Anton had been with the group when they first arrived. "I did a head count as the students filed off the bus, and I know I had the correct number."

"Could you have possibly miscounted?" Sandra asked gently.

Fern's eyes blazed. "No, Sandra, I do not miscount. I am meticulous about my head counts!"

No one was about to argue her point.

"Okay, then maybe he's still inside somewhere. We should do another sweep before they close," Maya suggested.

"All right, I'll come with you," Fern sighed. "Sandra, you and Lucas go with the kids back to the hotel. I made a six-thirty reservation at the restaurant. I will feel a lot better once I know the kids are back in their rooms for the night with full bellies."

Sandra nodded, clearly uncomfortable with being paired with Lucas, but she wisely chose not to challenge Fern's instructions, especially in her delicate state.

Coach Cavill let Sandra board the bus first and then followed; the swinging doors of the school bus closed and Clancy slowly drove away, nearly clipping a parked motorcycle as he pulled away from the curb.

Maya and Fern split up, Fern heading across the street to the Peterson House to make sure Anton had not gone there and Maya returning to the theatre to scour every inch for any sign of him backstage and up in the balcony. Twenty minutes later they reconvened back outside, having turned up nothing.

Maya requested a Lyft on her phone to drive them back to the hotel. Fern stared restlessly out the window the whole ride, collecting her thoughts, planning her next move to deal with this unexpected crisis.

"Are you going to call his host parents?" Maya asked.

"I have no choice. I have to let them know that he's missing," Fern said solemnly. "I had a sinking feeling ever since we left Portland that something like this was going to happen. I never should have tried to do this. It's just too much for me to handle."

"Fern, don't beat yourself up. We're going to find him. And there are twenty-four other kids on this trip who are reasonably well behaved and having a truly memorable experience. Watching them soak up all this history, their enthusiasm, it's downright infectious. Even I'm having a good time, and we all know how hard I am to please!"

Fern gave her a grateful smile.

She desperately needed this pep talk.

The Lyft dropped them off at the hotel, and Maya and Fern immediately took the elevator up to Maya and Sandra's room, where Sandra reported that all the students had been fed and were now tucked away in their rooms.

Unfortunately, there was still no sign of Anton.

Fern couldn't help herself. "Did you do a final head count?"

"Twice," Sandra said softly.

Fern grimaced in the open doorway, tortured. "Well, I suppose I should go to my room now and call the Kablers and tell them the exchange student they took in from Russia for the school year has mysteriously vanished . . . under my watch."

Maya wanted to give it a little more time, hoping he might turn up, but she knew Fern would never agree. Fern needed to let Anton's host parents know what was going on, and so she kept mum.

Suddenly the elevator bell rang at the other end of the hall, the doors slid open, and Coach Cavill came out, gripping a tense-looking Anton forcefully by the arm. He hustled him down the hall toward a slack-jawed Fern, who stood between Maya and Sandra.

"Look what I caught sneaking back into the lobby downstairs!" Cavill shouted.

Anton kept his eyes glued to the rug, refusing to make eye contact with anyone.

"Anton, what happened to you? Where did you go?" Fern sputtered, shocked and angry at the same time.

He shrugged. "Nowhere."

Maya cocked an eyebrow. "Wow, is that your strategy? No explanation, nothing? I would play it a little differently myself, maybe get down on my knees and beg for forgiveness after scaring everyone half to death."

Anton raised his eyes and studied Maya warily. He was a lot more intimidated by her than Fern, and so he offered up a weak, "Sorry."

"Still not cutting it!" Maya snapped. "You owe us a little more than that."

Anton knew he had to cough up more, so he muttered under his breath, "I just wanted to see some sights on my own."

Maya and Sandra exchanged a quick glance.

Neither one of them was buying it.

He was acting strangely.

Where had he gone?

What was the big secret?

And why was he acting so suspicious?

"Well, I hope you saw everything you wanted to because that was your last opportunity to see anything other than the walls of your hotel room," Fern growled. "You are to go to your room right now, and stay there for the remainder of this trip."

Maya half expected him to argue, but he didn't.

He just nodded and started to shuffle off down the hall.

Coach Cavill turned to Fern. "I'll go make sure he gets there and stays there."

"Thank you, Lucas," Fern said, still furious.

"Night, ladies," Cavill said, smiling at Maya but too embarrassed to glance quickly at Sandra. He hurried off to stay close on Anton's heels.

Halfway down the hall, Anton abruptly stopped and spun around. "Please don't call Bob and Susan and tell them what happened."

Bob and Susan Kabler, Anton's host parents.

A sweet retired couple who never had any children of their own and so were happy to open their home to foreign exchange students.

"I will be good from now on, I promise; I won't break any more rules," Anton added in a lame attempt for leniency. "They are so nice, I do not want to stress them out."

"You should have thought about that before you took off without anyone's permission!" Fern snapped, then paused. "But I will think about it."

That was as good as he was going to get.

Coach Cavill cuffed him by the neck with his hand to keep him moving down the hall. "Let's go, champ."

Sandra turned to Fern. "What do you think you'll do?"

"I'm not sure yet. He needs to be punished. But maybe it can wait until we get home. Let's just get through this trip first. But don't tell Anton. I prefer holding the threat of calling the Kablers over his head in order to keep him in line."

"Good plan," Maya agreed.

"I'm going to bed; I'm exhausted," Fern whined. "Good night."

"Night, Fern," Maya said as she followed Sandra back into the room they were sharing, her mind racing. She was burning with curiosity to know where Anton disappeared to and why.

Chapter 14

"You tried taking the bus through the McDonald's drive-thru?" Maya asked Clancy incredulously.

"Yup, who knew there was a height limit?" Clancy shrugged as he handed out Egg McMuffins and hash browns to the students boarding the school bus for today's sightseeing tour.

"Um, everybody?" Maya remarked.

Clancy chuckled. "I almost made it, but the clearance bar was a little too low and I scraped the hell out of the roof of the bus. But I'm not too worried. It's not like the school board is going to grab a ladder and inspect the top of the bus. Nobody's ever going to know." He glanced at Maya and Sandra suspiciously. "Unless you tell 'em, of course."

"Our lips are sealed, Clancy," Sandra assured him, working hard to refrain from adding her prayers that he just get them home in one piece.

"After the manager got tired of yelling in my face for chipping the paint on that clearance bar, I just went inside and stood in line to give 'em my order," Clancy explained. "You should have seen the eye rolls I got when I asked for thirty-five Egg McMuffins."

When the last of the students had grabbed their breakfast and were on the bus, Clancy hustled up the steps and plopped himself down in the driver's seat. "Let's hit the road!"

"Hold on," Maya said. "We're still waiting on Fern. I think she's giving Anton another warning about not leaving his room for any reason while we're out."

"She found a way to track his phone," Coach Cavill said, passing them and hopping on the bus. "Kids feel naked without their phones, so it's a safe bet he's not going anywhere today."

Sandra's own phone buzzed and she glanced at the screen.

It was Stephen's staffer Suzanne.

She answered, "Good morning, Suzanne."

"Sandra, I'm so sorry to bother you . . ."

"No, please, don't worry about it. What's up?"

"I have been trying to reach Stephen, but he's not answering my calls or texts. He's been at the Capitol all night waiting to vote on that legislation, and from what I can see on C-SPAN, both parties are still debating it with Stephen front and center."

"What's wrong?"

"I'm worried about Tess. She didn't come home last night."

Sandra's stomach flip-flopped.

"Even though she keeps to herself most of the

time, she always texts me if she's going to be late coming home, but last night she didn't, and she never showed. I didn't think much of it until this morning when I got up. She's usually up ahead of me and has the coffee brewing before I drag myself out of bed, but this morning, nothing. There was no sign of her and her bed looks like it hasn't been slept in."

"When was the last time you saw her?"

"At work last night. I was meeting some friends at a bar for drinks and I invited her along, but she said she had to deliver some papers to Stephen's apartment. He prefers hard copies of his reading material. She said she would see me at home later. After that, nothing. She never made it."

Sandra felt a twinge of dread in her gut.

"Okay, I'm not too far from Stephen's condo. I'll go check it out, see if she ever dropped off the paperwork. You keep trying Stephen. He probably turned his phone off while he's on the Senate floor. He's the only politician I know who does that!"

"Thank you, Sandra."

She ended the call.

Maya noticed the worry lines on Sandra's forehead. "Whatever it is, it doesn't sound good."

"I have a bad feeling," Sandra said to herself.

Fern rushed out of the revolving door of the hotel. "Okay, we need to get moving; we are already twenty minutes behind schedule. Where's my Egg McMuffin?"

Sandra stopped her. "You go on ahead. I will catch up with you later."

Fern's eyes popped out. "What? Why?"

"It's a personal matter. Go, I'll meet you at the Smithsonian."

Before Fern could object, Sandra spun around and asked one of the hotel bellhops to hail her a cab. Maya followed close on her heels. "I'm coming with you."

Sandra was actually relieved.

The cab took seven minutes to reach the upscale seven-story building in a leafy, quiet neighborhood off the beaten path of the hectic city avenues. Maya and Sandra jumped out and hurried into the lobby where they were greeted by a friendly African-American doorman with a beatific smile and sweet demeanor. He wore a crisp gray uniform with red trim.

"Well, look who it is, so nice to see you again, Mrs. Wallage."

"Lovely to see you, Cliff," Sandra said.

"If you're here to see your husband, I don't think he's home. I've been on duty all night and haven't seen him come in."

"He's working. I just have to check on something."

"Sure thing, you need me to let you in?"

Sandra rummaged through her purse. "No, I believe I still have my key." She plucked it out and held it up.

"Go on up then," Cliff said, nodding at them as he pressed a button behind his desk to unlock the elevator.

"Thank you, Cliff," Sandra said, scurrying to the elevator before stopping and turning around to the doorman. "Cliff, you mentioned you were here all night?"

"Yes, working a double shift. Andy, who usually takes over for me at midnight, is at the hospital. His wife is having twins."

"Did anyone from Stephen's office show up here to drop something off?" Sandra asked.

"No, not that I recall. It was a pretty quiet night. But I do my rounds every couple of hours, so if anyone had their own key, or if someone up there buzzed them in while I was away from my desk, I might have missed them."

"Okay, thanks," Sandra said as she and Maya boarded the elevator and rode it up to the top floor.

"It sounds like she never made it here," Maya said.

"We still better make sure."

They stepped off the elevator and dashed down the hall to the corner unit. Sandra inserted her key and cautiously opened the door. There was an eerie foreboding stillness as they entered.

Sandra spotted a half-eaten sandwich on the kitchen table. "Someone was here last night. Stephen's too anal retentive to not wash the plate when he's done eating."

"Sandra, look," Maya said, directing her attention to a manila envelope sitting on top of the built-in bar adjacent to the living room.

Sandra walked over, picked up the envelope, and unsealed it. She pulled out some papers and quickly perused them. "It looks like the reading material Suzanne said Tess was going to bring over here for Stephen."

"Then she *was* here," Maya said.

Sandra had a sinking feeling. Without saying another word, she marched past Maya to the master bedroom, stopping suddenly in the doorway, gasping in shock, throwing a hand to her mouth. Maya rushed to her and stopped short as well in the doorway.

The two women gaped, horrified, at Tess's body lying on top of the king-size bed.

Sandra instantly noticed a small pill vial tipped over next to a nearly full twelve-ounce bottle of water on the nightstand. A few of the pills were scattered on the rug. Otherwise, the vial appeared empty.

It looked as if Tess might have swallowed most of them.

Maya hurried over and grabbed Tess's limp wrist, desperately feeling for a pulse.

Sandra stood frozen.

The wait was excruciating.

Finally, Maya looked up at Sandra, her face stricken. "She's dead."

Chapter 15

Sandra quickly grabbed for her phone to dial 911. Adrenaline coursed through her entire body, throbbing in her veins as Maya slowly stepped away from the corpse and began searching the bedroom for any clues. Within minutes, they could hear sirens approaching. Sandra used the intercom by the front door to call down to Cliff at the reception desk and alert him to what was happening, and instructed him to let the officers up to Stephen's apartment just as soon as they arrived.

When Sandra returned to the bedroom, Maya was kneeling next to the nightstand, examining the empty vial, being very careful not to touch anything.

"Sleeping pills, prescribed to Tess. This is starting to look like a suicide," Maya said solemnly.

She then stood back up and walked back over to the bed, staring down at the young woman's body lying faceup, studying it intently.

Sandra watched her. "What? Did you find something?"

Maya didn't answer. She leaned over, eyes fixed on Tess's lower neck.

Suddenly there was a loud banging at the front door, someone yelling, "Police! Open up!" Sandra rushed to let them in. Seconds later, officers were swarming throughout the condo, pushing Maya out of the way to assess the situation. Maya and Sandra were both escorted to the living room and told to sit down on the couch until the detectives arrived. Sandra quickly concluded that the cops already knew these were highly sensitive circumstances given who the apartment belonged to; someone in the department must have known a powerful US Senator lived here.

A heavyset grizzled detective in his late fifties with waxen jowls who appeared to have stepped right out of the pages of an old Dashiell Hammett novel ambled in, conferred with two officers, then settled his beady eyes on Maya and Sandra as he wiped the sweat off his brow with a white handkerchief before stuffing it back into his jacket pocket. He then strode over and squeezed himself into an armchair across from them.

"I'm Detective Lonsdale. So you two discovered the body?" he asked, new beads of sweat forming on his brow.

"Yes," Sandra answered.

"What were you doing here?"

Sandra calmly explained the call of concern she received from Tess's roommate, Suzanne, how she still had her own key to the condo even though she and Stephen were separated, and how she and

Maya had stumbled across the body in the bedroom.

Lonsdale took it all in and then glanced at Maya. "And you are?"

"A friend," Maya said in a clipped tone.

"Whose friend? Hers?" Lonsdale asked brusquely, pointing in Sandra's direction.

"Yes. I did not know the victim, if that's what you want to know," Maya sighed. "I was just tagging along."

Sandra could tell Maya was no fan of Detective Lonsdale.

Maya had purposefully omitted the fact that she and Sandra were themselves private detectives. It did not seem pertinent to the investigation at this juncture.

The detective nodded, his jowls jiggling. He reached for his handkerchief again to sop up more sweat from his face. "Does this place have air conditioning? It's hot as Hades in here!"

"On it, Detective!" a junior officer called out before looping around the condo in search of a thermostat.

"It's on the wall next to the bathroom in the hallway!" Sandra yelled.

"Thank you!" the young officer responded, and seconds later a blast of cold air was blowing out of the vents, much to the relief of the discomfited Detective Lonsdale.

He peppered them with a litany of questions.

Why were they in DC.

Any previous encounters with the victim.

Where was Stephen?

And then, the one they had been waiting for.

What did they do for a living?

Maya knew things were about to get a whole lot more complicated, but she had no choice but to answer the detective's question. She opened her mouth to speak when suddenly the young officer who had trotted off in search of the thermostat popped his head back in the living room. "Senator Wallage is here."

"Sit tight," Lonsdale said to Maya and Sandra. "I will be right back."

He hauled himself up out of the chair and shambled over to the front door to the condo where Stephen stood just inside. Sandra had a clear view of him. He was visibly shaken, his face pale, eyes bloodshot and tired. Suzanne must have finally been able to reach him at the Capitol Building and informed him of what was happening and he had immediately rushed home.

As Detective Lonsdale explained what was going on, Sandra could see tears pooling in Stephen's eyes as he learned of poor Tess's fate. He stared at the detective, listening intently, and then, caught off guard, cried, "She was found in my bed? By whom?"

Lonsdale pointed a pudgy finger over at Maya and Sandra sitting together on the couch in the living area. Stephen blew past him and a couple of officers and bounded over to them.

"Sandra, what the hell is going on?"

Sandra shot up and hugged him. "I'm so sorry, Stephen. Suzanne couldn't reach you, so she called me, and I still had a key, so I didn't think you would mind if we came over to see if she was here . . ."

"Oh my God!" Stephen wailed. "Why would she take her own life . . . in my bedroom?"

Lonsdale placed a hand on Stephen's arm. "I would like to ask you a few questions, if I may, Senator Wallage?"

"Of course," Stephen whispered, still in a state of shock at all the pandemonium around him in his own home.

Lonsdale zeroed in on Maya. "Don't go anywhere, ladies. I'm not through with you yet."

Sandra caught Maya rolling her eyes and whispered in her ear, "He's just doing his job."

"I know, but it's the patronizing tone I cannot get past," Maya muttered, sitting back defiantly and crossing her legs.

Sandra watched Detective Lonsdale lead Stephen over to the kitchen table, where they both sat down and started talking. Stephen rubbed his eyes incessantly, nodding occasionally, answering the detective's questions. She surmised by the suspicious look on Lonsdale's face that he was having trouble with some of Stephen's statements. Stephen was usually a master at maintaining control, keeping a lid on his emotions, doing what he had to in order to solve an urgent problem. But this tragedy had walloped him. He appeared confused and unfocused, utterly despondent. Who could blame him? One of his employees had possibly killed herself, not only in his own home, but in his own bedroom. If she had done so intentionally, was she going for some kind of symbolic statement? Sandra was not sure she even wanted to know. And by the look on Detective Lonsdale's face, he was thinking the exact same thing.

Sandra analyzed her husband's body language.

She knew him well enough to know he was spiraling, an emotional mess at the moment. She glanced at a couple of police officers hovering nearby, listening, both of them with skeptical looks on their faces as they eavesdropped on Lonsdale and Stephen's conversation. They weren't buying a word of what he was saying.

And Sandra feared that could spell a whole lot of trouble for poor Stephen.

A few minutes later, Stephen's aide Preston arrived, pushing his way through the front door as the junior officer tried to stop him. "Excuse me, I work for the Senator; I demand you let me through."

Stephen stood up from the kitchen table. "Please, let him in."

The officer relented, and Preston plowed his way into the kitchen and to his boss's side, his irritating voice loud enough for everyone in the condo to hear.

"There's already a gaggle of press outside blocking street access. They nearly trampled me when I arrived, but I refused to make a statement. We need to get ahead of this, Stephen. Tell me everything so I can figure out how to spin this!"

"Not now, Preston. She's dead. Tess is dead!" Stephen cried, grief-stricken.

"Yes, I know; it's all over the news," Preston lamented. He turned to a group of officers huddled together and yelled, pointedly, "Somebody already tipped off the press!" He then turned back to Stephen. "What was she even doing here?"

"She was dropping off papers, or so I'm told," Stephen said, his voice cracking. "I just don't understand . . ."

He broke down in tears and had to sit back down. Preston recoiled, apparently not used to outward displays of human emotions.

Sandra turned to Maya and whispered softly, "Go ahead. I know you want to ask me."

Maya sat upright. "Ask you what?"

"If I think Stephen's being insincere."

Maya glanced around to make sure none of the police officers were within earshot. "The thought did cross my mind given his history, but I did not want to upset you."

"I'm worried . . ."

"Worried he's not being completely truthful?"

"I hate not trusting him, but I can't ignore the pattern, the long, long pattern."

"So you think it's possible he was romantically involved with Tess, which may have been what caused the rift with Deborah at the restaurant the other night?"

Sandra paused, considering all the evidence. An officer passed by and so she waited a few seconds before continuing. "It pains me to say this, but it's not just possible; it's probable, based on my own experiences."

She looked over at Stephen again. He was hunched over at the kitchen table, hands covering his face as Preston savagely tapped a text or tweet on his phone.

If the worst-case scenario was true, and Tess was

more to Stephen than just a hardworking intern, and Deborah somehow found out about it and demanded he end it, what if he had just broken up with her? If she took it hard and was distraught and fragile, then overdosing in Stephen's bed would certainly send a clear message.

A message that would end Stephen's life as he knew it.

Chapter 16

When Lonsdale finally finished questioning him, Stephen rose and, on wobbly feet, made his way over to the bar to pour himself a bourbon, desperate to take the edge off. Sandra joined him, mostly to keep an eye on him. She had told Maya that when Stephen was under too much stress he had a troubling habit of trying to fix it with too many shots of liquor.

Maya watched Lonsdale conferring with a couple of the officers, before wandering back over to where the paramedics were carefully lifting the body up on a stretcher. Maya hustled over to him and tapped him on the shoulder. "Excuse me, Detective Lonsdale?"

He turned toward her, irritated, as if she were a tiny gnat buzzing around his face that he wanted to swat away with a brush of his hand. "What?"

Maya took a deep breath. "I just wanted to know

if you noticed the odd bruising on the victim's neck?"

He stared at her stupidly, scratching the stubble on the side of his face. "What are you talking about?"

Apparently he had not.

So Maya plowed ahead.

He had to know.

It was a significant clue.

"When we were waiting for the police to arrive after calling 911, I had the opportunity to examine the body . . ."

His eyes flared up.

Maya held up her hand. "I did not touch it or disturb it in any way; I just happened to see contusions around the neck, which might suggest some kind of an assault."

"Just who the hell are you?" he barked.

"Maya Kendrick."

"Yeah, I got that; I jotted down your name when I questioned you. Are you a cop or something?"

"Something. Detective."

"Homicide?"

"Private."

Lonsdale rolled his eyes. "Oh, God, not another one of those."

"Not a fan of private eyes?"

"Anyone with an internet connection fancies themselves as detectives nowadays, or at least hosts their own podcast; mostly they just get in the way, in my opinion."

"I am licensed in the state of Maine," Maya said evenly.

"Good for you. I got a fishing license in Maryland; that doesn't make me Captain Ahab."

"Charming," Maya spit out with a forced smile. "I also worked fifteen years as a police officer, so I have been around a few crime scenes—"

"Let me stop you right there! You are way out of your jurisdiction, so any idea you've got about helping me out or teaming up is not going to fly, you hear me?"

"Trust me, I have zero interest in teaming up with you; I just wanted to make sure you are aware of what I saw."

He scribbled on his notepad something illegible. "And here I am writing it down. So duly noted, *Detective.*" He sneered at her, his words dripping with condescension and sarcasm. "But in my humble opinion, this is not a crime scene. This looks more to me like the sad tragedy of a troubled young woman taking her own life, so since you're not in Maine and you're in DC, I would appreciate you keeping your opinions to yourself."

"Fine," Maya seethed.

Lonsdale sighed loudly and walked back over to the female officer now guarding the door in case anyone tried to bolt without his explicit permission.

The paramedics wheeled Tess's body strapped to the stretcher and covered with a white sheet past Maya. One corner of the sheet was dragging across the floor, so Maya stuck out her foot and stepped on it. The whole sheet slid off the stretcher, uncovering Tess, whose eyes had been shut, the bruising on her neck purplish and very noticeable.

Lee Hollis

As one of the paramedics bent down to scoop up the white sheet, Maya seized the moment before he had the chance to cover her back up again.

"Huh, did anyone else notice the bruising on her neck?" Maya asked loudly, pointing.

Both paramedics studied the body, as did a nearby officer, who nodded as he stared at the obvious marks.

She had done it.

At least enough people knew about the bruising now so Detective Lonsdale would have to take it into consideration during any investigation.

She glanced over at the now red-faced Lonsdale, steam practically coming out of his ears. He barked something at the female officer and she hustled over and took Maya firmly by the arm. "You're free to go, so I suggest you leave now."

"I'm still waiting on my friend," Maya explained, gesturing toward Sandra, who was still consoling Stephen at the bar.

"Then you can wait downstairs; we need to clear the premises," the officer said rigidly, squeezing Maya's arm tighter.

As she was escorted out, Maya called back, "Good luck with your investigation, Detective Lonsdale!"

He did not bother responding.

The moment she crossed the threshold and was out in the hallway, the door slammed loudly behind her.

Chapter 17

Maya and Sandra had barely been back in their room at the hotel for five minutes when there was a loud banging on the door. Sandra opened it to find Ryan, spooked and dismayed, standing there next to Vanessa, who had a comforting hand on his arm.

"Mom, tell me what's going on," Ryan said tremulously. "It's all over the news. Are they going to arrest Dad?"

"What? No! Come in here," Sandra ordered, pulling them both inside the room and shutting the door.

"I'm calling an Uber. I need to be with Dad now," Ryan said, frantically tapping the screen of his phone.

"Ryan, slow down," Sandra demanded. "We just came from your dad's condo. He is still with the police. You will just be in the way. Let's wait a little bit until things calm down."

"He needs to get ahead of this. They're already speculating on the news that he's somehow involved with what happened to that poor girl!" Ryan cried.

Vanessa turned to her mother. "So that girl, Tess, they were saying on TV that the police believe she committed suicide. Is that true?"

"Maybe," Maya answered.

Sandra shot her a look.

Ryan rushed over to Maya. "*Maybe?* Why maybe? What do you know?"

"Nothing definitive," Maya said.

Sandra sighed. "Maya, please . . ."

"I think they're old enough to hear this," Maya said sharply.

Sandra knew she was right and so she stepped back and did not try to argue with her anymore.

"I don't speak for your mother, Ryan, but frankly, I am convinced there is more to this story than a depressed young woman taking her own life by swallowing a bottle of sleeping pills."

"You think someone *killed* her? In Dad's condo?" Ryan gasped.

Vanessa, wide-eyed, gaped at her mother. "Why would you think that?"

Maya recounted the bruising she had noticed on Tess's neck as Ryan and Vanessa listened with rapt attention.

Ryan spun around to Sandra. "Someone's trying to frame Dad for murder!"

"We don't know that yet, Ryan, okay? Let's just give the police a chance to investigate first," Sandra warned.

"But why else would they lure her to Dad's condo? He's got a lot of political enemies who would like to see him go down!"

"There might be another reason besides murder that would explain the contusions on her neck," Sandra said.

Vanessa folded her arms. "Mom's never wrong about these things. Remember the case that first brought you two together back home in Portland? Same thing, as I remember. Bruising on the neck. And she was right about that! It was murder!"

Sandra threw her arms up in the air. "I give up!"

Ryan crossed over to his mother and put an arm around her shoulders. "Look, Mom, we can't leave Dad twisting in the wind as he's convicted in the court of public opinion. We should go to him now, circle the wagons, as a family, to show our unwavering support and belief in his innocence."

Sandra stared at her son, flabbergasted.

He was in full damage control mode.

Like a highly paid crisis manager.

And he was only seventeen.

Like father like son, she supposed.

Sandra hesitated.

"Mom, please, listen to me; we have to bust a move before it gets worse," Ryan pleaded.

"It already is," Vanessa muttered, eyes fixed on her phone.

Sandra's stomach knotted. "Why? What's happened?"

"Zoe Rush," Vanessa whispered.

Sandra was familiar with the name Zoe Rush.

She was a top-notch political reporter Sandra had known for years. A personal friend, in fact. Smart, intrepid, tenacious. She had started out at the *Portland Press Herald* in southern Maine but had recently moved to DC to start a new gig at the gossipy *Washington Insider*. Her column had quickly become a must read for the Beltway movers and shakers.

Vanessa slowly handed the phone to Sandra.

Sandra stared numbly at the screen.

It was even worse than she had imagined.

There were news alerts popping up from every major publication. The *New York Times*. The *Washington Post*. *USA Today*. Even the BBC in the UK, all linking to a freshly posted article on the *Washington Insider* website by Zoe Rush, breathlessly offering up proof that there was more going on between Senator Stephen Wallage and the pretty young intern who had just been found dead in his king-size bed.

There were photos.

Lots of photos.

Stephen and Tess having a quiet, romantic, candlelit dinner at an out-of-the-way DC restaurant. Snapped by a sharp-eyed paparazzo just a few nights before Tess's untimely death. One even captured Stephen touching her hand with his. Gazing into her eyes as she smiled at him longingly.

As Sandra scrolled through all the photos, one after the other, she slowly became sick to her stomach.

Zoe's breathless prose all but confirmed what everyone was already thinking, that Senator Wallage was conducting an inappropriate relationship with one of his interns.

There was just no way to spin this.

It was already achingly bad for the Senior Senator from Maine. And no strong show of support from his soon-to-be ex-wife and relentlessly devoted son would do much to help him now.

Chapter 18

Stephen opened the door a crack to his executive suite at the historic Hay-Adams Hotel in Downtown Washington, DC, to see who was at the door. A wave of relief washed over his face at the sight of Sandra.

"The Hay-Adams, Stephen? I thought you wanted to keep a low profile," Sandra said. "You couldn't have chosen a hideout that's a little more discreet?"

He opened the door and waved her inside. "I didn't have much of a choice. I know the manager and he was able to sneak me in through the kitchen of the Lafayette Room. They checked me in under an assumed name."

"Were you followed by the press from your condo?"

"It took three separate black Range Rovers leading them on a wild-goose chase all around DC before we managed to shake them off and get me over here undetected. But they have eyes and ears everywhere, so I'm basically stuck up here in this room."

A suitcase was open on the bed, carefully packed with an array of pressed dress shirts, slacks, and an assortment of colorful ties. A room service table had been delivered and there was a half-eaten Roasted Scottish Salmon and a few scattered brussels sprouts and asparagus on a pristine white plate. Stephen's phone was charging on top of a desk in the corner.

"How long do you plan on staying here?" Sandra asked.

"Indefinitely. I could not fathom staying at the condo after what happened there; it's too upsetting."

"What about work?"

"I've already been in contact with Senator Briggs to be my proxy vote if need be. I can't go to the Capitol right now; it'll just be a circus."

Senator Phil Briggs was a close friend of Stephen's who represented New Jersey. They had worked on countless bills together.

"This is a nightmare," Stephen moaned. "I have been sitting here watching cable news all morning. Half my colleagues from the opposing party are gleefully trashing me; the other half are dodging the cameras or yelling, 'No comment!' It doesn't look good."

"You need to call Ryan; he's very worried about you," Sandra said.

Stephen nodded solemnly. "Where is he now?"

"Touring the Smithsonian with the rest of his class. He just posted a selfie with Bill Clinton's saxophone on Instagram. He's keeping on a brave face, but I can tell he's rattled."

"This is all Zoe Rush's fault," Stephen hissed. "If she hadn't put those photos out there, I'd still have some kind of control over this scandal."

Sandra silently wished he had not used the word "scandal."

Because even if overblown by a rabid press, there usually was at the very least a modicum of truth to your typical Washington political scandal.

Stephen noticed Sandra's sour face instantly.

"It is not true what Zoe is implying, Sandra; I want you to know that."

"Okay," she responded tentatively.

"I'm serious. There was nothing sordid going on, despite what Zoe is implying in her column."

"She's doing a bit more than just implying, Stephen. And she's using those photos of you and Tess to bolster her case."

"My relationship with Tess was purely platonic!" Stephen bellowed forcefully, slamming his fist down on the room service cart, rattling the plates and saucers, startling Sandra enough that she took a step back.

Stephen quickly realized that losing his temper would do neither of them any good, so he softened his tone. "Look, I was simply mentoring her. She was having trouble adjusting and I took her under my wing and offered her some advice. That's all. We never, not once . . ." He could read the skepticism written all over Sandra's face. "I understand why you might doubt me given all that I've put you through over the years, but Sandra, you have to believe me, there was nothing physical between us, nothing, not even a kiss."

"Then why did she swallow a whole bottle of pills at your condo?"

Stephen shook his head. "I have no idea, honestly. I know it looks bad, but none of it makes any sense."

"I can only imagine what Deborah must be thinking," Sandra noted.

Stephen flicked his eyes guiltily in Sandra's direction.

It was obvious he had not thought about his girlfriend, Deborah Crowley, since this whole ordeal began.

Stephen heaved a sigh. "I'm not going to lie. Deborah was threatened by Tess. She was convinced Tess had a crush on me and it was making her uncomfortable."

"So that's what you two were fighting about at Dauphine's?"

Stephen nodded sheepishly. "It was becoming an issue. I was trying to explain to her she was being paranoid, but she wouldn't listen to reason; she just kept assuming the worst."

Stephen plopped down on the luxurious king-size bed and hunched over, rubbing his eyes with the palms of his hands. "Try as I might, I just could not convince her otherwise," he mumbled.

Can you blame her? Sandra thought to herself.

She wanted to say the quiet part out loud but wisely chose to keep mum.

He was too tortured, too unraveled, at the moment.

But Stephen could hardly be surprised by Deborah's reaction to his time spent with his comely young intern.

The fact was, in Sandra's mind, Deborah had every right to assume the worst-case scenario, especially given Stephen's checkered history. And it was common knowledge that most politicians did not hesitate to lie.

And Stephen, after all, was a world-class politician.

Chapter 19

After departing the Hay-Adams, Sandra texted Maya to have her meet her at Suzanne's apartment near Dupont Circle. When Sandra finally managed to book an Uber and get herself over there, Maya had beaten her to the tasteful, contemporary two-bedroom apartment on Pierce Street with deep cherry cabinetry, stainless-steel appliances, and frosted-glass accents. No doubt too steep for Suzanne to afford on her own, but manageable with a roommate. Sandra remembered Suzanne telling her recently that her roommate had left DC to return back home to California to work for the Governor in Sacramento, which would explain why Suzanne could take Tess in when she needed a temporary residence after arriving in town to work for Stephen.

Sandra found Maya already sitting at the round white table next to the kitchen when Suzanne welcomed her inside.

Sandra noted how tired Suzanne appeared. She had probably spent most of the night and day worrying about Tess. A flat-screen television on the wall in the living area was muted, but just from a quick glance at the screen Sandra could tell Suzanne had been watching CNN and its wall-to-wall coverage outside Stephen's condo building reporting every salacious rumor that was floating out there involving the Senator and his sadly deceased intern.

"Sorry it took so long; traffic was a nightmare as usual," Sandra explained.

"I just got here," Maya said. "I was asking Suzanne about Tess's family."

"I'm sorry, I wish I could be more help," Suzanne sighed, distressed. "But again, she's been living here the past three months, but we never really bonded. I do remember her mentioning back in college that she didn't speak to her parents. They have been estranged ever since she turned eighteen and could leave home to go to Penn on a full scholarship, so I have no idea how to get in touch with them, and there was an uncle and his husband she liked to visit on holidays, somewhere in the Pacific Northwest, maybe Spokane, I'm not sure."

"Don't worry, we will track them down," Maya assured her. "Suzanne, would you mind if I took a look in the spare room where Tess was staying?"

"No, of course, it's the room directly across from the bathroom, but I have to tell you, she didn't show up here with a lot of possessions. Just a small suitcase and a travel bag."

Maya stood up and scooted off.

Suzanne turned to Sandra. "Any useful contact information would probably be on her phone. The police must have found it on her."

Sandra shook her head. "No, I heard one of the officers mention that they could not locate it anywhere in the condo. Not on her person or the nightstand next to the bed, or in her bag."

"That's really odd. She wouldn't be caught dead without her phone," Suzanne bemoaned, then realized what she had just said. "I'm so sorry; that sounded like an awful joke." Her eyes pooled with tears.

Sandra gently rubbed her back. "It's okay, Suzanne; this is a lot to deal with."

Maya returned from the bedroom, frustrated. "You were right. Except for a few outfits and a makeup bag, it's like she wasn't even staying here."

"No phone?" Sandra asked.

Maya shook her head. "No iPad, no laptop."

"Tess did everything on her phone. She didn't have any other computer or device. At work, she'd use the office desktop."

The missing phone did not bode well for Stephen.

If her death was indeed a suicide, the phone almost certainly would have shown up at the scene.

Someone must have taken it.

Sandra's sense of dread just kept growing.

Suzanne took a deep breath. "I know this is not my place to say, Sandra, but . . ."

Sandra girded herself for what might be coming. "But what?"

"I can see the pained expression on your face, what you must be thinking, but let me tell you, I don't believe for one minute Stephen had anything to do with this."

Sandra gave her a tight smile. "Thank you."

"No, it's logical to have doubts and you're probably asking, 'Why should I listen to her? She's just a legislative assistant.'"

"Suzanne, I think you're the most rock-solid person in Stephen's orbit. I trust you completely," Sandra insisted.

"Good, because I have worked for the man for three years; I have put in a lot of hours, too many, which is probably why I don't have a boyfriend. But when you spend that much time with your boss, you really get to know him. We all know Stephen's a very flawed human being; who isn't? But I never, ever saw him act inappropriately around Tess. From my vantage point, and it's a pretty good one, their relationship was all business, strictly professional."

Comforting words, indeed.

As well as genuine and sincere.

Sandra was definitely inclined to believe Suzanne because she was right. She knew him better than probably anyone else.

Even Sandra.

But if Suzanne was right, then how did that poor girl end up dead in Stephen's bed?

Chapter 20

"We still have the riverboat tour along the Potomac to Mount Vernon, George Washington's estate, the Holocaust museum, the Arlington National Cemetery Tour, and now we're hit with this!" Fern cried in her hotel room, where she had gathered Maya, Sandra, and Coach Cavill for an emergency meeting. Clancy was downstairs in the restaurant supervising the kids as they ate their dinner.

"I don't see how the sudden death of Senator Wallage's intern directly affects us, Fern," Cavill noted, a puzzled look on his face.

Fern shot him an icy stare. She did not appreciate being challenged when she was in the middle of making the major news story of the day all about her. "I would say having the son of the Senator, not to mention his wife, as a part of our group absolutely affects us, Lucas!"

"Ex-wife," Cavill corrected her.

"What?" Fern snapped.

"Sandra and the Senator. They're divorced."

"Not officially. At least not yet," Sandra quickly added.

"But you're separated, right?" Lucas asked.

"What does it matter?" Fern blustered, throwing her hands up in the air. "I cannot allow my charges, these innocent kids, to be somehow dragged into such a white-hot tawdry scandal. The school board will have my head. Why did I have to pick this week to come to Washington? I have always had the worst timing ever, my whole life!"

Again, she was making it about her.

And Sandra could see it was annoying Maya, who finally piped in.

"Look, Fern, dial it back a bit, okay? This has nothing to do with you, or the students. It just happened."

"Two of my chaperones discovered the body. And we can quibble about whether the divorce papers have been signed yet or not, it doesn't matter, Sandra is smack dab in the middle of this whole ugly mess, and it's only a matter of time before the press connects the dots to this class trip and starts hounding us."

Maya shook her head. "Fern, you are too much."

"No," Sandra said quietly. "Maybe she has a point. They will find out I was the one who discovered the body. I should distance myself from the group so as not to draw attention to you. That way, you can continue with your tour as scheduled and I can be more available for Stephen. Believe me, he's going to need all the support he can get."

"I can take over and cover for you; the kids tend

to behave better around me anyway, must be my deep masculine intimidating voice," Lucas said with a laugh. "You too, Maya, I know you want to stick close to Sandra and help her out."

"Wait just a minute!" Fern protested. "I can accept losing one chaperone, but two? I promised Principal Williams—"

"Principal Williams is over five hundred miles away; she'll never know," Cavill argued.

"Thank you, Lucas," Maya said with a grateful smile.

Fern was still torn, running all the angles in her mind, imagining the worst-case scenario that could result in a wrong decision at this extremely critical moment.

"What about Ryan?" Fern asked.

"He's one of twenty-five kids. If we continue on like normal, stay together as a group, the press will probably never even have to know he's here in DC," Lucas said.

"I don't know . . ." Fern whined.

"Come on, Fern, you know you can handle this. From the moment I met you, I have admired how good you are at what you do; running roughshod over a bunch of rowdy students is right in your wheelhouse," Lucas said, poker-faced.

Sandra had to admit Coach Cavill was a charmer.

He was working Fern hard and she was starting to fall for it. Hard.

She flashed him a girlish smile. "As long as you are here to help me, Lucas."

"You got me. And Clancy. That old codger certainly won't take any guff from those kids, believe me."

Fern turned to Maya and Sandra. "Okay, go. Do whatever you have to do. We'll continue the tour without you."

"You're a rock star, Fern," Lucas said with a playful wink.

She practically melted on the spot.

Sandra was beginning to see Coach Cavill, or Lucas, which he had continually begged her to call him, in a whole new light. And she liked what she saw. She had been so reluctant to reengage with any man, especially a single and available man, since the debacle last year with Henry Yang, the tech billionaire. But maybe she had reacted too hastily. Maybe when they were through the eye of this storm, when she was back home in Portland and life was once again near normal, or her version of normal, maybe she might just give Lucas a chance.

She was suddenly distracted by Zoe Rush's face on the television behind Cavill and Fern. She was talking to a pretty blond anchor on Zoom from her office at the *Post*. Sandra scooped up the remote from the desk and turned up the volume. Maya joined her as Fern and Coach Cavill discussed tomorrow's full itinerary.

"My source in the police department tells me we are probably dealing with a homicide," Zoe gushed. "The leading detective on the case noticed bruises on the victim's neck."

Sandra saw Maya grimacing at the fact that Detective Lonsdale had twisted around the facts of who actually found the marks on Tess's neck. But this was not a contest. Maya was just relieved they were finally taking her discovery seriously.

"Obviously this does not bode well for Senator Wallage," Zoe said, a gleeful look on her face.

"Do you believe the police consider him a suspect?" the wide-eyed anchor asked.

"Of course he's a suspect, Claire," Zoe said in a patronizing tone, which seemed to slightly throw off the anchor, who pouted, insulted, as Zoe breathlessly continued. "Her body was discovered in the Senator's condo. The optics of that can't look any worse. I would not be surprised if the police are at this very moment preparing an arrest warrant."

"Oh, Zoe," Sandra sighed, shaking her head.

Sandra's phone buzzed. She glanced at the screen.

It was Stephen.

Sandra tapped the screen to answer the call. "Hi. What's up?"

"Somebody already tipped off the press that I'm here at the Hay-Adams. They're camped out everywhere. I'm trapped."

"Well, just stay put in your room. They can't get to you if you don't leave."

"No, I'm going stir-crazy. It's like the walls are closing in. I need to escape."

"I'm not sure what you want me to do."

"Get me out of here."

"And take you where?"

"Anywhere. I can't stand staying here another minute."

"Stephen, I . . ."

"*Please*, Sandra, I'm begging you."

He had always been claustrophobic. Even in a palatial five-star hotel suite, if he knew he could

not leave, or the exits were blocked barring an escape, he would suddenly be gripped by fear and
anxiety. She had lived with it their whole marriage.
He had nearly passed out one summer when they
hiked into a cave in Acadia National Park and
nearly got trapped inside when the tide rose faster
than expected. Even entering a walk-in closet was
sometimes too much for him.

"Okay, let me talk to Maya; I will call you back."

Maya looked at her curiously.

"We need to plan a rescue mission," Sandra
said.

Ten minutes later, after a quick taxi ride to the
Hay-Adams, Maya and Sandra swept into the or-
nate, historic lobby that had hosted such famous
guests ranging from Amelia Earhart to the Oba-
mas. Sandra quickly zeroed in on a young bellhop,
about Stephen's size and height, loosening his tie
and waving goodbye to a similarly uniformed doorman who was greeting guests by the entrance as
they came in, and made a beeline for him. Maya
hustled to catch up with her.

"Excuse me, are you off duty?" Sandra asked the
bellhop.

"Uh, yeah, as of two minutes ago," he said with a
quizzical look. "Can I help you?"

"How much would it cost to rent your uniform
for an hour?"

"My uniform? Um, I don't know; we're not supposed to . . ."

"A hundred?"

"Dollars?"

"For just an hour. I will have it right back to you
and I will also pay to get it dry-cleaned for you."

He gaped at her, utterly confused.

"Two hundred?" Sandra offered.

"*Dollars?*" he repeated, this time more emphatically.

Sandra reached into her bag and extracted two crisp one-hundred-dollar bills, glanced around to make sure no one was watching them, and then pressed them into the palm of his hand.

The young man stared at the two bills and then ripped off his tie and handed it to Sandra. "Deal."

He led them to the employee lounge, where he shed his uniform and slipped on some street clothes, stuffing the uniform in a large blue plastic garbage bag he got from the cleaning staff. Sandra exchanged numbers with him and then took the bag up to Stephen's suite. She rapped on the door. It was a long wait before the door finally opened a crack and Stephen peered out, worried it might be some intrepid reporter who had conned someone at the reception desk to fork over his room number, so he was enormously relieved to see Sandra and Maya.

Sandra shoved the bag at Stephen. "Here, put this on."

He opened the bag and stared at the contents. "What is this?"

"Your only way out of here," Sandra said. "Hurry up; the taxi waiting for us out front still has the meter running."

Stephen started unbuttoning his shirt as Maya and Sandra quickly filled Stephen's suitcases. Five minutes later, Maya and Sandra were marching through the lobby followed by Stephen, in full bellhop regalia, loaded down with his own luggage. None of the reporters hanging out in the lobby even took notice. As they passed the doorman, he did give Stephen a cursory look, vaguely recognizing him, but he did not confront him. He just tipped his hat. Once they were outside, Stephen breezed past the clump of news reporters and cameramen just to the right of the entrance. The taxi driver popped open the trunk as Maya and Sandra slid into the back of the vehicle. Once Stephen had tossed the suitcases in the trunk and slammed it shut, instead of returning to the hotel, he jumped in the passenger's seat, and the taxi peeled away. Not one eagle-eyed reporter noticed the bellhop leaving in a taxi with two guests of the hotel.

They were home free.

Chapter 21

Stephen emerged from the shower of Sandra and Maya's hotel room looking much less stressed out. He wore a white towel around his waist and padded over to a room service cart that had just been delivered. He lifted the tin and he brightened at the sight of a hearty club sandwich and French fries. Popping a fry into his mouth, he turned to Sandra, who was seated at the desk, scrolling through emails on her laptop.

"I feel so much better," Stephen said, grabbing another fry off the plate.

"Good," Sandra said, flicking her eyes toward him, surprised by how well in shape he still was long enough for him to notice.

"Judging my dad bod?"

"No," Sandra said quickly. "Quite the opposite. You look good."

He playfully flexed his right arm muscle. "Deborah got me a trainer twice a week for my birthday.

I guess she was trying to tell me something. What can I say, I love French fries." And with that, he picked up two more and stuffed them in his mouth.

"Well, whatever you're doing, it's working," Sandra said, trying to be casual, staring at him a bit too long before he smiled knowingly and she self-consciously averted her eyes back to the computer screen.

"I really appreciate you doing this, Sandra, letting me stay here, I mean, until we figure out my next move."

"Of course."

She worked hard maintaining a blithe, pleasant tone.

But this was not easy.

She had spent the better part of two years creating a new normal for herself, a life without Stephen. And just when she was starting to get comfortable, he blows right back in like a category five hurricane off the coast of Puerto Rico to upend everything.

The electronic lock on the door whirred and clicked and Maya breezed in, stopping short, startled by Stephen standing in the middle of the room, half-naked. She instantly looked away.

"Wow, I did not expect that . . ."

Sandra gave him an admonishing look. "Stephen . . ."

It took him a few seconds to even notice what was wrong, but then, as he glanced at Maya hiding her eyes and his bare chest, a bell in his head finally rang. "Oh right, sorry." He hurried to the closet, snatched a white hotel robe off a hanger, and slipped it on. "Okay, the coast is clear."

Sandra quietly shook her head.

In her mind, this could not get any more awkward.

Maya peeked through her fingers just to make sure, and then lowered her hand. "Okay, Fern's on board."

Stephen was now scarfing down the club sandwich. "Who's Fern?"

"Ryan's history teacher, she organized this whole trip," Sandra explained.

"I told her you snore like a foghorn and I can't sleep, so she offered me the sofa bed in her room," Maya said.

Stephen swallowed his sandwich. "I appreciate you doing that, Maya, allowing me to bunk with Sandra for the night."

"On the sofa bed," Sandra quickly added.

"Yes, dear, whatever makes you happy," Stephen sighed, slightly wounded. He replaced the tin on top of the uneaten portion of his club sandwich and sat down on the bed, adopting a more serious tone. "Now that Maya's back, I would like to discuss something with the both of you."

"Okay," Sandra said tentatively.

She had no idea what was about to come next.

"The press has already convicted me. I don't think the police are looking at any other suspects; I mean with those marks on her neck and the fact that they found Tess in *my* condo, it just looks bad, really bad." Neither of them was about to argue with him, so he continued. "So I want to hire you."

"*What?*" Sandra cried.

"You're private detectives and I need someone

working on my side to prove my innocence," Stephen said. "Before they arrest me for murder."

Sandra's mind reeled. The last client she would ever have imagined working for was her soon-to-be ex-husband.

"Please," Stephen begged. "Will you do it?"

"Yes," Maya said emphatically.

"N-No!" Sandra sputtered.

Maya spun around. "Why not?"

"Because . . ." Her voice trailed off.

She was at a loss for words.

Maya tried helping her out. "Because he's your ex?"

"Yes." Sandra nodded.

That was a good enough reason.

"If he doesn't have a problem with it, why should you? He's the one in serious trouble."

"I know; it's just weird," Sandra muttered.

"Whatever your going rate is, I'll double it," Stephen offered.

Sandra could see Maya already totaling the number up in her head, thinking about all the bills she could pay off with what they would make from this case.

Suddenly there was a pounding at the door.

Maya snapped out of the calculations in her head and hurried over to the door, peering through the peephole. "It's Vanessa and Ryan." She opened the door.

Ryan burst in, Vanessa behind him, and rushed over to his father, throwing his arms around him. "Dad!"

Stephen hugged him tight, eyes closed, grateful

for his presence. Vanessa hung back beside her mother.

Ryan finally pulled away. "I've been so worried about you! How're you doing?"

"I've had better days. Sorry to steal focus away from your class trip."

"Don't worry, Vanessa and I have seen enough monuments and museums to last a lifetime. Tell me what's going on. What's the strategy?"

Ryan was much more of a born politician like his father than his older brother, Jack, who was more singularly interested in sports.

"Don't you worry about a thing," Stephen said assuredly, patting his son lightly on the back. "I have got everything under control. It's all going to work out just fine."

Sandra could see Stephen shift into his perfect dad mode, fearless and untroubled, the unshakable king, feet firmly planted on his pedestal, not wanting his kids to fret even for one second that his life might unravel at any moment. But both boys were old enough now to see right through his act.

Noticing Ryan's incredulous look, he pivoted and pulled him down next to him on the bed. "Look, Son, I need you to know that what the press is saying, it's just not true. I'm not the man they're portraying me as."

"I know, Dad," Ryan said. "I have gotten used to all the lies and innuendos. It comes with the territory. I don't doubt you for a second. I support you one hundred percent."

Stephen stared at his son, awestruck.

He couldn't ask anything more from his own kid.

Unwavering devotion.

"You're more steady and confident than even I am," Stephen marveled, chuckling.

A phone buzzed on the night table.

"That's mine," Stephen said, standing up and crossing over to retrieve it. He glanced at the screen. "It's Jack, the other prodigal son."

"I'm sure he's seen the news in Boston and wants to know how you're doing," Sandra said.

Stephen pointed to the still steamy bathroom where he had just showered. "I'll take it in here." He tapped the screen and pressed the phone to his ear. "Jack!"

That was about all they heard once Stephen closed the bathroom door behind him.

Ryan instantly turned to his mother. "Are you and Maya going to help him?"

Sandra stood up from the desk, flabbergasted. "Did he tell you he was going to try and hire us?"

"What? No, I just figured you'd want to do everything you can to help clear his name. I mean, it's what you two do, right? Investigate crimes?"

He was right.

There was no denying that.

Sandra glanced over to where Maya stood, an expectant, hopeful look on her face.

She wanted this job.

Badly.

Working for a United States Senator was a big deal.

But she did not press the point because she knew at the end of the day, this was Sandra's call.

Sandra paused, but in the end there was no point dragging this out, considering all the pros and cons, because she knew ultimately what her answer would be, despite the long-running trust issues she had with her husband.

"Yes, Ryan, we're going to help him."

Maya could barely contain her glee.

Of all the clients she had reeled in since starting her own private eye firm, this was by far the biggest fish yet.

And Sandra knew it was going to be her job to navigate the choppy waters that were sure to come.

Chapter 22

Outside the J. Edgar Hoover Building, home to the Federal Bureau of Investigation in DC, an intrepid reporter from CNN with her camera crew in tow chased after two women who had just walked out of the building. One was tall, black, with gorgeous curly long black hair, serious looking, the other slightly shorter, silky auburn hair cut in a bob, white alabaster skin, just as serious looking. Both appeared to be FBI agents. They kept their eyes straight ahead as the determined blond female reporter hustled behind them, nearly colliding with a fire hydrant before jumping over it to keep up with them.

"Are you two working on the murder of Senator Wallage's intern?"

Neither spoke, just kept walking toward their car, a brown coupe, which was parked in front of the building.

All of this was playing out on the TV screen in

Maya and Sandra's hotel room. Vanessa and Ryan lounged on the bed, intently watching while Maya and Sandra talked quietly over by the window and Stephen was shaving in the bathroom, on the phone, the door half-open.

Vanessa, holding the remote, scoffed, "She has a *name*! Why can't they just say 'Tess Rankin'?"

On the television, the white woman circled around to the passenger's side of the car to get in as the black woman stopped and unlocked the coupe with her car remote.

The reporter managed to catch up to her and rudely stuck a microphone in her face as she was about to slide into the driver's seat. "Is Senator Wallage a person of interest in this case?"

The agent stopped, considered her next move, then slowly turned around to face the reporter.

Vanessa raised the volume on the television, making it louder.

"I cannot confirm or deny, but if you were to report that, the FBI would not dispute it," she said flatly, then hopped in the car, slammed the door shut, and moments later peeled away.

The reporter swiveled back around to the camera, breathlessly reporting to the anchor, "Wolf, that was Special Agent Tabitha Markey and her partner Jane Rhodes, and they are telling us that Senator Stephen Wallage appears to be a person of interest in this murder investigation!"

Maya, who was conferring with Sandra by the window, scooted over to the bed. "Vanessa, turn that down; the Senator is on the phone."

Vanessa pressed the button to lower the volume, but Stephen, phone clamped to his ear, had already noticed what was happening on the television. He put down his razor, wiped his face with a hand towel.

"Bill, I've got to go!" Stephen barked, hurling his phone down on the basin and marching out of the bathroom to join the others. "Who were those two women on TV?"

"They're FBI agents," Ryan said.

Stephen's eyes widened. "FBI agents? What are they doing talking to the press? That's against policy. What did they say?"

Nobody spoke.

There was an uncomfortable silence except for Wolf Blitzer at the CNN DC headquarters taking us into a commercial break.

"Come on, tell me, what did they say?" Stephen repeated, anxious.

"They basically confirmed that you're a person of interest, Dad," Ryan muttered.

"What? That's insane! What's going on here? Is the FBI out to get me? Why would they do that? Those two should be fired! I'm calling the Attorney General!"

Sandra rushed over and placed a hand on his arm. "Stephen, you need to calm down. Don't do anything rash. Give us some time to do what you hired us to do."

Sandra's soothing presence seemed to work.

One of her talents was talking Stephen down off the ledge. It's what made her so effective in all of his political campaigns.

He gave her a rueful smile and patted her hand with his own. "You're right. As always. Sorry. I'm a little on edge. That was Bill Kornish."

Maya couldn't help but be impressed. "The majority leader?"

Stephen nodded. "Not an easy call. It was very fraught. I can tell he's freaking out over this. He wants me to release some kind of statement."

"Maybe that's a good idea. It's a lot safer than a press conference. A simple statement extending your condolences to Tess's family, friends, and colleagues. Short and to the point. Nothing about the investigation," Sandra said, her mind racing.

"Yes, I agree. I will get on it right away," Stephen said before turning to Sandra wistfully. "You were always my best advisor."

"In the meantime, Sandra and I will get cracking," Maya said. "But we're going to need to find a place to work out of; it's too crowded here, and you need to stay put."

"Use my office. It's not like I can go back there right now, too much press. I'll text Preston and have him arrange security passes for you," Stephen said.

"Great," Maya said.

Stephen's phone buzzed. He walked over, glanced at the screen, and grimaced.

"What is it now?" Sandra asked, not sure she really wanted to know.

Stephen put down the phone and rubbed his eyes with his fingers. "The entire opposing party is calling for my immediate resignation in order to maintain the integrity and ethics of the United States Senate. They're not even waiting for any charges to be filed."

"No big surprise there," Sandra sniffed.

"So far, Bill's holding together our caucus. No

one's spoken out against me . . . yet. But if he senses any cracks, if any of my fellow Senators start to cave, then he's going to try and force me out."

"Then we better clear this up before that starts to happen," Maya said. "Let's go, Sandra; the clock is ticking." She spun around to Vanessa and Ryan, both sitting on the edge of the bed, hanging on every word. "You two go down to the lobby and join your classmates. The bus should be leaving soon for your next tour."

"How can we go sightseeing with all that's going on?" Vanessa protested.

"Because I said so," Maya warned.

"You too, Ryan," Sandra added. "I want you to do everything Fern says. If you don't, you know I will hear about it."

"Okay, whatever," Ryan moaned.

Maya then raced for the door, eager and excited.

This case was a very big deal.

Sandra lingered behind for a moment with Stephen, whose face was drawn, his shoulders slumped. "Are you sure you're okay?"

He gave her a reassuring smile. "I'll be fine. I will email you the statement before I send it out."

"You don't have to do that. I trust you."

"But I don't trust myself. I need your input."

"I will look it over; just don't go anywhere. You need to keep a very low profile right now."

Stephen, already formulating his press release statement in his head, gave her a brief nod.

She studied him, not sure if he was listening to her.

"I mean it, Stephen; I need you to promise me," she said more firmly.

"Yes, yes, I promise. I'll stay put."

He then hurried over to the desk, grabbed a pen and paper, and started scribbling.

She knew him well enough to know that sometimes when he got too much into his own head he tended to make rash, impulsive decisions that more often than not ended in disaster.

As she watched him hunched over the desk, crafting the perfect public statement, Sandra could not shake off her sense of dread about what was coming.

Her premonitions from the past were usually spot-on.

And she felt strongly in her gut that a cataclysmic storm was brewing.

With her own family in the eye of it.

Chapter 23

After arriving at Stephen's office in the Senate Building, and getting set up with the help of Stephen's Chief of Staff, Preston Lambert, Sandra left Maya behind to question all the staffers about Tess hoping one of them might provide a lead or key detail that they had not already learned, which they could follow up on while Sandra headed to Georgetown. Stephen had provided her with the home address of his girlfriend, Deborah Crowley, who had not been returning Stephen's calls ever since their ill-fated dinner at Dauphine's several nights earlier. When Sandra called her office at the Commonwealth Fund, she was told by an assistant that Deborah was not working today, so Sandra was going to try and catch her at her townhouse.

As Sandra hurried out of the Senate Building to find the Uber she had ordered to take her to Georgetown, she stumbled upon the slimy Senator

Charles Grisby, surrounded by the press pool, a smug look on his face, relishing the rapt attention.

"When did it become acceptable for a public servant to completely shed all ethical responsibility? What happened to decency, honor, integrity? Can we not expect that from our politicians anymore? Are all of those traits just relics of the past?"

Sandra stopped, infuriated. She knew Grisby was talking about Stephen. Grisby's eyes flicked toward Sandra and his snakish smile broadened even wider. He was thrilled that she was there to witness his performance, and he brazenly winked at her.

It made Sandra's skin crawl.

"I believe it is vitally important for the Senate to respond to this kind of behavior, and so I plan to introduce a formal statement of disapproval for the whole body to vote on, censuring Senator Wallage, and if the facts lead to where I think they will, then if he refuses to resign, we should go ahead with a full expulsion," Grisby gleefully announced.

A Fox reporter shouted, "Do you think he did it?"

Grisby pursed his lips contemptuously. "That is for the police and the district attorney of DC to say, not me . . ." He paused for dramatic effect. "But let me just say this. It's not the words that define a man's character, it's his actions, and we only have to look at the actions of Senator Wallage to see the truth of his character. Thank you very much!"

Grisby extracted himself from the swarm of reporters and headed back up the steps to the Russell Senate Office Building, stopping when he reached Sandra, who glared at him disdainfully.

"Too much?" he sneered.

"Not for you, Charles."

"They were all over me to say *something*; what could I do?"

"Your hypocrisy is a wonder to behold."

"How is Stephen? I haven't seen him around today."

"He's holding up pretty well. He knows the knives are out. Believe me, Stephen can handle a bloviating rival trying to take him down."

"Oh, my dear, I don't have to take your husband down. He's doing a commendable job doing that all by himself." He paused, giving her the once-over. "You look lovely, by the way; Clementine always wanted to know what was your secret?"

"I would have told your dear late wife that the key to staying young is to not be married to you."

Grisby chuckled. "Touché."

He continued on up the steps flanked by his small army of aides. Sandra spotted the Uber logo on the windshield of a black Lincoln Town Car and waved at the driver. Within fifteen minutes, they were rolling down a quiet tree-lined street where up ahead Sandra could see a large moving truck parked outside the townhouse address Stephen had given her.

The Lincoln pulled over to the curb and Sandra hopped out as Deborah followed a mover, who was carrying a brown suede chair, out the front door. Behind them, two more movers emerged lugging a leather couch.

Sandra walked up to them. "Hello, Deborah."

The voice startled her and she whirled around, shading her eyes from the sun with her hand. "Sandra? What are you doing here?"

"I came by to talk to you."

One of the movers banged a couch leg against the loading ramp of the moving truck.

"Careful!" Deborah scolded.

The mover mumbled an apology and clattered up the metal ramp, lifting the couch leg higher in order to avoid hitting anything else.

Sandra watched as a fourth mover walked out the front door with a tall black iron floor lamp. "I see you're moving."

"Yes. I'm going back to Birmingham."

Sandra's eyes widened in surprise. "Oh, you're actually leaving DC?"

"I'm going to go work for a small law firm there. The same one my dad started out at," she said. "As far away from the glare of the Washington spotlight as possible."

Sandra could see the bitterness and weariness on Deborah's face. "I saw many people get hopelessly disillusioned by the brutal sport of politics when I lived here."

"And I'm done with all the lying politicians, both in my professional life . . . *and* my personal life."

"So it's definitely over between you and Stephen?"

Deborah laughed derisively. "You could say that."

"I'm sorry."

"Don't be."

The movers clomped down the rattling ramp and marched back into the house for more furniture.

Deborah looked at Sandra impassively, unsure she was someone to be trusted. "What did you want to talk to me about?"

"Stephen swears he was never romantically involved with Tess Rankin."

"He *would* say that," Deborah scoffed. She then stared at Sandra incredulously. "Don't tell me you believe him?"

"I am not sure what to believe at this point."

"Oh, come on, Sandra, how many times during your marriage did you hear Stephen say, 'Nothing is going on,' or 'Our relationship is strictly professional'? He's practically made an art form of denial."

"Of course. He's lied before. But do you honestly believe that Stephen, the man you have been dating for almost two years now, is capable of murder?"

Deborah stood silent.

Sandra cocked an eyebrow. "*Do* you?"

Deborah let out a long sigh. "I wish I could say emphatically no, but I have been so beaten down by this town, by all the snakes and vermin masquerading as purveyors of justice and equality and freedom, frankly, I am just not sure of anything anymore."

This chilled Sandra to the bone.

The fact that the one woman who had spent the most time with Stephen during the last couple of years was refusing to vouch for his innocence was unsparing and telling. She was so stunned by Deborah's assertion, all she could muster up to say was a barely audible, "Wow."

She had found one person, a critical person in Stephen's life, who was actually entertaining the idea of his guilt. Which brought up another even more disturbing question in Sandra's mind.

Were there more?

Chapter 24

On her way back to the hotel from Georgetown in the Uber, Sandra received an ominous text from Maya, requesting that she meet her in the lobby as soon as she could get there.

What could it be now?

There was heavy midday traffic, but Sandra finally arrived fifteen minutes later, rushing into the lobby to find Maya waiting for her near the concierge desk.

When Sandra scurried up to her, Maya blurted out, "He's holding a press conference in the hotel ballroom!"

"Who?"

"Stephen."

"What?"

"He was already on his way down from the room when I got back here. I tried talking him out of it, but he wasn't going to listen to anything I had to say, he barely knows me, and you weren't here."

"What on earth possessed him to do something so stupid?"

"He said something about getting too many calls from frantic Senators urging him to deny the rumors, that it was imperative to get ahead of the story publicly."

"What part of keeping a low profile did he not understand?"

"You tell me; he's *your* husband."

They hurried through the lobby and down a long, carpeted hallway toward the main ballroom. The large oak doors were open, and they could hear Stephen speaking into a microphone. As they entered, they could see a small podium set up for Stephen and a crush of reporters and photographers gathered around.

Stephen gripped the sides of the podium as he spoke. At the moment, he appeared refreshed and confident. "There is zero truth to the rumors that are floating out there about me and that poor young woman . . . Ms. Rankin. And anyone who suggests otherwise is just making things up. It's as simple as that."

An ABC reporter shot her hand up and Stephen pointed to her. "Yes, Mary?"

"Your office claims that you were at the Capitol Building debating a bill on the night Ms. Rankin died in your apartment, is that correct?"

"Yes," Stephen said forcefully.

"And yet there is a two-hour window when no one saw you, according to our reporting. Where were you?"

Stephen's jaw tightened. "I took a nap in the

Marble Room outside the Senate Chamber. I was exhausted and needed to recharge a bit."

"Was anyone else in the Marble Room with you?"

"Maybe at some point, I don't know; like I said, I was asleep," Stephen said warily.

"I haven't found anyone so far who admits to seeing you. Two hours is more than enough time to leave the Capitol Building, go to your nearby condo, and get back in plenty of time to resume your duties."

"I don't like what you're suggesting, Mary," Stephen seethed. "Next question."

A sea of hands shot up in the air. Stephen pointed to someone near the front, whose face was blocked by a cameraman. When she stepped forward, his face fell at the unwelcome sight of Zoe Rush. The regret on Stephen's face showed he deeply wished he had chosen someone else.

Zoe flashed a wickedly sardonic smile. "Senator Wallage, I appreciate your firm denials of engaging in an inappropriate relationship with your intern, Tess Rankin, but can you appreciate the obvious skepticism permeating this room?"

The question threw Stephen off balance.

He cleared his throat, buying himself some more time to come up with a proper answer that would not give Zoe Rush the upper hand.

Sandra could see him starting to sweat.

"First of all, Zoe, I'm not sure why anyone should be skeptical. I pride myself on being completely honest with my constituents, the press . . ."

Zoe's eyes narrowed. "What about your wife?"

"I-I'm not sure what you're getting at? M-My wife?"

"Isn't it true you once had an extramarital affair and lied about it?"

Sandra could feel her cheeks burning.

Zoe Rush had once been a friend she had regularly confided in. And now she was using that personal relationship to make Stephen look guilty. It was underhanded, unfair, and, in Sandra's mind, reprehensible.

Stephen was starting to look less refreshed and more puffy.

And guilty.

"Don't let her trip you up," Sandra whispered under her breath.

"Whatever transpires in my marriage is a private matter between me and my wife," Stephen said evenly. A bead of sweat rolled down his forehead, but he didn't dare wipe it away out of fear of looking too nervous.

"So you're not willing to admit you cheated?"

The cameras were flashing wildly now, everyone excited to get a shot of Stephen's deer-in-the-headlights expression.

"I think you're out of line here, Zoe."

"I am just trying to establish a pattern of deception that might be instructive as we connect the dots to what exactly happened to Tess Rankin, who was a victim of murder apparently, in *your* home."

"I did *not* kill Tess!" Stephen cried. His shoulders immediately sank. He knew he had blown it. Big-time. That would be the quote that would lead all the newscasts tonight coupled with an unflattering photo of his sweaty, puffy face and beady eyes filled with abject fear. The photo alone would twist his strong denial into something more akin to a desperate lie.

"Thank you all for coming," Stephen muttered, defeated, as he stepped away from the podium as reporters shouted more questions, which he ignored on his way out. As he pushed his way through the throng of the press, his eyes locked on Sandra, who was near the entrance with Maya, incensed.

He raised a hand and sighed. "I know what you're going to say. Huge mistake."

"What possibly made you think, in your frame of mind—?"

He cut her off. "I can't do this now. I'm going up to the room." He brushed past her and raced off down the hall toward the lobby, several reporters on his heels, chasing after him.

Zoe, a self-satisfied grin on her face, ambled over to Sandra. "I thought I might get him to say something slightly incriminating, but I certainly did not expect him to self-immolate in such a spectacular fashion!"

"You must be so proud of yourself!" Sandra snapped scornfully.

"Frankly, I am," Zoe retorted. "He thought he could control the narrative, paint the picture that he wants us to see, and now he knows we are not going to capitulate to his political ends."

"You were out to get him long before he stepped in front of that microphone, Zoe."

"Maybe." She shrugged. "But I'm surprised you're

not cheering me on. After all, in a sense, you were his first victim."

Sandra was knocked back on her heels. "You're nothing but a jaded muckraker, Zoe. I want nothing to do with you anymore."

She stormed off, furious, determined more than ever to prove Zoe's slanderous and unproven allegations to be totally false, even though she had just been profoundly rattled by their unpleasant encounter and her husband's impulsive, ill-advised actions, which most certainly did not help his case.

Things were quickly going from bad to worse.

Chapter 25

"Of course you can see the security footage," Cliff, the doorman at Stephen's condo building, said to Maya and Sandra as they stood in front of his desk in the front lobby.

"I sure appreciate it, Cliff, thank you," Sandra said warmly. "We promise just to take a quick peek just to see if anyone somehow slipped in here while you were off making your rounds."

"You know I support Senator Wallage one hundred percent. I think the press is giving him a rough time, and I want to show my support and help out in any way I can."

"I will make sure Stephen knows that," Sandra promised.

Cliff sat back in his chair. "Absolutely. He's a good man and I don't like to see nice people railroaded." He paused. "But the thing is, you're going to have to wait your turn."

Maya cocked an eyebrow. "Wait our turn?"

Cliff nodded and gestured toward the door that led to a private office off the lobby. "I just let somebody else go back there and take a look at the footage."

"Who? The police?" Maya asked.

Cliff shook his head, holding back a grin. "Nope."

"FBI?"

Cliff reached for his now cold cup of coffee and took a sip from the mug that said "World's Greatest Grandpa." "I don't want to get anyone in trouble."

This only piqued Maya and Sandra's curiosity even more. "Who's back there, Cliff?"

He hesitated, then sighed, realizing he had no choice. He glanced at Sandra with a knowing smile. "Your son."

"*Ryan?*" Sandra gasped.

"Yeah, he showed up here asking the same thing as you. Said it would only take a few minutes. Had a very pretty young girl by his side too."

"That would be my daughter," Maya groaned.

Cliff studied her. "She does have your brown eyes."

"And they're back there right now?" Sandra asked, aghast.

"Yes, ma'am."

Sandra gestured toward the ring of keys on the desk and said, fuming, "Would you mind?"

Cliff hauled himself up to his feet, grabbed the keys, and circled around the desk, ambling to the door and unlocking it. He swung it open and Maya and Sandra brushed past him into the private office where they found Ryan sitting behind a desk, Vanessa leaning over him, as they watched the video footage on a large computer monitor.

"Just what do you think you're doing?" Sandra seethed.

Both kids raised their eyes, their mouths dropping open in surprise at the sight of their mothers.

Sandra marched forward. "You are supposed to be back at the hotel with the rest of your classmates! You two are breaking curfew!"

"Mom, I couldn't just sit idly by and do nothing while Dad's convicted in the press and he hasn't even been arrested or charged with anything!" Ryan protested.

Maya whipped her head around and glared at Vanessa. "And *you*?"

"I'm here for moral support," Vanessa mumbled.

"Look, Mom, somebody has to be on Dad's side to prove his innocence!"

"Yes, and your father has asked me and Maya to investigate, not you two! Once Fern finds out you two left the hotel without permission, she's going to have a freak-out, a nuclear meltdown."

"We don't have to tell her," Ryan suggested.

Maya snapped up her phone and began tapping on the screen.

Vanessa eyed her nervously. "What are you doing?"

"Calling you two an Uber. You're going to go straight back to the hotel immediately. We will discuss this little outing of yours later."

"Mom . . ." Ryan whined.

"I don't want to hear it," Sandra warned sharply.

Maya lowered her phone. "Three minutes. It's a white Prius. Driver's name is Mohammad."

Ryan and Vanessa wavered momentarily.

"Go wait outside! Now!" Maya barked.

The two kids sprang up and hurried for the door. Ryan suddenly stopped and turned back. "We only got about an hour into the footage before you showed up, but there's a blip about forty-two minutes in. Cliff said there was a brief power outage for about five minutes when he was on his seven o'clock rounds, probably during the same time Tess showed up, because we haven't seen her on any of the security footage, just so you know."

"Goodbye!" Sandra blurted abruptly.

"Okay, I'm going!" Ryan cried, scooting out the door after Vanessa.

Maya looked at Sandra. "We are going to punish them for this, right?"

"Oh, yeah, big-time," Sandra said.

They took their kids' place behind the desk and reversed the security footage, starting from the beginning. Sure enough, at seven sharp, Cliff got up from his desk and grabbed his key ring and hustled off to make his rounds. At seven fifteen, just as Ryan had described, there was a break in the footage. When the image of the front of the building reappeared, there was a five-and-a-half-minute gap in the footage, and no sign of Tess arriving. Cliff returned at seven twenty-two and sat down to read his James Patterson paperback. No one arrived before eight thirty, when Cliff got up and wandered into the private office, presumably to use the bathroom. At eight thirty-four, a slender man, medium height, in jeans and wearing a gray hoodie, approached the building. He loitered outside for about a minute waiting for the guard to let him in, but Cliff was still preoccupied. The man's back was to the security camera and so they could not see his face.

He wandered over to the call box outside the building and studied all the names. He pressed a number and waited. It looked as if someone answered, because the man leaned in and said something into the speaker. Whoever he was talking to buzzed him in and he entered the lobby and looked around before heading to the elevator.

Maya stared at the back of the man's head. "Come on, turn around, turn around."

"There are dozens of condos in that building; he could be visiting anyone," Sandra said.

But then, after pressing the button to the elevator, he slowly turned around as Cliff came shuffling out of the private office.

Sandra gasped out loud.

It was Anton.

Anton Volkov.

The Russian exchange student.

He slipped on the elevator and the doors closed, carrying him up to Stephen's floor, security guard Cliff none the wiser.

"This is not good," Sandra groaned.

Maya fast-forwarded the footage.

Ten minutes later, according to the time code, Anton appeared again, but instead of arriving in the elevator, he emerged from the stairwell so the guard would not hear the bell indicating someone coming down to the lobby. Cliff was on his cell phone, chattering away with someone, while stuffing his face with a Subway sandwich. He was facing away from the front door, so he never saw the boy sneak back out and into the night.

They now had a number one suspect.

Chapter 26

When Ryan opened the door to his hotel room and saw his mother and Maya standing there with stern looks on their faces, his shoulders slouched and he audibly groaned. "Seriously, Mom? Do we have to do this now? Can't we all just get a good night's sleep and you can yell at me in the morning?"

"Is Vanessa here?" Maya asked.

"No, she's in her room where she's supposed to be!" Ryan cried. "We figured we were in enough trouble already. Why are you here?"

Sandra pushed her way past him. "We need to talk to Anton."

Ryan stepped aside. "Anton? What did he do?"

They looked around, but there was no sign of him. The bathroom door was ajar and inside the light was off. Maya checked it anyway just in case he was in there hiding behind the shower curtain. She returned and gave Sandra a shrug.

Sandra spun back around to her son. "*Where is he?*"

"Relax. He didn't run off again. He just went down the hall to get some ice. He's coming right back."

Sandra folded her arms. "Planning a little after-hours party, are we?"

Ryan sighed. "No, Mom. I bought us some sodas downstairs when I got back to the hotel, and they were warm, so Anton just went out for a bucket of ice so we can chill them. What's going on?"

Sandra stayed mum, which frustrated Ryan.

"Come on, Mom, tell me . . ."

Then, it suddenly dawned on him.

"He was on the security footage, wasn't he? He was at Dad's condo the night—"

They heard a thud in the hallway.

Maya dashed outside to the hallway and saw an ice bucket upended on the rug, ice cubes scattered everywhere, and Anton dashing down the hall toward the elevator at a clip.

"Anton! Wait! Stop!" Maya yelled. As she took off running after him, she heard Sandra tell Ryan to stay in his room as she scurried off after Maya.

By the time Maya reached the elevator doors, they were already closing and she only caught a glimpse of Anton pressed up against the back mirrored wall, praying she would not be able to jam an arm between the doors and stop him from escaping. Lucky for him, the doors closed before Maya could reach them.

She whipped around to Sandra, who was just catching up to her. "Come on, we can take the stairs!"

They were on the seventh floor, and they scrambled down the seemingly endless flights of stairs, Maya like an Olympian long-distance runner, Sandra more awkwardly, trying to stay steady on some cumbersome heels.

When they finally reached the hotel lobby, they spotted Anton darting through the hotel's revolving door out onto the street. They sprinted across the lobby, nearly colliding with a bellhop pushing a luggage cart and almost plowing down a startled couple just arriving to check in. Outside the hotel, they saw Clancy standing next to the parked school bus, his eyes glued to his phone.

Maya raced up to him. "Clancy, have you seen Anton?"

Clancy glanced up from his phone, confused. "I've been texting with my granddaughter. Who are you looking for?"

Maya scanned the entire area and each end of the street, her eyes locking in on Anton just in time to see him disappear around a corner, fleeing down a side street.

Maya spun back around to Clancy and Sandra. "We're never going to catch him on foot!"

Clancy lit up like a Christmas tree. "Come on, we'll take the bus!"

Maya and Sandra hesitated but knew they did not have much of a choice if they wanted to catch up to the kid. They all piled on, and Clancy excitedly plopped down in the driver's seat and flipped the ignition switch.

"I was just about to take it to the overnight parking garage when you two showed up! Let's go!"

He shifted the gear and the big yellow school

bus lurched forward, tossing Maya and Sandra around like rag dolls. The bus nearly sideswiped a Lyft driver waiting for a fare as it roared off down the street. Maya and Sandra held on to the vinyl seat covers for dear life. Clancy, knuckles white from gripping the steering wheel so tight, eyes scanning like the Terminator searching for his prey, slammed his foot down on the accelerator as the bus barreled down the street, swerving left onto the side street where they had just seen Anton fleeing.

Although it was left unsaid between them, Maya could tell that both she and Sandra were mighty impressed with how adept Clancy was at expertly maneuvering the big bus in and out of traffic when he was focused on a mission, a far cry from the doddering old senior driver he at least pretended to be on the trip down to DC.

As if reading their minds, Clancy called out from the driver's seat, "I did two tours as a truck driver in an Army convoy in Vietnam back in '68, so I was constantly dodging rockets and mortars and small-arms fire!"

"Let's pray he's not having a flashback right now," Sandra muttered, her eyes clamped closed.

They heard the bus's tires screeching as they rounded another corner. It was dark outside, and Maya and Sandra could only see Clancy hunched over the wheel, bopping up and down, totally in the zone. He jerked the wheel again, speeding up, and then jerked it again, so Maya and Sandra crashed into each other, their shoulders bumping, before he slammed on the brakes.

The bus squealed to a stop, and Clancy jumped

out of his seat and opened the door to the bus and hurtled down the steps as fast as his nearly eighty-year-old body could carry him. Before Maya and Sandra even knew what was happening, Clancy returned with a shell-shocked Anton, holding him by his shirt collar.

"I saw him take off down an alley, so I sped around the block to cut him off before he came running out the other side," Clancy announced proudly. He then shoved Anton toward the two women. "He's all yours, ladies."

Anton slumped down in a bus seat, exhausted and defeated.

Maya and Sandra exchanged stunned looks.

There were a lot more interesting layers to Clancy the bus driver than either of them had ever imagined.

Chapter 27

It was a typical strategy of "Good Cop, Bad Cop." Sandra, who was by nature more sensitive and understanding, played her "Good Cop" role to the hilt, asking if Anton would like her to run into a corner market to buy him a snack and something to drink. Maya, with her years of experience interrogating lowlife drug dealers and lying robbery suspects, was much more comfortable as the "Bad Cop," shouting over Sandra, threatening to get Anton's host parents on the phone right now to let them know just what a holy terror he had been on this class trip, how a full expulsion and a deportation back to Russia might be in order since he was unwilling to follow a few simple rules.

Anton, for his part, once again begged for leniency, just like he had with Fern after his first vanishing act. Sandra quietly explained that she might be willing to go easier on him if he just fessed up and confessed the truth about why he was on that

security tape, but Maya pretended she did not want
to hear any more of his lies. It was obvious to her
now that this kid was utterly incapable of telling
the truth and so they might as well turn him over
to the police and be done with him.

Clancy, who was enjoying the floor show as he
drove the bus into the overnight parking structure
and up a ramp to find a vacant guest parking spot,
suppressed a chuckle as Maya brutally laid into the
now pale-faced, panic-stricken boy.

"Please, I'm telling you, I didn't do anything to
Tess, I swear; I just . . ."

"Just *what*?" Sandra asked calmly, placing a
motherly hand on his arm.

"I just went there to talk to her, that's all."

Sandra leaned in closer. "About what?"

Anton dithered some more, eyes flicking from
sweet Sandra to monstrous Maya.

Clancy watched them through the rearview mirror, a big, knowing grin on his face.

"Why are we wasting our time here?" Maya
snapped. "Let's just call the cops and have them
book him."

His eyes widened in fear.

"Give him a chance to explain," Sandra sighed,
pretending to give Maya an admonishing look.
"He's just nervous."

"You need to stop coddling the spoiled brat.
Maybe a night in a cold, dark jail cell will get him
to focus!"

Clancy couldn't help but audibly snicker.

Maya shot him a stern stare through the rearview mirror.

She felt they were getting close to wearing Anton down enough so he might start telling the truth, and she certainly did not want Clancy screwing it up now.

Anton shifted uncomfortably in the front seat of the bus just behind Clancy where Maya had pushed him down to question him. "The other day at the Capitol Building, when we went to visit Mr. Wallage—"

"*Senator* Wallage," Maya corrected him.

Anton nodded. "Right. Senator Wallage. When we were introduced to the staff, and I saw her for the first time . . ."

"Tess?" Sandra asked.

Anton nodded again. "I thought she was the most beautiful girl I had ever seen. I could not take my eyes off her. When we were shown out, I kept thinking about her, I couldn't get her out of my mind, I had to see her again, talk to her, find out more about her, and so when we got to the Ford Theatre I peeled away from the group when no one was looking, and took the Metro back to the Capitol Building."

"How did you get back inside?" Maya barked.

"I didn't. I waited outside for like three hours. I was about to give up, but then I saw her. She was all alone, but I couldn't work up the nerve to say anything. She walked right past me, didn't even recognize me, and so I followed her. She took the Metro to Mr., I mean Senator Wallage's apartment, and went inside. I stood outside like an idiot, practicing over and over in my mind what I would say; then when I finally worked up the courage to go for it, and went to the front entrance, the guard was gone from his desk, so I used the call box to ring upstairs."

Maya folded her arms, incredulous. "And she just let you right in, without even knowing who you were?"

Anton shook his head. "No. I said I was Ryan."

Sandra rubbed her forehead with her hand. "Anton, no."

"It was the only thing I could think of that might get me inside the building and it worked. She buzzed me right in. I took the elevator up, and when I got to the apartment, she was already there with the door open waiting for me. She knew right away I wasn't Ryan, and she suddenly looked really rattled."

Maya angrily threw her hands up in the air. "Of course she was rattled! You lied your way inside the building! You could have been anyone! The poor thing was probably scared half to death!"

"I tried to explain why I was there, that I only wanted to talk to her, how pretty I thought she was, but she didn't want to hear it. She just wanted me to go."

Anton lowered his eyes to the floor, hurt.

"And did you?" Maya snapped.

"Did I what?" Anton mumbled.

"Did you go, or did you force your way inside so you could talk some more?"

"No!" Anton yelled. "She stepped back inside and shut the door in my face, so I left. That was it. Then I walked all the way back to the hotel because I was out of money and couldn't buy another Metro card."

"How convenient you took another hour to walk from the condo to the hotel. And I'm fairly certain no one who may have passed you on the street that night will ever remember seeing you. That leaves quite a big chunk of time left with no discernible alibi," Maya growled.

"I did not kill Tess!" Anton cried, near tears. Convinced Maya was now a lost cause and would continue doubting his story, Anton turned all his attention toward Sandra. "Please, Mrs. Wallage, you have to believe me!"

He hurled himself at Sandra, throwing his arms around her, sobbing. Sandra comforted him.

"For what it's worth, I believe the kid," Clancy announced from the driver's seat as he pulled the school bus into an empty parking space.

Sandra tended to agree.

And she could tell from the softening expression on Maya's face that despite her best efforts to play "Bad Cop," she was leaning in that direction as well.

Chapter 28

When Maya and Sandra escorted Anton back to the hotel room he was sharing with Ryan and marched through the door, Ryan popped to his feet from one of the double beds to greet them.

"What happened? Are you okay, Anton?"

"He's fine," Maya said gruffly before shoving Anton down in the chair next to the small desk with the leather-bound guest services book. "Now you listen to me, if I catch you even poking your head out that door, it's over. I will bring a whole world of hurt down upon you, so don't you dare test me."

"I know a couple of Capitol Police officers who moonlight as security guards that I could post outside your door," Sandra said.

"You don't have to do that," Anton tried assuring her. "I won't try to sneak out again, I promise. You can trust me."

"I don't have to trust you because I'm counting

on Ryan here to make sure you stick to your word, because if you don't, then it's on *both* of you," Sandra explained calmly.

Ryan's eyes nearly bulged out of his head. "What?"

"It's like the old buddy system. You're both responsible for each other. One screws up, you both pay the price," Sandra said sharply.

"But I didn't do anything wrong—" Ryan stopped short, catching himself, realizing that wasn't quite true.

"This way, you're both invested in playing by the rules, and speaking up if one of you gets any bright ideas to break them again."

"Mom, will you please stop? Nobody's going to break any more rules," Ryan sighed.

There was a quiet knock at the door.

Ryan's face fell as Maya crossed the room and opened it.

Vanessa stood in the doorway, startled to see her mother.

"It's past curfew. You should be in your room."

"I . . . uh . . . I . . ." Vanessa stammered, drawing a complete blank as to how to explain why she was there.

"If you keep your mouth shut, don't say another word, and just turn back around and head straight to your room and don't try to come back when we're gone, I will pretend you were never here," Maya said evenly.

Vanessa opened her mouth to speak, thought better of it, and then scooted away.

Maya leaned out the door and called after her, "Remember, these halls have security cameras!"

Sandra shot Ryan a hard look.

"We were just going to watch a movie together," Ryan mumbled, looking at his mother sheepishly.

Sandra jabbed a finger in Anton's direction. "Stay put."

"Yes, Mrs. Wallage," Anton whispered, contrite.

Then she walked over and joined Maya, who was staring down the hall, making sure Vanessa actually got on the elevator to go back to her room. As they stepped out into the hall and Sandra grabbed the door handle to swing it shut, she heard Anton ask, "What happens now?"

She poked her head back in the room. "What do you mean?"

"To me? I am seen on camera going into the building. Are the police going to take me in for questioning? Am I going to have to stay in DC until they find out who did this?"

"I don't know, Anton, we'll probably know more tomorrow, so just try to get some sleep now, okay?"

He was scared.

Sandra could not be sure if he was more frightened of being a murder suspect or of his host parents finding out about the major trouble he was in.

Sandra shut the door and followed Maya down the hall where Maya pressed the button to call the elevator. Sandra's phone buzzed and she glanced at the text on the screen.

"I just pray Fern's already asleep when I get back to the room so I don't have to stay up and listen to her stress out about tomorrow's schedule, which will just stress *me* out," Maya said, sighing.

Sandra reached out and touched Maya's arm. "You don't have to go back there. I just got a text from Stephen. They moved him to another room upstairs. I called earlier this morning and requested that he be put on a waiting list. I didn't want him to get too comfortable bunking with me." Sandra grinned as she read over his text again. "Maybe I'm reading between the lines, but he doesn't seem too happy about it."

"Of course he's not," Maya remarked. "He was over the moon sharing a room with you. It was just like old times. He could have moved back to the Hay-Adams after giving away his whereabouts by stupidly calling that press conference. He just wants to be near you."

The elevator bell rang and the doors opened.

They stepped on and went up two floors.

When they reached the room and Sandra inserted the key card and opened the door, she instantly tensed up. In the reflection of the wall mirror, she could see someone sitting on the bed, and it wasn't Stephen. It was a woman, who she didn't recognize at first.

Maya brushed past before Sandra could stop her and breezed down the short hall past the bathroom and stopped suddenly. She gasped, stopping in her tracks at the sight of not one, but two intruders in the room, one sitting on the bed, the other leaning against the wall in the corner next to a floor lamp.

"What are you doing here?" Maya shouted.

Sandra was about to call 911, but something stopped her; the woman sitting on the edge of the bed looked vaguely familiar. Sandra had seen her before.

By the time she joined Maya and got a look at the

two trespassers, she knew exactly who they were. She had seen them on television.

Tabitha Markey and Jane Rhodes.

FBI agents.

"How did you get in our room?" Sandra demanded to know.

Markey and Rhodes exchanged smirks before Markey answered, "We're FBI. We can pretty much get in anywhere we want."

"Without a warrant?" Maya seethed.

Rhodes chuckled. "Want to call a cop?"

"We just came to have a little chat," Rhodes said pleasantly, staring at Sandra. "By the way, that's a lovely shade of lipstick you're wearing, kind of an orangey red. Perfect for your warm skin tone."

Sandra knew this fed was being condescending to her, so she refused to engage. "What exactly do you want to chat about?"

"We just came from your husband's condo where Cliff the night guard was kind enough to show us the security footage from the night of Tess's murder, which apparently not only have you two watched already, but so have your kids," Markey sneered. "We had no idea your little private detective endeavor was a family business."

"Yeah, well, we can't help it if we work faster than the FBI," Maya said pointedly.

Markey gave her a tight smile. "We're going to need to talk with Anton Volkov."

"He's downstairs in his room. We'll take you to him," Sandra said.

Rhodes held up a hand. "No need. We know where to find him. We just stopped by to give you a little piece of advice."

Maya breathed through her nose. "And what might that be?"

Sandra could tell Maya was about to lose her temper, and casually touched her arm to bring her back from the edge.

"Back off," Rhodes said with a contemptuous sneer.

"Let us do our job," Markey said. "You didn't come here to solve a murder; you're chaperones on a class trip. None of this should be any of your concern."

"It is my concern if you're going to suggest to the press that my husband is to blame for what happened to Tess Rankin," Sandra said sharply.

"We're not pointing fingers; we're just investigating at this point, following the trail of clues wherever they might lead us," Markey said.

Rhodes nodded in agreement. "And right now, they've led us right here and to your Russian exchange student who has a knack for escaping like a teenaged Houdini."

Markey stood up from the bed and signaled Rhodes that it was time to go. "What room is he in?"

"Seven-twelve," Sandra said. "But let us come with you. I think he would be more comfortable if we were there with him when you question him."

"Our goal is not to make him feel more comfortable; it's to get him to tell us the truth!" Rhodes barked.

"She's right; you two should probably stay right here," Markey said, then in an even more patronizing tone added, "After all, at the end of the day, you're soccer moms, not FBI professionals."

And then they waltzed out of the room.

Sandra could almost feel the burning rage bursting out of Maya. She grabbed a pillow from the bed and held it toward Maya. "Here, scream into this. Don't give them the satisfaction of hearing you all the way down the hall."

Maya swatted the pillow away.

She took a deep breath and turned to Sandra. "If they think we're going to just walk away . . ."

"We made no promises to leave anything alone, Maya," Sandra assured her. "As far as I'm concerned, nothing's changed."

Maya nodded. "Except now we have a little competition."

Chapter 29

Early the following morning, Maya and Sandra went down to join the other chaperones and students in the hotel dining room for the breakfast buffet before their last day of touring. They both opted for some fresh fruit, yogurt, and coffee and wandered over to a large round table in the corner where Fern was eating with Coach Cavill and Clancy. Fern's back was to them, but they could see Cavill staring at her with a distasteful look on his face, the food on his plate untouched. Clancy, on the other hand, was scarfing down a bowl of oatmeal and raisins with gusto before moving on to a made-to-order omelette stuffed with all kinds of meat and cheeses. When Maya and Sandra arrived at the table to sit down in the two empty seats, they immediately noticed what had made Coach Cavill lose his appetite. There were big red splotches all over Fern's face, neck, and bare arms. At the moment, she was madly scratching her left shoulder, which was covered in a rash of little red bumps.

"My God, Fern, what happened to you?" Sandra gasped, pushing her fruit and yogurt away from her, unable to eat.

"Hives," Fern moaned. "They broke out all over my body last night, right about the time I found out Anton Volkov was being questioned by the FBI! I was up all night worrying, my heart was thumping like a war drum, and the itching has gotten even worse this morning!"

"You should see a doctor," Maya advised, sipping her coffee.

Fern moved from scratching her shoulder to attacking her elbow, which was also covered in red bumps. "We are on an extremely tight schedule; there's no time. I'll make an appointment with my own doctor when we get home to Portland tomorrow."

"Fern, no, you need to take care of this now," Sandra said.

"I know how to take care of it. This is completely stress related, and once I get all these kids back home safe and sound tomorrow, I will be significantly less stressed and I am sure these hives will finally start to go away."

"So you are just going to suffer until tomorrow?" Sandra asked.

Fern nodded, moving from her elbow to her right arm. "It's not that painful; it's just itchy, very, very itchy!"

"Fern, I don't think you should wait until tomorrow; why don't you cut the trip short and head home today? It's only one day," Sandra suggested.

"The kids have seen and learned so much in the time they have been here, more than most people ever do; you have done a stupendous job. They're going to remember this trip for the rest of their lives . . . but maybe now it's time to go home."

Fern shook her head, still violently scratching herself. "What? But we still have the Holocaust Memorial Museum and the Renwick Gallery and—"

"They can always come back with their families or on their own someday. You've already given them such an education on American history in everything you've already shown them. Do yourself a favor, please; just go home," Sandra urged.

Fern looked to Coach Cavill, who shrugged. "I think they're right. I know I'm ready. I was done after the Air and Space Museum."

Clancy polished off his omelette and put his fork down. "All I need to do is gas up the bus and we can be on our way."

Fern hesitated but was seriously tempted. "What about Anton? Those FBI agents who showed up at the door told me he's a suspect in what happened to that poor intern."

"They also know he's a minor who needs adult supervision, which he will have back in Maine. They know where to find him if they have more questions."

Fern finally stopped scratching. "You know what? I'm starting to feel better already."

"Good," Sandra said. "Then it's settled."

"I will make the announcement after breakfast, then give them a half hour to pack their bags so we can check out," Fern said. She then glanced at her watch. "Can you all be ready to leave by nine thirty?"

Coach Cavill jumped to his feet. "Honestly, I've been ready ever since we pulled out of the school parking lot." He turned to Maya and Sandra. "How about you, ladies?"

"We're not going," Maya announced.

"What do you mean you're not going?" Fern asked as she resumed scratching her face, both cheeks at the same time.

Maya picked up a strawberry from her plate and tossed it in her mouth. "Sandra's ex-husband needs our help, so we're going to stick around and see this thing through."

"But I promised Principal Williams I would deliver *everybody* home safely," Fern whined.

"I'm sure she won't have a problem with us staying behind, especially given the unfortunate circumstances," Sandra said.

Coach Cavill looked deflated as he turned to Sandra. "But I was going to save you a seat on the bus next to me."

Sandra ignored the comment. She was too distracted watching Ryan and Vanessa eating breakfast a few tables away with Anton and a couple of other students. She turned to Cavill. "Do me a favor though, Lucas. When Fern does the last head count before you leave, make doubly sure that my son Ryan's butt is in his seat and he's accounted for."

"Vanessa too," Maya added.

"Sure thing," Coach Cavill said with a wink.

Sandra ignored that too, and he awkwardly walked away after mumbling something about brushing his teeth.

Sandra knew she had a major battle ahead with her son.

Ryan was not going to appreciate being shipped off home to Maine when his dad was in the midst of a monumental crisis. He had already made it loudly known he wanted to be here for him. But this wasn't her first time at the rodeo. She knew things could get more complicated, even dangerous, and she was determined to keep Ryan out of it, whether he liked it or not.

Chapter 30

The South Portland High School bus had barely pulled away from the hotel with Maya and Sandra waving goodbye to their fellow chaperones and charges when Maya's phone started buzzing. She glanced at the screen and Sandra noticed her grimacing.

"What now?" Sandra asked with a sense of dread.

"Senator Grisby's about to hold a press conference. Apparently he's going to make some major announcement about Stephen."

"Probably more of the same, requesting the Senate Ethics Committee investigate or some drivel like that."

Maya read the news alert, troubled. "No, it sounds way bigger than that. Zoe Rush is also teasing it's going to be a bombshell."

Sandra got a sickening feeling in the pit of her stomach and raced through the revolving door back into the hotel lobby, rushing across the marble floor, heels clacking, with Maya chasing after her. They hurried onto the elevator and took it back up to their room, where Sandra switched the television on to a cable news channel just as Senator Grisby stepped in front of a microphone with a smug, smarmy smile on his face.

Sandra sat down on the edge of the bed and braced herself for what was about to come.

"Good morning," Grisby said; his toothy smile, made brighter and whiter by some polished dentures, slowly faded as he adopted a more somber, serious tone. "Trust me, I take no joy in what I have to tell you today. I have always been a staunch believer in a man's individual privacy. Our Constitution mandates the right for personal freedom and the pursuit of happiness. And you all know I have long been a devoted scholar of our beloved Constitution . . ."

"Get to the point, you creepy old windbag!" Sandra heard herself yelling, causing Maya to snicker.

Grisby took a dramatic pause. "But the citizens of this great country deserve leaders who are forthright, honest, and of strong moral character, and it is with great sadness that I must demonstrate to you that my esteemed colleague from Maine, Senator Stephen Wallage, has been recently lacking in all of those qualities." He pointed a crooked finger at the crowd of reporters. "He is a hypocrite and a liar and unworthy of his position as a United States Senator!"

Another dramatic pause.

Silence except for the flashes and clicks of dozens of cameras.

A tall, handsome man in his early thirties, who

was similar in looks and stature to the actor Gerard Butler, except with soulless eyes and a contemptuous sneer and an off-putting air of superiority, slid in next to Senator Grisby, who reached up to put an arm around him, since he was about a foot and a half taller. "My son, Kyle, who also happens to be my communications director . . ."

"Because nobody else would hire him," Sandra muttered.

"He has come into possession of some emails, emails first obtained by the website TPL."

Everyone had heard of TPL, which stood for "Truth to Power Leaks," started by a purveyor of justice whose mission was to publish classified documents that would expose government corruption around the world. A noble goal, at least in the beginning, but the site's content had subsequently morphed into attention-getting clickbait, more interested in wallowing in trash and scandal and humiliating a plethora of public figures. The "Truth" in its title had become far less important when it came to its salacious subject matter.

"I must tell you, the substance of these emails is quite disturbing, some are hard to digest, but without a doubt, they do give you a clearer picture of Senator Wallage and his troubling relationship with the truth."

Maya's phone frenziedly buzzed with more and more news alerts. "Zoe Rush just released the first batch of emails."

Sandra fumed at the timing and coordination of the attack. Zoe obviously made some kind of deal with Grisby to be the first news reporter to release the emails.

But what were they?

How incriminating could they be?

Maya speed-read through them as Sandra watched her, almost too scared to know what was in them.

"How bad?" Sandra gulped.

Maya frowned, raising her eyes up to Sandra.

Sandra right away detected the pity in them. She shot a hand out. "Give me the phone."

Maya hesitated, but Sandra jumped to her feet and crossed over to her and snatched the phone out of Maya's hand.

She began frantically scrolling down through the newly released emails from Stephen's personal account.

Long exchanges between Stephen and Tess.

From Stephen: *It was so hard at the office today not being able to hold you and kiss you. I kept wanting it to be Sunday again when we spent the whole morning cuddling in bed.*

From Tess: *When are you going to tell Deborah about us? It's killing me keeping "us" a secret. I want to tell the world!*

From Stephen: *Please, sweet pea, be patient. I will tell Deborah, it just needs to be the right time.*

From Tess: *I think she suspects. She can barely look at me when she comes by the office. She's always so rude too. She doesn't even say thank you when I fetch her coffee. I can't stand her.*

From Stephen: *I know, she's a smart woman, I'm sure on some level she senses the love between us.*

Sandra's mouth dropped open as she read the emails.

Love?

He *loved* Tess?

A fling was one thing, but love?

She was less than half his age.

On the television, it was chaos as a crush of reporters shouted questions at a gleeful Senator Grisby, who could barely contain himself, he was so excited about blowing up Stephen's lie about his relationship with his intern Tess being strictly platonic. Grisby's son, Kyle, casually took a step back behind his father, far less thirsty for the spotlight.

Sandra returned to scrolling down the endless email exchanges.

From Tess: *I worry when she finds out, she's going to try and break us up, try and convince you what we have is somehow wrong.*

From Stephen: *I promise that's never going to happen. You get me. We're good together. And it would be stupid of me to ever let you go.*

Sandra could feel the bile rising in her throat.

She threw a hand over her mouth, fearing she was about to be sick, but luckily, it eventually passed.

Maya put a comforting arm around her. "You okay?"

Sandra nodded, but she wasn't okay.

He had lied to her.

Blatantly lied.

Again.

Deborah Crowley had been right all along.

Sandra had forgiven him for his past indiscretions.

Although their marriage had not survived, they had found a way to make their relationship work for the sake of their boys.

And she had been impressed with how hard Stephen had tried to regain the trust of his family.

But it was all a sham.

In the end, he was just another lying, cheating politician.

Self-serving.

Self-involved.

Self-sabotaging.

It was yet another gut punch from her soon-to-be ex-husband. Sandra was embarrassed, humiliated, and, above all, furious.

It was time for her to quit Team Stephen.

Permanently.

Chapter 31

"It's not true!" Stephen blurted out as he yanked open the door to his hotel room to find Maya and Sandra standing there. He looked exhausted with the sleeves of his white dress shirt rolled up, the bright blue necktie Sandra had given him one Christmas loosened and askew. He had dark circles under his eyes, and Sandra noticed he had been chewing on his fingernails, a nervous habit she had spent years trying to break him of with little success. Behind him in the room, his key staff had set up a makeshift office safely away from the chaos of their usual Capitol digs. Preston paced back and forth by the window, phone clamped to his ear, trying to do damage control, and Suzanne sat at the small desk, on her laptop, typing away, pretending everything was business as usual. The television was on mute, but they could see it was currently wall-to-wall coverage of Stephen and his emails.

Stephen waved Maya and Sandra into the room and shut the door behind them. "They're making things up now out of whole cloth! I swear, they are hell-bent on destroying me!"

"Who's *they*?" Sandra asked.

"Grisby and his allies. They smell blood in the water, and they're coming after me with everything they've got," Stephen said, rubbing his temples with his two index fingers.

Preston lowered his phone. "My PR contact, Olivia Kennedy, thinks you should do another presser, issue a full-throated denial that those emails belong to you."

"He has already done that," Sandra interjected. "If he keeps holding press conferences, that's only going to make him look desperate. I would just issue a brief statement about the emails being fake."

Preston glared at Sandra. He did not appreciate being ordered about by the wife, nearly ex-wife, of the boss. "With all due respect, Mrs. Wallage, our situation *is* desperate, and we need to start getting aggressive . . ."

"Then be aggressive with a statement," Stephen said. "Sandra's right. Another press conference is a bad idea." Nobody wanted to say it, so Stephen said it himself. "I can't screw things up with a simple statement like I did the last time I stepped in front of a microphone."

Preston forced a smile. "Fine." Then he went back to talking to his PR contact, deliberately turning his back to everyone.

Stephen crossed over to Suzanne and hovered

over her. "Suzanne, can you stop what you're doing and start working on that statement?"

She nodded. "Sure, what do you want me to say?"

"That Senator Grisby is a liar, those emails are a fantasy, and have nothing to do with me, or Tess . . ."

Suzanne hesitated.

Stephen cocked an eyebrow. "What?"

"There are reports popping up on both CNN and FOX that those emails have been confirmed as coming from your personal account."

Stephen's face went white. "That's impossible . . ."

There was an uncomfortable silence.

Finally, Stephen cleared his throat. "Okay, everybody clear out. I need to talk to Sandra."

Nobody moved at first.

Stephen raised his voice. "Now. Take a break. Go down to the lobby and get some coffee. I need to have a conversation with my wife."

Suzanne jumped up first, offering Sandra a sympathetic smile as she scooted out. Preston moved a bit slower, still gabbing on the phone by the window as Stephen marched over, gripped him by the arm, and physically escorted him out the door while Preston continued his conversation with his PR contact.

Maya hung back, then spoke softly. "I'll be down in our room if you need me."

"Thanks, Maya," Sandra whispered.

After Maya slipped out, Stephen shut the door and turned to her. He studied her face. Sandra struggled to maintain an inscrutable expression, but they had been married too many years, knew each other far too well, for Stephen not to be able to detect the festering doubt in her eyes.

"What, Stephen?"

"When it comes to being completely honest and truthful with you in the past, I know I have some-what of a spotty track record."

At least he was self-aware enough to recognize it, Sandra thought to herself.

"So you can understand why I might be a little skeptical now in this particular moment?" Sandra said evenly.

"Yes." Stephen smiled. "Of course. You have every reason in the world to be suspicious. I would be, if I were you."

Sandra knew where this was going.

They had had this exact same conversation several times before during the course of their marriage. She decided to help prod him along. "But you swear, on your life, on the life of your sons, that this time is different? That you are one hundred percent innocent of these latest accusations?"

Her sharp tone wounded him, but he knew he had very limited credibility at the moment to offer up any indignation.

"Yes," Stephen moaned, lowering his head and staring at the floor. "Sandra, I will say it over and over until you finally believe me. My relationship with Tess was strictly professional; nothing inappropriate ever happened between us, *nothing!*"

"What about the emails?"

"I didn't write them!" Stephen wailed.

"Then who did?"

"My guess is Grisby's kid. He's like his father's

enforcer, a real bad actor. I'm certain he's behind all of this!"

"So they hacked your account?"

"Yes, that's the only way . . ."

Now it was Sandra's turn to study Stephen.

She could tell he was panicked and on edge, but in the past when he had lied to her there was an underlying smugness, a cocky confidence, like the last thing he ever expected was to actually be caught out in a lie. But now that part was missing, which suggested to Sandra that he might, just might, be telling her the truth.

But she certainly wasn't about to give him the satisfaction, at least at this point, of letting him know that she was ready to believe him again, the first time in a long while. No, she had been too hurt by the previous myriad of lies.

Stephen stepped forward and grabbed her hands. "I know I have yet to earn back your trust, I know there's a possibility I never will, but I'm going to keep trying."

There were a million memory flashes going through her mind. All the good times with Stephen and their two sons, those happy family vacations and Christmas mornings, all the bad times, when she would happen upon the little clues that painted a clear picture of her husband's infidelities, the painful confrontations with him, the hollow denials.

She peered into his eyes and saw the sorrow, the misery, the anguish, and she felt sorry for him, not enough to tell him that she believed him wholeheartedly, but enough to continue helping him.

"Don't worry, Maya and I will get to the bottom of this," she said.

And she was confident they would eventually find the truth, whatever that truth might be.

But not knowing what they would find truly scared her.

Chapter 32

"So is it true?" Senator Abbie Cantwell asked after escorting Maya and Sandra into her Senate office and shutting the door behind them away from the prying eyes and ears of her young Congressional staff.

Sandra shrugged. "He says no."

Senator Cantwell folded her arms. "I'm not asking you what Stephen is telling you. Lord knows you can't trust a rooster who's already been caught in the henhouse."

Maya snickered.

Senator Cantwell's eyes narrowed as she stared at Sandra. "What's your gut telling you?"

Sandra took a deep breath. "My gut is telling me to believe what he's saying. But then again, my gut has been wildly off before."

"From where I sit, it looks to me like this whole thing is starting to spiral out of control. The press is feeding off it like a frenzied school of starving piranhas!"

Senator Cantwell certainly loved her colorful metaphors.

"He's going to put out a statement," Sandra said. "I discouraged him from doing another press conference."

"Good advice. That just opens the door to more scrutiny, but he's got to explain those emails. Just saying they're fake isn't going to cut it. In Washington, you're guilty until proven innocent, no two ways about it."

Abbie Cantwell had been a Congresswoman from Virginia when she and Sandra first met. They had first been introduced at the annual bipartisan Congressional baseball game where Stephen served as pitcher and Abbie played the outfielder position before either had decided to run for the Senate. Sandra and Abbie had immediately hit it off, becoming fast friends, going to the gym together and taking an art class on the weekends. When Sandra became pregnant with her oldest son, Jack, the same time Abbie was carrying her daughter, Sarah, they attended the same prenatal and childbirth class. Abbie had been an Army helicopter pilot in the Gulf War after 9/11. A rocket-propelled grenade struck her chopper, causing it to crash. Abbie lost a leg, which you could hardly tell now with her robotic prosthetic replacement. She was determined to return to normal with the help of her doctor and physical therapist. She wound up marrying the physical therapist who guided her through her recovery, and he was also the one who encouraged her to get into politics despite her early misgivings. But now Abbie was a rock star in Washington, focusing on veterans' issues. She and Sandra had remained close even after Sandra left Washington and moved back to Maine. Sandra also knew that Abbie was a plain talker, never one to sugarcoat anything, and so she was the first person Sandra thought she and Maya should talk to about Senator Grisby's troubling evidence against Stephen.

"What can you tell us about Senator Grisby?" Maya asked.

Senator Cantwell let out a derisive laugh. "Idiot. Opportunist. Infuriating sexist. His wife was lovely, when she was allowed to speak. Poor dear, may she rest in peace. She knitted me a reindeer sweater the Christmas before she passed. It was the tackiest thing I had ever laid eyes on, but such a sweet gesture. I wore it to the Virginia Holiday Reception at the Decatur House. She was so excited. I made a friend for life."

Sandra frowned. "Why do you think Grisby hates Stephen so much?"

"Oh, I'm sure he doesn't. He just saw an opening and took it. He wants his political party to retake the Senate majority in the next midterms, and knocking off a powerful Senator from the opposing party is just his small contribution to the cause. He's your typical craven, corrupt politician happily willing to brush the truth aside in order to achieve his goal. The trouble is, people are starting to believe him."

"We need to prove those emails are fake," Sandra said.

Maya grimaced. "Even though they apparently came from Stephen's personal account."

Senator Cantwell sat back in her leather chair. An American flag was hung behind her. "I never said it was going to be easy. My advice, focus on Grisby's son. He's worse than his father. There have been rumors going around for years that he's bad news, rubbing elbows with a bunch of unsavory types. He was a lawyer in Norfolk for a while until he got disbarred by the state of Virginia for bringing forth too many frivolous lawsuits on behalf of his lowlife criminal clients."

"Sounds like a real catch," Maya sneered.

"He will be the first one to tell you," Senator Cantwell joked. She leaned forward in her chair and offered a reassuring smile. "I know it looks bad, and maybe it is, but with Grisby's holy terror of a son intimately involved in all of this, I smell a setup. So I did my homework. Zoe Rush."

"What about her?" Sandra asked.

"She appears to have been the point person in this whole press rollout. She was the first to publish some of those incriminating emails, so she's probably working with Kyle."

"Zoe and I have been friends for years, but I hardly recognize her now. I just don't understand why she would ever get mixed up with someone like Kyle Grisby," Sandra lamented.

"Who knows? Maybe they have somehow convinced her that it's all true, and she's just trying to do right by Tess. But you need to trace those emails, find out how TPL got their hands on them, if they're legit, and who sent them to Zoe."

"How?" Sandra sighed.

"It just so happens, Zoe Rush has been trying to get me to sit down with her for months to get me on the record for a book proposal she's been working on about the challenges for women in all branches of the military. She's very passionate about it, and she's told me multiple times that my interview is key to the book being sold for a six-figure advance. She should be here any minute."

Maya was one step ahead of her and chuckled. "So you will agree to the interview *if* she coughs up an IP address for us?"

"Sandra, you've hitched your wagon to one smart PI," Senator Cantwell said, grinning. The phone on her desk buzzed and her assistant outside the office spoke through the intercom. "Senator, your one o'clock is here."

"Zoe is always very punctual," Senator Cantwell noted, checking her watch. "Send her in, Mary Beth."

A few seconds later, the door opened and Zoe sauntered in, trying to act cool but clearly excited to be securing such a pivotal interview for her book project.

"Senator Cantwell, thank you for finally agreeing . . ." Her eyes drifted across the room and stopped at Maya and Sandra, who were standing off to the side. "Sandra . . ."

"Hello, Zoe, congratulations on your new book. I'm sure it will be a number one *New York Times* best seller."

Zoe glanced at Senator Cantwell, confused. "I'm sorry, I don't understand what's happening here."

Senator Cantwell clasped her hands together and flashed Zoe a knowing smile. "Well, then, let me bring you up to speed."

It was less than five minutes later when Zoe Rush was reluctantly giving up the IP address for all those emails to Maya and Sandra. She had made a few noises about how she didn't appreciate being blackmailed, how she was a principled journalist and was just doing her job, but in the end, she did not have much of a choice.

Six figures was quite a lot of money.

Even for a principled journalist.

Chapter 33

The Cyber Crimes Unit of the South Portland Police Department was pretty much just one guy. His name was Oscar Dunford, and as a rumpled, slow-talking, socially awkward millennial with a lazy eye and a propensity for wearing stupid T-shirts that said things like "Math—The Only Place Where People Buy 73 Oranges and No One Wonders Why." He wasn't your typical idea of a dedicated, hard-nosed cop. Still, he was the best resource the department had when it came to investigating computer-related issues and crimes, a bona fide wunderkind. He had all the talent and know-how of a top Russian hacker, but without the malicious intent.

He'd also had a massive crush on Maya ever since he saw her bent over retrieving a Snickers bar at the vending machine on his first day at work. Maya left the department just a few months after Oscar had been recruited, but she had made a lasting impression on the newbie officer, and he had made it his personal mission to stay in contact, even after she put up her own shingle as a private detective. Oscar was more than willing to moonlight, helping his imaginary girlfriend Maya whenever she needed him. And for Maya's part, she was happy to take advantage of Oscar's crush, if it meant getting key information she needed on a particular case.

Such as tracing the IP address Zoe had forked over.

"Talk to me, Oscar," Maya said into her phone in Stephen's empty office at the Senate Building where she and Sandra were hanging out while the rest of his staff worked remotely to avoid the increasingly rabid press, not to mention all of his opportunistic colleagues across the aisle, eager to exploit his dire situation.

"I had a dream about you last night," Oscar whispered excitedly into the phone.

"Was it the same weird one you had last month after binging *Lost* where we're both on a plane that crashes on a remote island after an apocalyptic event, and we're the only two survivors left on earth, and we discover that it's all just an illusion created by some aliens so they can watch us to see how we reproduce?"

"That was so awesome, I actually wrote everything down after I woke up from that one. Maybe I'll turn it into a short story, but no, this one was based more in reality. I dreamed we were getting married—"

"That's not based in reality, Oscar, but I'm flattered I'm like the Scarlett Johansson of your REM sleep cycle."

"You would have made such a great Black Widow! I'm picturing you right now in that black leather jumpsuit. . . ."

"Oscar, focus. What do you have for me?"

"Why do you have to be so bossy? Don't get me wrong. I'm incredibly turned on right now . . ."

"Oscar!"

"You're not really much into foreplay, are you?"

"Foreplay suggests a back-and-forth that ultimately leads somewhere, and trust me, as much as I adore you, Oscar, this foreplay here is going to hit a dead end. Do you understand me?"

"I miss the days when you would at least pretend to flirt with me in order to get what you want out of me."

Maya sighed. "I know, but we're in a bit of a time crunch down here, and so I don't have a lot of time for our usual flirty repartee. Now, did you trace the IP?"

"Yup."

"And?"

There was a long pause.

Maya rolled her eyes. "Are you pouting, Oscar?"

"Maybe a little."

"If I agree to have dinner with you when we get back to Portland, will that make you happier and speed things along here?"

"Absolutely! But no fast food, not like last time, no Five Guys near the mall. I want a real restaurant in the Old Port, with a pricey wine list and maybe a fancy raw oyster appetizer with lemon and a mignonette sauce and stuff."

"Fine, I'll let you pick. Whatever you want. I'm

actually impressed you know what a mignonette sauce is. Now can we finally get down to business?"

"If we must. Okay, I talked to one of my contacts over at Truth to Power Leaks, and he said that what Senator Grisby claimed about TPL first obtaining Senator Wallage's emails was a lie. They had nothing to do with it."

"Why didn't they issue a denial?"

"Why would they? They were happy to take the credit. It's free publicity for their cause."

"Then who did get their hands on those emails?"

"Nobody."

"You're confusing me, Oscar."

"Nobody stole them because they're not real."

Maya noticed Sandra pensively staring at her from across the room, waiting impatiently for some kind of news that might clear Stephen, and so Maya gave her an encouraging smile.

"How do you know they're not real?"

"Because of the IP address you gave me. TPL didn't forward those emails to that reporter Zoe Rush; they came from a company called Freedom Fighters, Inc."

"And who are they?"

"According to their website, they consult with companies to rout out corruption, make sure everyone stays aboveboard, but in reality, they do just the opposite, because the whole operation is fake, it's a farce, it's literally just one guy with a shell corporation."

"Let me guess. Kyle Grisby."

"Yeah, he uses it as a cover for all sorts of nefarious political games and misdeeds. I guess he thinks he's covering his tracks, but man, it was so easy tracing everything right back to him. He's not nearly as smart as he thinks he is."

"So *he* wrote the emails?"

"He probably had someone he knew, a hacker type, slip through the firewall and hack Wallage's email account. I can't imagine he's bright enough to do it himself. Then, he could just mirror the Senator's account and write whatever he wanted."

"So not only did he pose as Stephen; he also wrote all the lovestruck emails from Tess."

"Yeah, which is why they sounded so stilted and forced. Let's face it, he's not exactly Tennessee Williams."

"Again, you've impressed me with a Tennessee Williams reference."

"I'm young, but smart. I took an American Playwrights course at Bates."

"Oscar, I don't know how to thank you!"

"Yes, you do, I'm on OpenTable right now making a reservation for two for next week."

"I will even let you order dessert."

"I know a place with a life-changing Key Lime crème brûlée that we could share—"

She ended the call before he could finish and quickly updated Sandra. Maya could see the tension draining from Sandra's whole body as she listened, relieved. Sandra then grabbed her phone.

Maya stepped toward her. "Who are you calling?"

"Zoe Rush. She needs to know she's been used as a pawn. It was all a setup."

Maya thrust out a hand. "Wait. Not yet."

"But we have the evidence to prove it was all a sham. We need to get it out there."

"We may have enough to blow up Senator Grisby's plan to ruin Stephen's career, but we still don't know who it was who killed Tess. What if Kyle is somehow connected? If we tip him off at this point, if we spook him and he runs scared, we may never know the truth. We need to keep all of this under wraps. If he is involved, and he thinks he's getting away with it, he may get cocky and make a mistake."

"And we'll be there when he does," Sandra said with a sly smile.

Chapter 34

There were no surprises in the life of Kyle Grisby. At least not for a good chunk of his day.

When he ambled out of his townhouse near Dupont Circle at six the following morning, in a tight-fitting tank top to show off his thick, muscular biceps and short shorts to draw attention to his sculpted calves, the gym rat had no idea his daily routine was under surveillance. He hopped in his sporty Papaya Metallic Macan Porsche that was parked out front and sped away.

Maya and Sandra, who had been sitting across the street for two hours in a rented nondescript blue Toyota Camry, pulled out from the curb, did a quick U-turn, and zipped off after the racing Porsche. Luckily, there was enough early morning traffic to slow down the speedster and they were able to keep pace, crawling along two cars behind him. In two blocks, Kyle pulled up to a parking valet stand outside a very exclusive-looking gym, got out, and wagged a finger in the face of the attendant, apparently warning him to take very good care of his vehicle. The young attendant nodded vigorously with a forced smile. He was probably used to dealing with a lot of these entitled jerks. This was Washington, DC, after all. Satisfied the attendant wasn't going to take his beloved Porsche on an impulsive joyride, Kyle pressed a twenty in the palm of the guy's hand and headed inside, a gym bag slung over his shoulder.

Maya, who was behind the wheel, found an empty parking space directly across the street and maneuvered the Camry into it. They could see through the large picture window that looked into the reception area Kyle meeting with a large muscle bear of a trainer in a bright blue tank top. They exchanged a few words and then Kyle turned and said something to the receptionist. She smiled awkwardly, completely turned off by whatever he was saying. Then he disappeared into the men's locker room.

Sandra watched the trainer flirt with the girl behind the check-in desk, who was much more receptive to the hunky bear than Kyle. "If you think one of us should go in there, it should be you. He probably knows who I am, and let's face it, you know your way around a gym a whole lot better than I do."

Maya laughed. "I think we're good. His trainer doesn't look like a savvy political operative or Russian hacker who we should be worried about. We'll just wait for him to finish his workout."

Sandra glanced out the passenger side-view mirror and frowned. "Maya, did you notice—?"

"The red Jetta. Yes, it was parked four cars behind us at Grisby's townhouse, and now it's across the street just down from the gym."

"Do you think someone else is following Kyle Grisby?"

"Maybe, or they could be following us."

Sandra jolted up in her seat. "Really?" She started to crank her head around to get a better look, but Maya stopped her.

"Don't look. You'll just tip off whoever's in that Jetta to the fact that we know it's there."

Sandra whipped her head back around and stared straight ahead. "Sorry, sometimes I feel like such an amateur when it comes to this whole PI thing."

"You're doing fine," Maya reassured her.

Sandra waited for more, but nothing came. Maya wasn't the most effusive person, mostly she was all business, so Sandra decided to take the "doing fine" comment as at least a passing grade.

"It's way too much of a coincidence that Jetta keeps popping up everywhere we go," Maya said.

"Do you think it's those two FBI agents, Markey and Rhodes?"

Maya adjusted her rearview mirror, pretending to check her lipstick but studying the Jetta down the street. She shook her head. "No, it's just one guy. He looks big. And bald. Kind of like a low-rent Vin Diesel."

"What should we do?"

"Nothing right now. We keep one eye on Kyle Grisby and the other on Chrome Dome, and see what happens."

Precisely one hour later, Kyle Grisby emerged from the gym freshly showered and wearing a sleek Brooks Brothers suit. When the attendant brought around his Porsche, Kyle meticulously gave it a once-over to ensure there were no new dents or scratches. Satisfied, he jumped in and sped off. Maya and Sandra followed in the Camry, with the red Jetta still behind them, tailing them at every turn.

Kyle Grisby's day post-workout consisted of coffee with a political hack reporter known to promote baseless conspiracy theories, a meeting at a political action committee raising reelection funds for his father, lunch with his father's comely Chief of Staff. There was nothing out of the ordinary to note for a Senator's communications director, not until the early evening after Kyle stopped by his townhouse to change into a more casual Ralph Lauren white open-collar dress shirt, pressed jeans, and dark sports coat, got back behind the wheel of his Porsche, and drove out to Georgetown. The closer they got to his destination, the more noticeably nervous Sandra got.

Maya glanced over at her. "What's wrong?"

"I have a sick feeling I know where he's going."

"Where?"

"Just up ahead."

Sure enough, Kyle parked his Porsche in front

of a very familiar Georgetown townhouse, one Sandra had been to recently. Kyle sprang out of the Porsche, popped a mint into his mouth, grabbed a bouquet of fresh flowers from the passenger's seat, and then bounded up to the front door and rang the bell.

When the door opened, just as she suspected, Deborah Crowley, in a lovely simple black cocktail dress, lit up at the sight of the flowers. When Kyle handed them to her, he reached in to steal a kiss. She blushed.

"Your husband's girlfriend is just full of surprises now, isn't she?" Maya cracked.

They watched as Deborah invited him inside the empty house that had no furniture since the movers had already been there. They could see through the front window Deborah making Kyle a drink as he stared at her lasciviously; then they disappeared into another room and were no longer visible. Twenty minutes later, they emerged and drove a short distance in Kyle's Porsche to a nearby restaurant and had dinner. That lasted less than an hour. After Kyle drove her home, he followed her to the door and she gave him a sweet albeit brief kiss good night before she disappeared inside and promptly closed the door on his face. He looked frustrated, as if the evening had not gone as planned. He stalked back to his Porsche and sped off, Maya and Sandra barely managing to keep up. He returned home, armed the car alarm in his Porsche, and skulked inside, apparently for the night.

It had been a long day.

But it had not been wasted.

They now had a tangible connection between Stephen's biggest political enemy and his disgruntled ex-girlfriend, which was troubling, to say the least.

"Should we split up tomorrow? One of us tail Deborah, the other Kyle?" Sandra asked.

"First, let's find out who's been tailing *us* all day," Maya said quietly, her eyes flicking up to the rearview mirror again.

Sandra almost spun around but caught herself. "Is it the Jetta?"

Maya nodded. "How well do you know this area?"

"I know every inch of Dupont Circle. I used to jog this whole neighborhood every morning when I lived here."

"Good. Then you can tell me how we lose this guy."

Sandra lit up with a smile. "Just drive. I'll tell you where to go."

Maya slammed her foot down on the accelerator and the Camry shot down the street. The driver of the Jetta, apparently caught by surprise, nearly crashed into a mailbox trying to catch up to them. Maya swerved down a side street, careening left onto a residential street, and then Sandra yelled for her to take a sharp right. They squealed into an alley and Maya quickly turned off all the lights in the car. They waited a few seconds and then saw the red Jetta zip by in hot pursuit. Maya backed out of the alley and followed the Jetta, which circled the block five times trying to locate the blue Camry, the bald driver having no clue it was right behind him.

Finally giving up, he headed toward Connecticut Avenue and then George Washington Memorial Parkway. Once they were on the freeway, it was easy for Maya to maintain a safe distance, staying a few cars behind the Jetta at a time. About a half hour later, the Jetta finally took an exit at Alexandria, Virginia. From there, he drove to a sprawling colonial-style home. He parked in the circular driveway and got out. Maya rolled the Camry to a stop on the opposite side of the street, far enough away from a streetlight so the car was hidden in the shadows.

It was late, but there were lights on inside the house. The bald man walked up and knocked on the door. A few minutes later, the door opened and a man in a bathrobe and slippers stepped out onto the porch to confer with him. When his face was in the light, Maya and Sandra recognized him immediately.

It was Senator Charles Grisby.

Maya scoffed. "So we're following his son, and he's got one of his security detail, I presume, following us."

"He knows we're helping Stephen," Sandra said. "I know the Senator. He likes to have eyes and ears everywhere so nothing ever surprises him."

Senator Grisby was yelling now, clearly upset.

"I'm guessing he just found out his guy lost us," Maya said. "So how do we deal with this? He's not going to give up. No matter what we do, where we go, he is going to find us."

"Precisely, so why fight it?" Sandra suggested. "If Senator Grisby wants to keep a watchful eye on us, let's make it easy for him . . . by getting right up in his face."

Chapter 35

Maya and Sandra swept into the East Room of the White House over an hour later after first arriving at the Southeast Gate and enduring an endless security cattle call, including no fewer than three metal detectors.

"I thought we'd never get in here. We had to prove everything, name, date of birth, Social Security number. I thought for sure they were going to ask for a blood sample," Maya joked.

"Luckily, Suzanne's sorority sister works for the First Lady's social secretary and managed to get us on the guest list at the last minute," Sandra said as Maya gawked at the impeccable decor of the People's House.

They had scored the invite mere hours earlier and had to work fast to get ready, which meant buying new outfits at a trendy DC boutique. Sandra opted for a sexy Zac Posen off-the-shoulder metallic party jacquard dress and Maya selected a

Lela Rose square-neck sleeveless floral-jacquard fit-and-flare dress, although Maya was prepared to just don some jeans and an off-the-rack JCPenney plain black crew-neck elbow-sleeve blouse after glancing at her new outfit's price tag. That's when Sandra insisted on putting both dresses on her credit card. It was important they fit in with the fashionable dress code at this high-powered soiree the President was hosting to celebrate the signing of a bipartisan infrastructure bill.

Maya had never imagined in a million years that she would ever step foot in the White House in her lifetime, but here she was, rocking a designer cocktail dress, gawking at the impeccable decor. Buffet tables with lamb, lobster claws, cauliflower mac 'n' cheese, were set up in the East Room and State Dining Room for those who were hungry; a jazz band played a Duke Ellington classic off to the side; guests milled about with their wine and cocktails gossiping and networking.

Maya glanced around. "So where's the President?"

"He and the First Lady usually hole up in the residence at the beginning of the reception before descending the Grand Staircase, making a big entrance. You'll know when because the crowd will go wild. Then they'll say a few words and head straight for the photo line, where they will spend most of the evening taking pictures with everybody."

"Max will freak if I get a photo with the President."

"The trick is to avoid the picture line at first," Sandra advised. "I jump in at the last minute when there's just a few people left so there is much less of a hassle."

Maya grinned. "You're a real pro at this."

"Sandra, my dear, what a lovely surprise seeing you here," a woman said from behind them with a melodious southern drawl.

Maya and Sandra turned around to see a skeletal woman, way too thin, in her mid-sixties, a face so tight from plastic surgery her eyes bulged out, almost too big for her face. She was in a very Audrey Hepburn—style modest black sheath dress with pearls and Tidewater perfume.

"Babe, it's been a while," Sandra said through gritted teeth. She obviously was not a fan of this woman. "Maya, this is Babe Grisby."

Babe was the widow of Senator Bob Milley of Louisiana, a Washington socialite for decades. When her husband died from pancreatic cancer, she did not waste any time hitching her wagon to another Washington power player. Lucky for her, Senator Charles Grisby was available after his first wife, Clementine, passed, so after suffering through an appropriate grieving period Babe and Charles finally married, once Babe managed to get rid of the young woman Charles was seeing on the sly during the final months of his wife's life. Babe was the polar opposite of Grisby's sweet-natured late wife. She was malevolent. Just like her new husband.

"Nice to meet you," Maya said with a fake smile.

Babe never made eye contact with Maya; she just nodded blithely in her direction, keeping her focus squarely on Sandra. She pouted and then shook her head with fake sympathy. "You poor thing. No one ever thinks about what the wife must be going through."

"I can assure you, Babe, I am just fine."

Babe reached out, her bony fingers grabbing at Sandra's. "I'm here if you need to talk. I know our husbands are not exactly golfing buddies, but we wives need to stick together, bridge that poisonous political divide."

"I appreciate your concern, Babe," Sandra said, forcing a smile.

"Has Stephen made any decisions yet?"

"About what?"

Babe licked her lips. "About resigning?"

Sandra stiffened. "Who says he's thinking about resigning?"

Babe's eyes tried to grow wider, but it was a nearly impossible task given how much they were bulging out already. "Oh, my dear, everyone here is talking about it. It's unfortunate, but we are in the Beltway. It's bound to happen."

"Well, you can report back to everyone who sent you over here with your well-wishes and condolences that reports of my husband's political demise are greatly exaggerated."

"We all hope, for Stephen's sake, and yours, of course, that this ugly situation manages to sort itself out."

Lie.

"We only want the best for you and Stephen."

Another lie.

"I have always said Stephen was a rising star who could be President someday."

Which is why he must be brought down.

"Well, your husband is doing everything he possibly can to ensure that Stephen moving here to the White House never becomes a reality," Sandra said curtly.

This comment caught Babe off guard.

She was not used to being confronted, especially with the truth. She hemmed and hawed before brushing it off with a wave of her hand. "That's just politics, I suppose."

Sandra did not respond.

Maya enjoyed watching Babe squirm.

Finally, Babe pursed her thin rouged lips and retracted her hand from Sandra. "I better go. I want to find someone to snap a photo of me next to Jackie O's portrait in the Gold Room. Excuse me." She then scurried off.

"I'm surprised you two haven't stayed in touch since you left Washington," Maya cracked.

"Oh, this is just the beginning. Look around. There are dozens more just like her circling like sharks, working up the nerve to come over here and trash Stephen to my face, fish around for some nugget of information about his impending resignation so they can leak it to the press."

"Why did you ever leave this paradise?"

Sandra chuckled. "I say bring 'em on. I've got my armor on; I'm ready for battle."

Maya noticed a bald man loitering near the bar, Grisby's security guy who had followed them the night before. She turned back to Sandra. "Vin Diesel's here. I'm going to go over and say hello."

Sandra peered across the room to see him just as a trio of dolled-up ladies sipping cosmos descended upon her. "Go. I'm about to have my hands full with the Real Housewives of DC."

"Good luck slaying those dragons," Maya joked as she scooted off toward the bar, past Vin Diesel, who was slurping down what smelled like whiskey. Maya quickly conferred with the bartender and then stepped aside as Vin turned and slammed his empty glass down on the bar. The bartender already had one poured and handed it to him.

"You must have read my mind," Vin said.

"No, she did," the bartender replied, nodding toward Maya.

"You looked thirsty, so I took the liberty of buying you another drink."

Vin gaped at her, surprised to see her, then grumbled, "It's an open bar."

"Lucky me. Now I'll have tip money for the valet."

"What are you doing here?" Vin growled.

"I hope making your job easier. I'm right here in front of you so you don't have to run around town looking for me."

"I don't know what you're talking about . . ." Vin muttered unconvincingly. "I work for—"

"Senator Grisby, I know."

He flinched, clearly rattled.

How did she know so much about him?

It was obvious he thought he had been so careful when he tailed them the previous evening.

Maya suddenly sensed someone sliding in close behind her.

"Beck, why don't you introduce me to your friend?"

Another heavy southern accent.

There was little doubt in Maya's mind who the

voice belonged to, and so she turned around, now face-to-face with Senator Grisby.

"Maya Kendrick," Maya said with a bright smile, and shot out her hand to shake.

Senator Grisby lit up like a Christmas tree at the sight of her. He grabbed her hand, lifted it up, and softly kissed it. "A pleasure, Ms. Kendrick. I'm Charles."

He didn't know who she was.

And Maya could only imagine the frantic signals his security guy Beck was trying to send at that very moment. Maya noticed Grisby's eyes flick in Beck's direction and then give him a puzzled look, but he soon gave up on what Beck was trying to tell him and returned his gaze to Maya. "Now I pride myself on knowing every gorgeous young lady in these rarified Washington circles, but I must say, you are a fresh discovery."

"I crashed," Maya said.

"And I must say, we're all the better for it."

He still clasped her hand, squeezing it tighter.

A woman's sharp voice suddenly cut through the air.

"Charles!"

Grisby deflated.

His new wife, Babe, was back from having her photo taken with Jackie O's portrait.

He quickly released Maya's hand, much to her relief.

Babe kept one suspicious eye on Maya as she spoke to her husband. "Walt Farrady is looking for you. He wants to discuss the appropriations measure."

"Right, yes, where is he?"

"Over there." Babe pointed with her bony finger.

Across the room, far away from Maya.

"I won't take up any more of your time," Maya cooed, bounding off with a flourish.

She saw Beck speaking intently with Grisby as he escorted him through the throng of guests to his colleague Farrady, no doubt explaining to him en route just who Maya was and alerting him to the fact that they were now being watched by the same woman he was supposed to be watching.

Which was exactly what Sandra and Maya had wanted.

Two could play this game.

Grisby needed to know he was pinned down under a microscope like an insect in a high school biology class. And they could make him writhe like the skewered worm he was.

Chapter 36

Deborah Crowley looked smashing in an off-white one-shoulder cutout cocktail dress, sipping a Manhattan while chatting up a glassy-eyed Montana Congressman in a cowboy hat who'd probably had one too many shots of free bourbon. Out of the corner of one eye, Deborah caught a glimpse of Sandra standing a few feet away, watching her. She managed to extricate herself from the obviously boring exchange, bid a quick adieu to the slavishly enthralled politician, and scooted over to join her.

"You're still here," Sandra said with a bright smile.

"Yes." Deborah nodded. "I'm here for another week tying up loose ends. I didn't exactly plan my exit strategy seamlessly. I scheduled the movers way too soon, so I'm sleeping on a blow-up mattress and I had to borrow this dress from a girlfriend who's the same size."

"Well, you look lovely," Sandra noted.

"Thanks," Deborah sighed. "It's not every night you get invited to the White House. Trust me, I'm not one of those jaded Beltway insiders who act blasé about coming here and getting a photo with the President and First Lady. I was not going to miss this for the world."

"Have you finished up at the Commonwealth Fund?"

"Last Friday, which has been a blessing, because now I have time to say a proper goodbye to all the people I am actually going to miss, which is only a handful, to be perfectly honest . . ."

"I'm sure they're all going to miss you as well. Is Kyle one of those friends?"

"Kyle who?"

"Kyle Grisby."

There was a long silence.

"I'm sorry, aren't you two—?"

The cocktail glass suddenly slipped through Deborah's fingers and smashed to the floor. A waiter was on the scene in a heartbeat with a hand broom and dustpan to clean it up. Deborah reached out and touched his shoulder. "I'm so sorry . . ."

"No problem, ma'am, accidents happen," he said, bending over to sweep up the shards of glass.

Shaken, Deborah returned her attention to Sandra. "How did you know?" Before Sandra had the opportunity to answer, Deborah raised an index finger to stop her. "Wait. I forgot. You're a private detective now. It's your job to know these things."

"Is it serious?"

Deborah's eyes widened. "What? God, no! It was just one date. And a lousy one at that. He had been chasing me for a while, knowing full well I was with Stephen, but after I began suspecting Stephen was cheating on me, I said to myself, 'Oh, the hell with it, I might as well see what else is out there.' And there was Kyle, looking handsome in his expensive Brooks Brothers suit, eagerly waiting for me to finally say yes to going out with him. So I did."

"For better or worse."

"Worse, to my dismay. Definitely worse." Deborah wandered over to the bar with Sandra and ordered another Manhattan to replace the one she had just spilled. "I admit, I found him attractive at first, on the outside at least. But I was completely in the dark about his personality. Why judge him right off the bat? It was no secret his father was a royal pain in the you know what, but in some cases there are apples that fall far from the tree. I was hoping maybe he took more after his mother, who I had met once. She had such a kind heart. So I gave him a chance."

Sandra smirked. "I can see where this is going."

"Within five minutes, he was making my skin crawl. He was the worst version of every smug, smooth-talking K Street cretin I have ever come in contact with. We had one date."

"I suppose you couldn't very well cook dinner for the two of you with no pots and pans."

"No, I invited him to my place for just one drink before our dinner reservation. Wait. How did you know he came to my townhouse and we went out to dinner? Have you been spying on me, Sandra?"

Sandra shook her head. "No, Deborah. I promise. We were tailing Kyle; he's involved in some pretty heavy stuff I can't get into right now. He just happened to lead us to your place in Georgetown."

This seemed to satisfy her. Deborah chuckled. "I served him cheap red wine in plastic cups and we had to sit cross-legged on the floor because I had no furniture, which he didn't like very much. Then he noticed the blow-up mattress in my empty bedroom as he went to use the bathroom and when he came back he made a crack about how it probably wasn't going to be big or sturdy enough for later. Yuck. What a pig. Just the idea of that made me shudder. By the time we arrived at the restaurant, I was already done. I went through the motions for a while because I was starving and was craving an expensive steak that I knew he was going to pay for, but I finally shut the whole thing down before dessert feigning stomach cramps, anything to make my escape. He drove me home and that was it."

"I am so sorry you had to go through all that."

"It was my own fault. I never should have agreed to go out with him. I only did it because I guess I was out for some kind of revenge."

"Stephen despises Senator Grisby as well as his son, and you knew that word would somehow get back to him."

"I made sure we dined at a very popular restaurant with a lot of Washington insiders. Not my proudest moment. I was just so hurt by Stephen's betrayal. Now I feel utterly foolish for living up to that awful woman-scorned stereotype."

"Deborah, the reason I am following Kyle Grisby around is because we, my associate Maya and I, believe that Senator Grisby and his son, with the help of some very powerful allies and associates, might be setting Stephen up."

"For Tess's murder?"

"For all of it. The murder, the affair . . ."

"Hold on. You honestly think Stephen is telling the truth about not being intimately involved with that poor girl?"

Sandra knew how surprising this was.

The soon-to-be ex-wife who was divorcing her husband because of his past infidelities, working hard to prove him innocent of a scandalous romantic affair.

The irony would not be lost on anyone.

"We are just following the facts wherever they lead us, and so far, there is a lot of smoke but definitely no sign of fire."

Deborah sucked down her Manhattan, stunned. "I was so certain he was lying to me, trying to cover up his bad behavior, I mean especially after everything he put you through."

Sandra winced, not wanting to relive any of that long-buried past.

Deborah frowned. "If he was telling me the truth the whole time, I would feel so terrible." She then thought of something and glanced up at Sandra. "You don't think I am involved in any way with Grisby's smear campaign, do you? Because I would never betray Stephen in that way!"

"No, Deborah, of course not."

"The truth is, even now that I have ended our

relationship, I would be lying if I said I don't still have some feelings for him. I will always admire the many good things he's trying to do for the people of Maine, for the whole country. It's hard to shut out that side of him. He has his failings, but he's still a decent man with a kind heart."

Sandra smiled and nodded.

She knew that better than anyone after twenty years of marriage. And right now she felt as if she was on an emotional roller coaster, unsure when this unpredictable thrill ride was ever going to end.

Chapter 37

After excusing herself and leaving Deborah Crowley, Sandra crossed the room, spying Zoe Rush engaged in a tense exchange with a pair of *Washington Post* reporters who had just won the Pulitzer Prize for their reporting on the last six months of the previous presidency, which was quickly followed by a New York Times number one best-selling book. As she approached them, Sandra immediately sensed that they were discussing the exploding scandal that was engulfing Stephen's political career. Zoe wagged an admonishing finger at the reporters, no doubt warning them off from taking on her story. Given her naked ambition and dogged determination, Zoe obviously had her eye on her own Pulitzer and she was not going to allow these two lauded scribes to snatch it away from her. The closer Sandra got, the more she could see the frozen smiles on the faces of the two reporters as Zoe prattled on, half joking, half threatening.

"Excuse me, I hope I'm not interrupting," Sandra cooed.

Zoe sighed, annoyed. "Actually, I was just—"

"No, not at all!" Paul, the male reporter, practically shouted, the relief on his face palpable. His colleague Cathy flashed Sandra a grateful smile and swallowed the rest of her white wine.

"I was hoping to steal away Zoe for a quick sec, if you two don't mind," Sandra said with a bright smile.

"We have to go anyway!" Paul blurted out. "We're meeting a source for a story we've been tracking."

"Maybe we can meet up for a drink at the Post Pub later and continue this conversation," Zoe said.

Cathy nodded agreeably. "We'll call you."

However, it was abundantly clear that the two reporters had no intention of ever doing that. Sandra had fortuitously just rescued them and they were not going to waste this opportunity for a speedy escape.

Paul waved a pudgy hand. "Bye, Zoe!"

"Nice seeing you, Mrs. Wallage. Paul and I would love to sit down with you at some point—"

Zoe stepped in front of Sandra like a Secret Service agent shielding the President at a campaign rally. "Back off, Cathy! I told you, this is *my* story!"

Undeterred, Cathy slipped her card into the palm of Sandra's hand. "Call me."

Before Zoe's hair burst into flames from burning rage, the two journalists skittered off.

"Those two are shameless! They have a Pulitzer, a best-selling book, and a sweet deal as political consultants at CNN; can't they just give me this one?"

"I assume you're referring to this fake news story you're peddling with the help of Senator Grisby," Sandra said coolly, folding her arms and glaring at her.

Zoe shrugged. "You can call it fake news all you want, Sandra; I am just following the facts."

"You may think you're following facts, but in reality you're being played."

"Look, it's no secret I harbor some personal animosity toward Stephen, I abhor hypocrisy, and I'm afraid your husband has it in his blood. He can't help lying. As a truth seeker, it's my job to expose him."

"If you're really a truth seeker, then why don't you seek the truth?"

"Isn't that what I'm doing?"

"No, not if you're peddling lies yourself."

"Look, Sandra, I have always been very fond of you. We've been friends for a very long time. But you're deluding yourself if you think—"

"Think about it. He betrayed me. Multiple times. I'm divorcing him. I have a whole new life now without him. Why would I go out on a limb and defend him if I didn't think he was being set up?"

Zoe paused.

Finally, a breakthrough.

If ever so slight.

But the reporter's nose had just gotten a whiff of something and she was now intrigued.

Zoe leaned in closer to Sandra. "What have you got?"

"I can't tell you here, but it's big."

"How big?"

"Watergate big."

She was totally hooked. "Can we go somewhere and talk?"

Sandra shook her head. "I need a little more time. But I will contact you when the time is right."

"Come on, Sandra, you can't leave me hanging like this. I will go absolutely crazy. Just give me a teeny tiny hint."

"Will you hold off on writing anything else damaging about Stephen, at least for a day or two?"

Zoe debated the pros and cons silently to herself before making a final decision and giving a quick nod.

Sandra glanced around to make sure no one in the vicinity was eavesdropping. "Senator Grisby, for a start."

Zoe cocked an eyebrow. "Really? You are not just trying to deflect attention away from Stephen, are you?"

"Trust me, Zoe," Sandra said confidently.

She knew that was all Zoe needed to hear because Sandra had spent all her years in Washington building up her reputation as an honest person of integrity and, unlike her husband, no one had ever found any reason to question it. A smart reporter like Zoe Rush knew Sandra's word was worth its weight in gold.

"Okay, twenty-four hours. But if by then I don't have a bombshell story, I hit send on my next Stephen Wallage piece."

They shook on it.

Zoe hustled off and Maya suddenly appeared at Sandra's side. "Look who just showed up."

She directed Sandra's attention to the entrance to the East Room where FBI agents Markey and Rhodes swept in, almost unrecognizable in chic designer cocktail dresses and sporting some very expensive-looking jewelry.

"Wow," Maya whispered. "They clean up real nice. Impressive given what they must make on an FBI agent's salary."

"The dresses are knock-offs and the jewelry is fake."

Maya turned to Sandra. "How do you know?"

Sandra gave her a sly smile. "Have we met?"

Maya chuckled. "I keep forgetting you come from this rarified world."

By now, Markey and Rhodes had zeroed in on Maya and Sandra and were making their way over to them.

"Good evening, ladies," Markey said with a thin smile. "I'm surprised to see you two here."

Maya folded her arms defiantly. "Why? She's the wife of a US Senator. She kind of belongs here more than the two of you do."

Both agents bristled at Maya's obstinance.

"So what are *you* doing here? Are you here under-cover, working some kind of angle in your case against Senator Wallage?" Sandra said pointedly.

"We are duty bound not to divulge any information relating to an active investigation," Rhodes said flatly.

"But that same law doesn't apply to civilians," Markey added. "Even civilians who have a PI license they probably ordered on the internet."

Sandra could feel Maya tensing up beside her.

These two women seemed to enjoy belittling them, blatantly ignoring Maya's years of experience in law enforcement.

"If you know any information about a crime and you don't share it with us, you're opening yourselves up to an obstruction of justice charge," Rhodes warned.

The threat landed with Sandra. It was one thing to try to clear Stephen from all the mounting accusations; it was quite another to break the law and risk going to jail. But before she could spill what they had found out about Kyle Grisby, Maya piped in. "If anything comes up, you will be the first to know."

Markey and Rhodes eyed Maya suspiciously.

Sandra was not a good enough actress to hide her nervousness, which the two agents immediately picked up on. They stood their ground a few more seconds, perhaps hoping Sandra might crack, but she didn't. She simply stayed mum and let Maya handle this.

"Enjoy the party," Maya said. "Be careful not to spill anything on those dresses; otherwise you won't be able to return them tomorrow.

Markey flared up. Rhodes smirked, appreciating Maya's humor.

Finally, the FBI agents withdrew and skulked away.

Maya turned to Sandra. "I totally thought you were about to come clean."

"I was!" Sandra wailed, her whole body shaking. "Maya, they were serious. We could get in big trouble withholding what we know."

"Please. Those two were just on a fishing expedition."

"But it's illegal to lie to the FBI."

"I know, but technically we did *not* lie; we just weren't completely forthcoming. If they had asked us directly about Senator Grisby and his son, we would have had to talk, but they didn't."

Sandra was still not convinced.

"I honestly don't trust them, Sandra. We have to be extremely careful right now about who we talk to, okay?"

Sandra gave her a tentative nod.

She wasn't sure about Maya's motives.

Was she shutting out Markey and Rhodes because she didn't trust them, or was it because of her ruthless competitive nature?

Either way, it was a dangerous move.

One they could come to regret.

Chapter 38

Maya stood just inside the lobby of the hotel, watching as her rental car turned out of the parking garage across the street and whizzed down the street. She could see Markey, behind the wheel of her car next to the curb outside the hotel with Rhodes in the passenger's seat, hit the gas and roar off in hot pursuit.

Maya quickly texted Sandra, who was upstairs in the room: **Coast is clear. I'm calling a Lyft now.**

Sandra texted back:

Be there in two minutes.

Like Senator Grisby's security goons, Maya knew Markey and Rhodes were staking them out as well, and if they were going to move freely around with the plan they were about to put in motion, they needed a distraction. So Sandra had enlisted the aid of Stephen's staffers Preston and Suzanne, who were happy to help them out. All they had to do was take Maya's rental car and drive it around all over DC for the next several hours leading Markey and Rhodes on a wild-goose chase to avoid them interfering in any way. By the time the agents figured out that it was not Maya and Sandra in the car, hopefully their mission would already be complete. Suzanne was blond, like Sandra, but Preston adamantly refused to wear a dark wig to more resemble Maya, opting for a floppy hat in order to remain gender-neutral. Maya chuckled to herself, imagining the comments from Markey and Rhodes about the gaudy hat she was supposedly wearing as she drove around town.

Sandra exited the elevator moments later just as a gray town car pulled up sporting the Lyft logo and they were off. It was a ten-minute drive to the Washington Bureau studio of Flash News, one of the top rising cable news networks that was giving Fox and CNN a run for their money.

The most popular show on Flash was a must-see two-hour early morning news program called *Morning Politics*, featuring a married couple, Jim and Rachel Nash. It was a combination of top news stories, political analysis, and cute couples' banter alongside an impressive roster of professional pundits and talking heads. Sandra knew Rachel Nash personally since she had roots in Maine and she and Jim had until recently spent summers in Bar Harbor at their sprawling seaside estate before selling and upgrading to a mansion in the Hamptons. Typically based in New York, *Morning Politics* was doing a week's worth of shows in DC currently interviewing on set a long line of Senators, members of Congress, cabinet officials, and lobbyists. Today's guests included the White House press secretary, the Surgeon General, *Post* reporters Paul and Cathy promoting their latest best seller, and, most notably for Maya and Sandra's purposes, reporter Zoe Rush and US Senator Charles Grisby, who had amiably agreed to appear in order to have another opportunity to trash-talk Stephen and further force the resignation issue.

Little did the Senator know, however, that he was walking right into a trap.

Convincing Zoe Rush to help them out had been easy, especially after presenting her with all the clear evidence of how she had been manipulated and played by Grisby, his son, and their allies. All it took was one phone call from Sandra to Rachel Nash to make sure Zoe would be on the set at the same time as Grisby. The Senator was more than happy to share his airtime with Zoe because in his mind she was a partner in his quest to destroy Senator Wallage. They had joined forces. He felt comfortable knowing she would be there to back him up with helpful "facts" further proving his case.

Maya and Sandra had been snuck in the back of the set by a production assistant and positioned behind the lights so the talent behind the large circular table in front of the cameras could not see them. Senator Grisby's face was shiny, so a makeup person dabbed him with some powder. Zoe sipped coffee next to him, chatting him up, dutifully laughing at his jokes, with seemingly not a care in the world. Word suddenly came from the control booth that they would be back from commercial in thirty seconds. Two other show regulars at the table, a former Senator from Missouri now a pundit and a young investigative reporter, put down their phones, while Grisby asked the makeup person how he looked and received a thumbs-up. He cleared his throat and licked his lips. Zoe put down her Starbucks coffee cup and smiled like a Cheshire cat as the stage manager counted down, "Five, four, three . . ." He counted off the last two numbers with his fingers and the red light on the camera flashed on.

Rachel shuffled some papers in front of her and spoke directly into the camera. "We're back at the top of the hour with a special guest, Senator Charles Grisby of the Commonwealth of Virginia. Good morning, Senator."

Grisby could see the red light on another camera blink to life and he slapped on a big, thoroughly disingenuous smile. "Good morning, Rachel, Jim, how're y'all doing, this morning?"

"Fine, thank you, Senator, we are so happy you're here. We have a lot to discuss. You have been noticeably in the public eye quite a bit lately."

"Yes, I have. My grandkids think I should start doing a few of those TikTok videos," he said, guffawing.

The rest of the table remained silent as Rachel plowed ahead. "You have been targeting Senator Stephen Wallage with some withering criticism—"

"All deserved," the Senator quickly interjected.

Rachel was unfazed by the interruption. "You have also been calling for his resignation."

The Senator's big smile faded and he leaned forward, choosing this moment to become grave and serious. "Yes, I have, Rachel, and that is not something I do lightly. Senator Wallage has been a colleague of mine for many years, but a few politicians, during the course of their careers, are sometimes led astray by their own personal failings and vices, and when that happens, I think as leaders, we have a moral responsibility to—"

Jim interrupted him. "But Senator Wallage has adamantly denied having any kind of inappropriate relationship with his intern Tess Rankin."

Grisby snorted. "You can't pull the wool over the eyes of the American people. They always know when you're lying."

Jim leaned back and folded his arms. "He also denies having anything to do with her death."

"Jim, come on, she was found in his apartment!" Grisby cried, huffily throwing his hands in the air.

"I'm not saying it doesn't look incriminating, but shouldn't we wait until the police finish their investigation before we draw and quarter him?" Jim asked pointedly.

Senator Grisby flinched slightly. He had not been expecting any pushback. Up until now, he had always been addressing a friendly, supportive, easily persuadable audience. But he knew coming on this show would be a bit more challenging because this crowd was on the opposite end of the spectrum politically, and so he worked extra hard to maintain his veneer of genial charm.

"Jim, Jim, Jim," Grisby said with a slightly admonishing drawl. "Everyone is innocent until proven guilty, I'm a lawyer, so that's ingrained in me, but come on, facts are facts. We have concrete evidence that he's lying."

Rachel knew it was her cue. "The emails?"

Grisby slapped a hand down on the table. "Yes! The emails!" Relieved to have his footing back, Grisby turned to Zoe next to him. "Zoe broke the email story. Perhaps she should talk about that."

Sandra nudged Maya.

This was it.

He had just opened the door for her.

Zoe pushed her glasses up the bridge of her nose and made direct eye contact with Rachel. "Yes, let's talk about the emails, the dozens of exchanges between Senator Wallage and his intern Ms. Rankin. Many of them salacious, disgusting, clear, and irrefutable evidence of sexual misconduct, I mean based on those emails, you have to ask yourself, 'What was that guy thinking?' "

Grisby smirked.

He was loving every minute of this.

"Those emails should be enough grounds to impeach the Senator, in my opinion. He used his powerful position to take advantage of that poor innocent girl, and who knows, he might have done worse. We don't know; we're still waiting on the police investigation. But even so, looking at those emails, there is no question he needs to go now."

Grisby was vigorously nodding in agreement.

"Except for one thing . . ."

Grisby ceased nodding.

The other two guests, the former Senator and the investigative reporter, suddenly sat up straight in their chairs, eager to hear more. Jim and Rachel never moved because they already knew what was coming.

Zoe paused for dramatic effect.

The suspense was killing Grisby, who blurted out, "What?"

She ignored him and kept her gaze squarely on Jim and Rachel. "The emails are fake."

"*What?*" Grisby screamed.

Zoe took a casual sip of her coffee and slowly turned to Grisby. "I said they're fake, as in not real."

"That's impossible. They came from Wallage's own account!"

"Wrong again," Zoe said matter-of-factly before spinning her chair back in the direction of the show's co-hosts and calmly detailing how Senator Grisby's son, Kyle, mirrored Stephen's account, wrote the emails himself, and used the TPL site to get them out into the world. It was a scam, a setup, all designed to bring down a Senator, all of it orchestrated by Senator Grisby and his loyal lapdog of a son.

Grisby wildly gesticulated with his hands, which were balled up into fists and bloodless. "Now wait just a minute! I don't know where you are getting your information, Zoe, but what you're purporting is libelous; I can sue you—"

"You can't sue me if it's the truth. And I have all the proof I need. And so does every major news outlet because I emailed them the evidence just before we went on the air."

"You . . . You can't just . . . This is an out-out-rage!" Grisby sputtered, eyes nearly popping out his head, so much spittle flying out of his mouth the young reporter had to literally duck to avoid getting hit.

Jim and Rachel Nash could hardly contain their excitement as they sat back and witnessed Grisby's on-air meltdown because they knew this moment was great television and would most certainly go viral and only spike the ratings of their show.

The investigative reporter decided to jump into the fray. "Did you pressure your son to come up with this dirt?"

"No, of course I did not! It was all *his* idea!"

Maya and Sandra knew it was over for Senator Grisby.

His career was already on life support given his direct involvement in this sordid scheme, but trying to foist all of the blame onto his own son? He had just pulled the plug.

"Bet he resigns by tomorrow," Maya whispered in Sandra's ear.

"*Tomorrow?*" Sandra scoffed. "He will be gone before Wolf Blitzer has time to reach the Situation Room this afternoon."

Maya laughed out loud, then quickly covered her mouth realizing they were still on the air.

The outburst caught Senator Grisby's attention as the cameraman moved position and a lighting guy adjusted one of the key lights, suddenly exposing Maya and Sandra to the on-air talent.

Grisby's mouth dropped open, stunned at the sight of them.

Sandra gave him a friendly wave.

In shock, he gaped at them, still unable to comprehend what had just happened. Jim Nash was on a rant about how corrupt politicians always believe they are somehow invincible, above reproach, but Grisby did not appear to be hearing a word of it. All of his attention was laser focused on Maya and Sandra, the bitter truth slowly sinking in that they had just beaten him. Soundly.

Chapter 39

Sandra emerged from the bathroom drowning in a plush white hotel bathrobe, slippers, and a towel wrapped around her head, surprised to find a large room service table with two salmon entrees, salads, a basket of bread, and a couple of crème brûlées for dessert. Maya sat on the edge of the bed in a pair of sweats and a pink T-shirt. The flat-screen television on the wall was broadcasting the Flash News channel but was muted.

Sandra's eyes lit up at the presentation. "What's all this?"

"I thought you might be hungry, so I ordered us room service. It arrived when you were in the shower."

Sandra's eyes flicked to a bottle of champagne nestled in a bucket of ice on the desk next to two long-stemmed glasses. "What are we celebrating?"

"I know we haven't cracked the case yet, but we

had a win today, a big one, which we desperately needed, so I thought we could toast to that."

Sandra walked over to the room service table and plucked a dinner roll from the basket and took a bite. "I like the way you think."

Maya climbed to her feet and went to pop open the bottle of champagne. "There's plenty of food. Should we call upstairs and invite Stephen to come down?"

"He's not there."

"Where is he?"

"The moment Senator Grisby resigned today, Stephen called his troops back to his office. They are going to burn the midnight oil and make up for the lost time when he was in hiding."

"It must be a relief to know he is finally off the hook."

"Well, he's not out of the woods yet, not by a long shot. Just because it's out now that the Grisbys were trying to frame Stephen, the press is not about to give him a free pass, especially given the lingering questions about what happened to Tess and why it happened in his apartment," Sandra said solemnly before cracking a smile. "But yes, we had a win today, so let's celebrate."

There was a loud pop as the cork shot out of the bottle, hitting the wall as fizzy champagne bubbled up and down the sides as Maya quickly poured some into the two glasses and handed one to Sandra.

They clinked glasses.

"To a good day," Maya said.

"Well played." Sandra chuckled.

They both took a sip.

Sandra glanced at the TV screen.

An image of Kyle Grisby's drawn face filled the screen.

"Maya, where's the remote?"

Maya scooped it up off the desk and pressed the volume button until they could hear the female news anchor speaking.

"Grisby was picked up by FBI agents this afternoon for questioning about his role in the scheme to paint Senator Stephen Wallage as a philanderer and, most unsettling, as a possible murderer . . ."

The anchor continued. "The two agents showed up at Grisby's home, where he voluntarily agreed to accompany them back to FBI Headquarters."

"You want to bet that the two FBI agents are named Markey and Rhodes?" Sandra asked.

Maya smiled knowingly and took another sip of her champagne.

The anchor continued. "Sources within the FBI say the younger Grisby has admitted to the political hit job in order to take down Senator Wallage and promote his father's political goals, but he is adamantly denying any involvement in the death of Wallage's intern Tess Rankin and claims to have never even met her."

"Of course he's going to say that. Fake emails is one thing; murder is quite another," Maya remarked.

On the TV screen, an unflattering photo of Charles Grisby looking as if he was foaming at the mouth replaced the one of his son, Kyle, as the anchor continued reading her cue cards. "Although Senator Grisby continued to deny any knowledge of his son's scheme, he resigned today, saying he did not want to be, and I quote, 'a distraction to the United States Senate getting on with the country's business.' Joining us now to discuss this very consequential day in American politics . . ."

Maya hit the mute button on the remote and observed Sandra, who had sat down in a chair and was picking at her salmon with a fork, a pensive look on her face. "Everything okay?"

Sandra finally took a bite of the salmon and nodded with a smile. "Yes, why?"

"You look a little troubled. You should feel good about this. It turns out Stephen was telling the truth."

"I know. I am happy about that; really I am. It's just that . . ."

"Just what?"

"I just keep thinking about something Deborah Crowley said. She was so conflicted about her relationship with Stephen. On the one hand, she admired him so much for the good work he was doing; genuinely caring politicians are a rare breed, and having been married to the man for twenty years, I know he's the real deal. But on the other hand, he's a flawed human being with a spotty track record when it comes to marriage fidelity." Sandra paused, then put her fork down and looked at Maya. "I understand why Deborah had to move on. Can he truly be trusted?"

Maya shrugged. "Is it really up to you to decide that?"

Sandra gave her a puzzled look. "What do you mean?"

"In a matter of weeks, days even, your divorce is

going to be final. It will no longer be any of your concern. You can just focus on him as first, the father of your boys, and second, that caring politician everybody seems to look up to. The loyal husband part will be moot."

Sandra stared off into space. "I guess you're right."

"Unless . . ."

Sandra snapped back into the moment. "Unless what?"

"Unless you are reconsidering going through with the divorce," Maya said, eyes boring into Sandra.

Flustered, Sandra pushed her plate of salmon away and stood up. "What? No, of course not."

"Sandra, we have been working together for almost two years now; I know that look, that indecision, like you're not sure what to do. Are you still in love with Stephen?"

Sandra hesitated. "No . . ." She let it hang there for a few seconds and then deflated, knowing the last person she could con was whip-smart Maya, before muttering, "I don't know . . ."

Maya let it go. She could sense Sandra was uncomfortable discussing her feelings. But there was no doubt what was left unspoken.

The door to a possible reconciliation was open.

At least a crack.

Chapter 40

Maya had never been to FBI Headquarters on Pennsylvania Avenue before, although Sandra had once taken their self-guided tour back when Stephen was first running for Congress. They had been summoned like students to the principal's office by agents Markey and Rhodes. Requesting that they come down to headquarters struck Maya as some kind of intimidation tactic, another attempt to scare them off from encroaching on their territory, but Rhodes seemed, if not friendly, at least cordial when she called Sandra and asked for the meeting.

In the lobby, Sandra went to check in with security as Maya's phone buzzed. It was Max. She hung back to take the call. "How's the painting project going?"

"I was done the day after you left. I'm a bored jobless ex-con with hardly any friends and my wife and kid were away from home. What else did I have to do with my time?"

"Are you feeling sorry for yourself?"

"No . . . Well, okay, maybe a little. But you'll be very impressed with the work I did. It looks like a brand-new house."

"Where's Vanessa?"

"In her room. The official story is she's doing her homework, but I think she's on the phone chatting with Ryan. If he's not over here, or she's over there, they're talking on the phone. I told her I think they're getting co-dependent, but she just rolled her eyes and laughed at me."

"Keep a close eye on her, okay? She thinks she can get away with more when it's just you around. You're the good cop."

"Ha, now there is the definition of irony."

Maya wanted to kick herself for the stupid comment. But Max seemed to be taking it in stride.

"I'm sorry, Max, that didn't come out right."

Max chuckled. "No, it's kind of funny. Funny and sad. At least as a parent I can be a good cop again."

Maya desperately wanted to change subjects. "So what have you been doing to keep yourself busy?"

"Besides watching all the drama you're mixed up in down in DC on TV? I had a job interview yesterday, working security at Maine Medical Center, the night shift."

Maya perked up. "That sounds promising."

"I didn't get it."

"Oh."

"The interview itself went great. I was my usual disarmingly witty and charming self," he joked.

"Don't forget 'modest,' " Maya cracked.

"Yeah." Max chuckled, then paused. "But given my criminal record, they didn't feel comfortable handing me a weapon despite all my training. I can't blame them."

"Something else will come along."

There was a silence on the other end of the phone.

Max clearly was not as confident as she was.

Sandra was waving at her by the elevators.

It was time to go up for their meeting.

"Max, I have to go . . ."

"Go save the world. I will be waiting for you when you get home."

"Thanks, love you."

"Love you too."

She hated ending the call.

He was trying to stay upbeat and positive, but it obviously was getting more and more difficult with each passing rejection. She wanted to help him somehow, but she also knew this was something he needed to do on his own.

She stuffed her phone in the back pocket of her pants and joined Sandra on the elevator up to the ninth floor, where they were met by an assistant and led to a private office where agents Markey and Rhodes awaited them. Once offers for coffee and water were dispensed with, Markey tried to make a little small talk by asking about how their kids' class trip had gone, but Maya was having none of it.

"Let's just cut to the chase and not waste each other's time. Why did you summon us here? Is it some kind of show of force? Maybe you thought once we were actually inside the J. Edgar Hoover Building with all these highly skilled FBI agents working on very important cases, we would realize we are in way over our heads and finally back off? Was that the plan?"

Markey and Rhodes exchanged smirks.

"Uh, no," Rhodes said. "But that's definitely worth remembering for next time."

"Then why are we here?" Maya demanded to know.

"Despite our initial misgivings, we now see that you two actually know what you're doing," Markey reluctantly admitted.

"You looked like you were in actual pain having to admit that," Sandra cracked.

Markey smiled. "Maybe a little."

"We thought we might be able to pool our resources, keep an open line of communication, at least while you're still here in DC," Rhodes suggested.

Maya held up a hand. "Wait a minute. First you threaten to arrest us if we get in the way; now you want to team up?"

"Not team up, the FBI is not in the habit of working with amateurs," Markey could not resist pointing out.

Rhodes, the more diplomatic of the two, shot her partner an admonishing look. "Civilians. But the FBI has learned some hard lessons in the past about not sharing information with other federal agencies . . . as well as independent investigators, and we are trying to change that."

Maya folded her arms. "Are we here to be interrogated by you, and then dismissed, or is this a two-way street? Are you willing to cough up anything you might know?"

Markey and Rhodes exchanged another look, pausing before Rhodes cleared her throat and said, "Two-way street."

"Okay, then," Maya said, satisfied. "You first."

Markey raised an eyebrow. "What?"

"Give us something. Show a little good faith."

Markey's face reddened. "That is not how this is going to work. You can't just order us to—"

Rhodes interjected. "Kyle Grisby's alibi checks out."

Markey sighed heavily, annoyed.

The FBI agents could tell that Maya and Sandra were hooked.

Rhodes continued. "He was having drinks with some old frat buddies at Archibald's Gentlemen's Club on K Street until the wee hours of the morning. We talked to at least a dozen people who confirmed it. He also never showed up on the security cam footage at your husband's condo that night."

"So he was telling the truth about never having met Tess Rankin," Sandra said.

"He knows we can charge him with lying to an FBI agent, and he's in enough trouble already for the fake emails, so my hunch is he's being straight with us. He was never there that night. He would have had to have arrived and left within that short five-minute gap when the power went out and the guard was away from his desk. Otherwise we would have seen him."

Sandra took a deep breath. "May I ask, do you still consider Stephen a suspect?"

"Of course," Markey sneered. "Just because those emails turned out to be bogus, that doesn't mean he's totally off the hook. There was serious bruising on Tess's neck. She didn't do that to herself. She may have overdosed, but somebody else was there, maybe to make sure she did."

Sandra's eyes narrowed. "It wasn't Stephen."

Rhodes softened a little. "Look, I understand you're loyal to your ex-husband . . ."

"Not yet," Sandra said firmly.

"Not yet what?" Rhodes asked.

"Not yet my ex-husband, it's still an ongoing process."

Sandra's clarification spoke volumes to Maya.

Her partner was in a state of confusion about her marriage.

Up to now, Sandra had drawn a hard line.

She had adamantly maintained that she was done and ready to move on. The trust issue between them was too messy and difficult to overcome. But something was shifting now after all the time they had been spending trying to clear his name.

Maya just hoped Sandra would not wind up getting hurt again. Because she had grown so fond of her over the last year and a half, considering her not only as her partner but also as a true friend.

In fact, her best friend.

Chapter 41

Preston leaned against the boss's desk, glued to the TV screen in Stephen's office. The disgraced Senator Charles Grisby and his second wife, the tightly wound Babe whom he was desperately clinging to, were both in full damage control as Gayle King interviewed him for her CBS morning show. Stephen was on the couch flipping through some paperwork, a child tax credit bill he had been working on, ignoring the television as Maya and Sandra entered, stopping to watch the interview.

Preston snorted and shook his head derisively. "He's talking about how his late wife Clementine used to knit these cute little Santa mittens every Christmas for all the grandchildren of his fellow Senators, like that's somehow going to help rehabilitate his image."

Stephen looked up from his papers. "Preston,

please turn that off. I'm tired of listening to his whining."

"You should be enjoying this," Preston said, picking up the remote. "You deserve to gloat a little."

Stephen glanced at the screen to see a tear roll down Charles Grisby's cheek as he talked about his late wife. "I take no pleasure in seeing the toll his son's actions have taken on his family."

Maya cocked an eyebrow. "You don't believe he knew what Kyle was up to?"

"If he did, it will all come out eventually."

"It must be killing Babe that she has to sit there and listen to him wax on about his first wife," Preston noted. "How can she do that?"

"Because that's what a good politician's wife does. She sticks by him and defends his good name no matter what, despite whatever despicable behavior he gets caught doing. That's part of the bargain."

Stephen, realizing the subtext of what he was saying, flinched slightly.

Preston grabbed the remote off the desk and flicked off the television. "Okay, so when you're done reading that boring legislation, can we finally talk about putting out a statement condemning Kyle Grisby's actions, making the point that you were right all along?"

Stephen, without looking up from his papers, shook his head. "No. I'm not going to take a victory lap just because it turned out I was telling the truth. I think the best course of action is to just keep my head down, work hard, and wait until the police arrest a suspect."

"I think that's a mistake," Preston warned. "We need to stay ahead of this, keep control of the narrative; otherwise people are going to continue speculating that you're somehow involved in Tess's death."

"People are always going to talk. I can't stop that."

"Stephen, now that the FBI has cleared Kyle Grisby, it's not like there are a lot of other suspects for them to consider. It's basically you, unless there is someone else they're keeping under wraps. It would be naive and frankly political malpractice to let the rumors keep spreading unabated," Preston argued.

"I appreciate your concern, Preston, but I'm going to overrule you here. The last thing I should be doing now is releasing statements or holding more press conferences. I should have listened to Sandra in the first place and just kept my mouth shut. I didn't do anything wrong. I just need to stand down and let the FBI do its work. They will find whoever's responsible."

Preston, frustrated, sighed loudly. "Fine."

He then flashed Sandra a contemptuous look.

When he saw her watching him, he instantly replaced it with an insincere smile. "He's the boss."

"I'm still confused about the timeline," Maya said. "Does anyone remember what time Tess left that night to deliver your papers?"

Stephen shrugged. "Security said they saw her leaving close to eight o clock."

Tess frowned. "But that doesn't make any sense."

"Why?" Preston asked.

"If it's a fifteen minute walk from here, she probably would not have arrived at your condo until around eight fifteen or eight thirty."

Stephen looked confused. "So?"

"We checked the security footage outside the building. She was never seen arriving. But there was a brief power outage around seven fifteen. The guard said he also left his station during the same time, so we concluded that was the time Tess would have had to arrive at your place."

Stephen shook his head. "No, she probably just used the back entrance."

Sandra spun around toward Stephen. "What back entrance?"

"There is a back entrance not a lot of people know about. Reserved for VIP residents. The Homeowners Association discourages us from handing out too many key cards because they prefer guests to use the front entrance for security reasons."

"Tess had a key card for the back entrance?" Maya asked.

"No, but that night I gave her mine," Stephen said.

"Is there a security camera in the back?" Sandra asked.

Stephen shook his head. "No. It's very private. I

think maybe three residents in the whole building are allowed to use it. We pay extra dues every month for the privilege."

Sandra's mind was reeling from this new startling piece of information. If she had been with someone, there would be no way to ever know who it was who might have accompanied her inside. And if she had been alone, then there was now the possibility that someone else could have entered the building from the back avoiding the security camera trained on the front entrance.

Sandra took a step toward Stephen. "The key card you gave Tess, is that the only one you have?"

"No, I have three."

Sandra's eyes widened. "Stephen, who has the other two?"

"Suzanne has one, in case of an emergency."

Sandra gestured toward Preston. "What about him?"

"No, Preston hasn't run any errands for me ever since I promoted him to Chief of Staff," Stephen said.

"Then who?"

"I gave one to Deborah," Stephen muttered. "When we first started dating, we agreed it was best to keep a low profile, I didn't want us to be splashed all over the gossip blogs, you and I were still not even officially separated, so I gave her a key card so she could sneak in the back when I wasn't there."

Sandra gasped. "Did she return it to you after she broke up with you?"

Stephen's face went white. "No, as far as I know, she still has it."

Deborah Crowley.

They had to find her.

Now.

Chapter 42

"Stephen, are the cards coded?" Sandra asked.

He looked at her, confused. "What do you mean?"

"Is there some kind of identifying information on each card, like a bar code, that would register whose card was being used?"

Stephen shrugged. "I don't know, maybe. You'd have to check with the building's security office."

Maya grabbed her phone. "Do you have a number I can call? Maybe someone can look up whose cards were used to gain entry to your building that night."

"Suzanne?" Stephen called out.

She appeared in the doorway to the office in seconds. "What do you need?"

"Do we have a phone number for the security office at my condo?"

"No, but I can get it."

"Good, give it to Maya when you find it."

"Right away." Suzanne turned to dash out before stopping and spinning back around. "Oh, by the way, the car service just called. The driver's stuck in traffic and is going to be a few minutes late picking you up."

Stephen looked puzzled. "Wait. What? I didn't call the car service."

"I was confused too because I didn't see anything on your schedule, but I figured maybe it was a last-minute thing and Preston had set it up."

"I don't arrange for car services," Preston huffed. "That's not my job anymore."

Stephen sighed, annoyed. "Suzanne, get that number for Maya. I will call the car service myself and see what's going on."

Suzanne dashed out with Maya on her tail.

Sandra and Preston watched curiously as Stephen picked up his phone and scrolled through his contact information, finding the service he normally used, then speed-dialed the dispatcher.

"Hello, Norm, this is Stephen Wallage . . . I'm fine; how are you? How're the kids?" He paused. "Dartmouth, really? Excellent school. Good for her. I know, they grow up so fast. Listen, Norm, I think there might be a little mix-up. Somebody from your company just called to let me know my driver is going to be late, but the thing is, I didn't order a car today . . . I see, where are they supposed to be picking me up? Oh . . . And where to? The airport? . . . When? . . . Do you have the flight information?" Stephen scribbled something down on a notepad. "Birmingham."

Sandra perked up.

Birmingham, Alabama.

Deborah Crowley's hometown.

She had probably used Stephen's car service account when they were together countless times and had absent-mindedly just called the service to take her to the airport, not thinking they might assume the car was for Stephen just leaving from her place. He had been using the company for years. Sandra was even friendly with Norm the dispatcher. Everyone was well aware of what was going on in Stephen's personal life just from driving him around the DC area nearly every day.

But Deborah had told Sandra at the White House reception that she was going to be in town for another week.

Why was she skipping out early?

Stephen lowered the phone and glanced up at Sandra. "The car's for—"

"Deborah, I know. Tell Norm we want two pickups. Have them come here to your office first, then go to Deborah's townhouse in Georgetown."

"I don't understand . . ."

"Please, just do it."

Stephen pressed the phone to his ear again. "Change of plans, Norm . . ."

Sandra rushed out of Stephen's office to where Maya was on her own phone, looking frustrated.

"I'm on hold," Maya sighed.

"Text or call me the minute you find out anything. I need to go out!" Sandra cried as she ran out of the office and down the marbled hallways, heels clicking.

Outside, she waited at the curb until she spotted

a black sedan approaching. When it pulled up next to her, the driver started to get out, but she waved at him to stay put and hopped in the back.

She recognized the driver immediately as Parv, a young Indian man from Mumbai, who had moved to the States after marrying his longtime American girlfriend, whom he met when she visited his home country with some college girlfriends one summer.

"Mrs. Wallage!" Parv exclaimed.

Sandra could see his eyes bulging through the rearview mirror. "Hello, Parv. I know you were expecting to see Stephen."

"Yes, I just assumed . . ."

Sandra could see sweat beads forming on Parv's forehead in the mirror. She knew exactly why he was suddenly so nervous. Senator Wallage's wife was in his backseat and his second stop was to pick up the Senator's girlfriend. He was barreling toward a supremely awkward situation.

"Mrs. Wallage, it's always lovely to see you, but I think I should tell you, I'm not sure how to say this—"

"It's perfectly fine, Parv. I know you're driving Deborah Crowley to the airport. We're friends. I'm just riding along to see her off."

He nodded with relief and beamed brightly. "Oh, good, that's good, very good."

Of course, she refrained from mentioning that Deborah Crowley had no idea that Sandra was going to be in the car she had ordered to take her to the airport.

Parv chattered on about married life and how he and his newlywed wife were expecting a baby, which was cause for much celebration by his large family back in Mumbai. Finally, after some more heavy traffic getting out of DC, they finally pulled up to the townhouse where Deborah Crowley stood on the curb with two large suitcases and a carry-on. Parv jumped out and loaded her luggage into the trunk. She could hear them exchanging pleasantries, but Parv never thought to mention Sandra because he just assumed Deborah already knew to expect her. When he opened the back door and Deborah slid in, he was taken aback by Deborah's startled gasp at the sight of Sandra sitting there waiting to greet her.

It took her a moment to collect herself. "Sandra, what are you doing here?"

"I couldn't let you leave town without saying goodbye."

Parv, who now sensed something was amiss, warily shut the door and circled around to the driver's side and got in the front seat. He didn't start the car right away because he was too distracted eavesdropping.

Deborah's eyes narrowed. "What's going on here?"

"As far as I can tell, you're on your way home to Birmingham to work at a small law firm, just as you explained to me. Except you're suddenly leaving a week earlier than planned."

"Yes, well, I changed my mind. I'm entitled to do that, aren't I?" Deborah sniffed. She checked the expensive-looking silver watch on her right wrist. "Parv, we better go; otherwise I'm going to miss my flight."

Parv shot up in his seat, embarrassed. "Right! Yes, sorry, Ms. Crowley!"

He squealed away from the curb and they sped down the tree-lined street toward the expressway.

Sandra glanced down at her phone.

There was nothing from Maya.

She was probably still on hold waiting for someone to deal with her. Sandra knew time was extremely limited. If Maya did not get back to her before they reached Ronald Reagan International Airport, then Sandra would lose her one opportunity to confront Deborah about whether she used her key card to enter Stephen's building on the night in question.

Deborah stared out the window at the passing cherry blossoms, lost in thought.

Sandra leaned across the seat closer to Deborah. "I need to ask, do you still have the key card to the back entrance of Stephen's condo?"

Deborah slowly turned, agitated. "Maybe. I don't know. Why?"

"But you didn't give it to anyone?"

"Of course not. Stephen was very adamant about that. The condo association is very strict about their rules."

Sandra's eyes flicked back to her phone.

Still nothing from Maya.

They were already swerving across lanes to take the Reagan National Airport exit off the George Washington Parkway. Sandra was running out of time.

She couldn't wait any longer for Maya to confirm it.

She had to bluff.

"I just got a text from Maya. She talked to the security office at Stephen's building. They just reported that your key card, the one Stephen gave you, was used to enter the back entrance of the building on the night Tess Rankin overdosed."

Deborah's mask of indignation held for a few more moments. "What? That's impossible . . ."

But her denial lacked conviction. Like a child caught stealing a pack of gum at the supermarket but still swearing innocence even though everyone could see it in his sticky little hand.

"If you did not give anyone else your card, like you just claimed, then who else could it have been?"

Sandra could see Parv's wide eyes watching through the rearview mirror, riveted. When she looked back at Deborah, who was now shrinking in her seat, that mask of indignation she had so valiantly tried to keep in place was melting away, fast.

Defeated, she said, her voice cracking, "Yes, I was there that night."

Chapter 43

Sandra could not believe her bluff had worked. Deborah had just admitted that she was one of the last people to see Tess Rankin alive. "Why were you there?"

Deborah swallowed hard. "After our fight at the restaurant, I was convinced Stephen and I were through. It was over. That made my decision to quit the Commonwealth Fund and move back to Alabama so much easier. But the next day, five minutes after I gave my notice, a big beautiful bouquet of camellias arrived at my office from Stephen along with a note of apology. I had to smile. Camellias are my favorite floral arrangement and they're the state flower of Alabama. He knew exactly what he was doing."

Sandra silently agreed. Stephen was a master at the personal touch, another reason why he was such an effective politician.

"I didn't call him back to thank him because I was still mad at him, but as time went by, I began to soften. On that day, I was stuck in meetings until eight, so instead of calling, I decided to just drop by his apartment and thank him in person. I had no idea he was on the Senate floor at the Capitol."

"So you let yourself into the private VIP back entrance with the key card he had given you, which is why you never showed up on the security cameras out front."

Deborah nodded. "Yes. I also had a key to the condo, but I knocked first and didn't hear anything. I thought Stephen might be in the shower or something, so I just let myself in, and that's when she came flying at me with a butcher knife."

Sandra gasped. "What? Tess?"

"I thought she was going to stab me with it. I screamed bloody murder and that startled her enough to drop the knife. I kicked it across the room and just started yelling at her for scaring me like that, demanding to know what she was doing there."

"What did she say?"

"She had this sullen, detached look on her face and fed me some lame story about how a boy had suddenly just shown up out of the blue, who was apparently stalking her, and she thought he had come back and she was just trying to defend herself . . . I mean, the girl was crazy!"

"She was telling you the truth," Sandra said quietly. "There was a boy who followed her there, but it was an innocent crush, totally harmless, and he left when she asked him to."

Deborah looked rattled by this. "Are you serious?"

"Yes. If I heard someone letting themselves into the apartment, knowing it wasn't Stephen, I might have grabbed a weapon to defend myself too."

Deborah covered her mouth with her hand. "Oh no. I thought she was playing games, trying to distract me from the real reason she was there, waiting for Stephen. She started to explain that she was just there to deliver some papers, but of course I didn't believe her. She was always so curt and rude to me whenever I was at Stephen's office, unlike Suzanne and even Preston when he wasn't in one of his moods, and so my suspicious mind always went to the same place. Why did she not like me? Was she jealous? Did she see me as a threat?"

"So when you saw her in Stephen's apartment, you assumed the worst."

"I said the most awful things to her. How girls like her always paid the price for going after rich, powerful men. I told her she was disposable, a plaything, too young to be taken seriously, and soon she would be tossed out with the trash like so many others. It sickens me now that I spoke to her like that. In what world is that okay?"

Sandra reached over and touched Deborah's arm. "You were upset."

"Yes. With Stephen. But I took it out on that poor girl. When I found out the next day that she had died from an overdose, at least that was the first rumor going around, I was consumed with guilt. I could barely breathe. The idea that I had driven her to commit suicide, well, I couldn't live with that; I wanted to die myself."

"But then, when the cops started making statements in the press about possible foul play, you got scared."

"I feared I might be a suspect. I was so close to escaping the toxic culture of DC politics, moving home, starting a new job, a new life, maybe meet a nice, simple local guy. But if I suddenly got swept up in a police investigation, my face all over the news, well, the partners at that small but influential firm in Birmingham might reconsider their offer, and my whole career, my new life plan, would be in jeopardy. So I made a vow to stay mum, not say a word about being there that night. And it's been eating me up ever since."

"Is that really why you stayed an extra week, after the movers left for Alabama with all your belongings?"

"I kept trying to work up the nerve to call the police and the FBI and just come clean. Tell them what happened. But in the end, I didn't have the guts, so here I am on my way to the airport, making my planned escape, and I will just have to live with that shame."

"It's never too late, Deborah. I know two very capable FBI agents you can talk to; the sooner you tell your story, the sooner you can move on from this."

"You believe I didn't kill Tess?"

"Yes, and I think they will too."

Deborah hesitated.

The town car had pulled up at the curb outside the American Airlines terminal at Ronald Reagan National Airport. Parv, having listened to the entire conversation from behind the wheel, waited for his next instructions.

Deborah glanced out the window.

There was a curbside check-in desk just a few feet away.

She stared at it longingly, but then after a long beat she sighed, knowing what she had to do.

She turned to Parv. "Parv, I would like to change my destination."

"Where to, ma'am?"

"FBI Headquarters."

As Parv typed in the new destination on his phone mounted on the dashboard, Deborah reached out and grasped Sandra's hand, whispering, "Thank you."

Sandra squeezed her hand in a show of support.

She knew that in the end Deborah Crowley would do the right thing.

Chapter 44

FBI agent Rhodes definitely had a sweet tooth. Maya watched in awe as she scarfed down a cinnamon coffee cake in three big bites. Agent Markey sat next to her, shaking her head, smirking at her partner. Just as Rhodes was done, she was already eyeing the half-eaten fudge walnut brownie that Sandra had left on her plate.

Rhodes stared hungrily at it and then said, "Are you going to finish that?"

Sandra looked at her, confused at first, then realized Rhodes's eyes were fixed on the brownie. She pushed the plate across the table toward Rhodes. "Knock yourself out."

"We just had lunch," Markey sighed.

Rhodes whipped her head in her partner's direction. "Are you fat-shaming me?"

"No, I'm not fat-shaming you. You're a tooth-pick. With a superhuman metabolism apparently."

Rhodes pouted and folded her arms defiantly. "No, she's right. I have already stuffed my face with a whole coffee cake."

"And half of my scone," Markey added before catching herself. "Sorry, that just came out. I wasn't that hungry anyway; why let it go to waste, right?"

Sandra grinned and then leaned forward, pushing the brownie even closer. "Just go for it. It's really good."

Rhodes debated with herself, then decided she didn't care what her partner thought and tore off a chunk of brownie and popped it in her mouth. Her eyes closed as she chewed and swallowed, practically in a rapturous state.

Maya wanted to laugh.

They were like an old married couple.

Always bickering but totally devoted to each other.

She was liking them more all the time.

But of course she would never admit that to them.

Maya had requested the two FBI agents meet them because she and Sandra had discovered some new information regarding Kyle Grisby and the fake emails and wanted to share it with them, now that they had called a truce and had actually decided to help each other.

Markey did not want any of her FBI colleagues to know they were getting help from two Portland, Maine, based private investigators, so she nonchalantly suggested they meet at a trendy coffee house just down the street from FBI Headquarters. After ordering coffees and desserts, they had found a corner table for a modicum of privacy away from the crowd of tourists who were busy studying their sightseeing brochures and the usual array of bloggers tapping away on their laptops.

As Rhodes polished off the rest of Sandra's brownie, an obvious sugar high was starting to take root. She suddenly got more energized, slapping a hand down on the table. "Okay, what have you got?"

Markey eyed her partner, who was buzzing, surprised she was the one taking charge this time.

"It's about the fake emails," Maya explained.

"What about them?" Rhodes asked, incessantly tapping her foot so fast her knee knocked the table, nearly spilling Markey's latte. Markey placed a hand on her partner's knee to get her to stop.

Maya plowed ahead. "I have an IT guy back in Portland who helps me with computer issues. He's like genius-level smart."

"He's also got a huge crush on Maya," Sandra piped in.

Maya tossed her an annoyed look. "Not relevant." Sandra suppressed a smile as Maya turned her attention back to Markey and Rhodes. "When he tracked the emails back to Kyle Grisby's shell company Freedom Fighters, he initially assumed Grisby had to have had some help penetrating the firewall and hacking Stephen Wallage's email account. He needed direct access in order to make it all look legit. But Oscar called me an hour ago to tell me he was wrong. He did a thorough deep dive into Stephen's hard drive and found no evidence of a hacker anywhere."

"Maybe the hacker was so good he or she didn't

leave a footprint. The Russians are really smart about that," Markey offered.

"Normally I would agree," Maya said. "But Oscar swears he would have seen something that might suggest a cyberpunk had been there, and there was nothing. Oscar is the best there is. I trust him implicitly. If he says Senator Wallage wasn't hacked, then I believe him wholeheartedly."

"Then what does that mean?" Rhodes asked, her eyes wandering over to the bakery case to see what was left after the post-lunch rush.

"It means someone had to have provided Kyle Grisby with Wallage's log-in information," Maya said solemnly.

Markey considered this. "Are you saying the call came from inside the house?"

"Exactly," Maya said.

"I just can't imagine who in Stephen's circle would do such a thing. They have all been with him for years," Sandra said, distressed.

"We're meeting with Grisby and his lawyer at three at headquarters; maybe we can coax him into telling us who this mystery person is," Markey said.

Maya checked the time on her phone, then stood up. "Good, it's quarter to three now. Let's go."

Markey cocked an eyebrow. "Whoa, where do you think you're going?"

"With you, back to FBI Headquarters. I want to be there when you question him," Maya said matter-of-factly.

"Sorry, not happening," Markey scoffed. "I appreciate the intel, but we are not a team of She Spies, some all-female special ops outfit. We can't just parade into that conference room en masse."

"But I am sure we can be helpful with the questioning," Sandra insisted.

Markey shook her head. "I don't doubt it, but the FBI director would have our heads if we allowed civilians to sit in on a meeting at FBI Headquarters."

"We have a video feed to the conference room in our office," Rhodes suggested. "There is no policy against them sitting in there quietly as our guests watching TV, and maybe texting us questions they think might be useful."

Markey did not dismiss the suggestion out of hand but was still on the fence. Maya, however, was already halfway out the door.

"Wait, hold up, I'm just going to grab a peanut butter cookie!" Rhodes called after them. "They're to die for! Anyone else want one?"

After settling into the office of Markey and Rhodes, Maya behind Markey's desk and Sandra on a drab scuffed leather couch that had seen better days, they watched intently a TV monitor on a credenza by the window. On the screen, Markey and Rhodes sat at a conference table across from an agitated Kyle Grisby and his flamboyant, hefty, blond curly-haired lawyer, a woman who was apparently very fond of loud bright colors and wild pink reading glasses. Maya guessed her clownish appearance was just a ploy to disarm her opponents, lull them into a false sense of security by not taking her seriously, so she could get the upper hand in any negotiations. Her theory proved to be true.

"I have advised my client not to answer any questions that may incriminate him."

Rhodes was chewing on that peanut butter cookie she just had to have. "That's his right, of course. But when he is charged, and believe me, he *will* be charged—"

The lawyer lowered her pink glasses to the edge of her bulbous nose. "Excuse me, could you not speak with your mouth full, please? It's very annoying."

Rhodes sat back, stunned by her gall, but it did little to throw her off her game. She chewed and swallowed, waited a few seconds, before spitting out, "Better?"

"Yes, much, thank you," the lawyer sniffed, folding her hands like an exasperated schoolteacher at the end of her rope with her unruly students.

"As I was saying," Rhodes huffed, eyeing the last piece of cookie but refraining from stuffing it in her mouth. "When the charges do come down, we will be requesting they add lying to an FBI officer to the list."

"Let's just toss in the kitchen sink at this point," the lawyer growled.

"But the fact is, your client *did* lie to us. He told us he was working alone," Markey said calmly.

Kyle practically jumped out of his chair. "But I didn't lie! My father had nothing to do with any of this! That's the God's honest truth!"

"I'm not talking about your father," Markey said.

Kyle sat back, confused. "I don't understand . . ."

"We have uncovered evidence that you had some help."

Kyle shook his head violently. "No, no, I wrote all those emails myself; there was no one else!"

The lawyer grimaced and squeezed his hand. It looked like she was trying to break it. "Kyle, I told you, you don't have to answer their questions. They could be bluffing."

Markey leaned forward, a snakish smile on her face. "Kyle knows we're not bluffing, don't you, Kyle?"

His bottom lip started to quiver.

"He knows who we're talking about," Markey said.

There was a long silence.

In the office, Sandra turned to Maya. "Have them ask if it was someone in Stephen's office!"

Maya texted on her phone.

They could see Markey on the TV screen receive the text and give it a cursory glance.

"We know it was someone in the Senator's office. Come on, Kyle. Hot? Warm? Cold? Things will go so much better for you if you just come clean with us."

His eyes blinked uncontrollably.

He was close to breaking.

"We're not here to play a game of Twenty Questions. When you have hard evidence, call me," the lawyer said, gathering up her papers and stuffing them in her colorful briefcase that looked like something out of *My Little Pony*.

"One name, just give us one name, and we could make half the charges you're facing just go away," Rhodes said sweetly.

The lawyer stood up. "Let's go, Kyle."

But Kyle stayed glued to his seat not sure what he should do.

"Have them throw out the name Suzanne!" Sandra shouted.

Maya's eyes widened. "Do you honestly believe it could have been her? You've always said she was so loyal."

"She is, but maybe he'll cough up the real name."

Maya texted Markey again.

They could see on the monitor Markey's eyes flick to her phone, then back up at Kyle. "Was it Suzanne? Did she give you the Senator's log-in information?"

Kyle said nothing but was involuntarily shaking his head no.

"Think of the awesome plea deal you could make with the DA if you gave us one name; just one little name, how hard could that be? Tick tock, Kyle, time's running out," Markey teased.

"Why are you talking plea deal? He hasn't even been charged with anything yet!" the lawyer bellowed, grabbing Kyle by the sleeve of his jacket, trying to physically yank him out of the conference room. She almost had him out the door when he suddenly grabbed the doorframe to stop himself, causing his lawyer to let go and stumble, nearly falling to the floor outside the conference room.

Beads of sweat were now pouring down Kyle's face as he screamed at Markey and Rhodes, "Preston! It was Preston! Preston Lambert!"

His lawyer was red-faced and ready to explode.

Rhodes casually reached for the lone peanut butter cookie left on the paper plate in front of her and picked it up. "Good boy, Kyle. Have a cookie."

Chapter 45

"He's lying!" Preston wailed defensively, eyes darting toward his boss, Stephen, who sat rigidly behind his desk in his office glaring at him. "Stephen, you have to believe me, I have never met Kyle Grisby!"

Maya pulled out her phone, held it up, and played a video of Preston entering a bar in the early evening. "Kyle told us where you met to hash out the plan. We got ahold of the security footage from the building across the street and that's clearly you going inside." Maya fast-forwarded the video on the phone. "And about an hour later . . ." She held up the phone again showing Kyle and Preston exiting the bar together, chatting. "You seem pretty chummy with a guy you claim to have never met."

Preston's composure was rapidly devolving as the reality of his situation began to sink in. "Okay, yes, I admit, I met with him once, just to find out if he had anything concrete he could use against you, Stephen. I wasn't conspiring with him, if that's what he's saying; I swear to you, it's a complete fabrication! I would *never* betray you!"

The more Preston implored Stephen to believe him, the less convincing he became.

"Stephen, please, you have to believe me!" Preston choked out, near tears, aghast at being in this position having to defend himself.

Sandra instinctively knew that Preston's high-strung emotional state was not because he had been falsely accused; it was because he had just gotten caught.

The security video stopped playing and Maya lowered her phone.

All eyes were on Stephen, waiting for him to speak.

He took a deep breath. "I don't know what to say, Preston. You have been a trusted confidant for so long, I really, really want to believe you; I do . . ."

There was a flicker of relief on Preston's face.

"But I'm not an idiot," Stephen continued.

And the look of relief just as quickly vanished.

"I-I don't understand," Preston stammered.

Stephen glanced over at Maya and Sandra, who stood near the door, a protective measure to make sure Preston did not try to bolt until they got what they needed out of him. "When they brought this new information to my attention, I have to say I was disappointed, but not surprised."

"Stephen . . ." Preston whispered, as if a dagger had just been thrust into his heart.

"All of us, you, me, Suzanne . . . Tess, we all worked in a very enclosed space here, on top of each other; it was hard to miss the signs."

"I don't know what you're talking about!" Preston cried.

Stephen cleared his throat, not entirely comfortable broaching this topic. "I know Tess had a crush on me. It was obvious to everyone in this office, hell, the whole floor. And it was painfully obvious you were jealous."

"What?" Preston squeaked out.

Sandra was stunned.

She had no idea Preston was in love with her husband, but she was in for a shock when Stephen spoke next.

"You were in love with her, but apparently she only had eyes for me, and that burned you up with an incalculable rage," Stephen said, pointing a finger at him.

Sandra could no longer stay silent and gaped at Preston. "Excuse me, I thought you were gay."

Preston stared at her with contempt. "What? No, I'm not gay. Sure, I may have experimented in college at a fraternity keg party my junior year, who didn't at some point, but in the end, I made the very firm determination, I like *girls*!"

As the words rolled off his tongue, Preston knew he was just further incriminating himself, so he suddenly stopped talking.

Sandra was reeling.

How could her gaydar be so off?

She had been so convinced about Preston.

And with her naive assumptions, she had immediately dismissed him as a possible suspect and compromised the whole case.

"You've been unhappy working here for a while now, Preston, anyone could see it, and for whatever reason you blamed me for your dissatisfaction, so when Tess came along and broke your heart, you wanted to take it out on me," Stephen concluded. "Maybe if you helped the Grisbys take me down, you'd feel better about yourself."

"I am not some pop psychology subject for your college thesis, Stephen," Preston retorted, eyes blazing.

Stephen ignored the comment. "Did Senator Grisby offer you a position with him if I ended up resigning?"

Preston refused to answer the question.

Which only confirmed the unspoken answer.

Stephen nodded slowly, deep in thought, and then he took a deep breath, exhaled, and stood up from behind his desk. "You're fired, Preston."

Preston stood frozen in place.

"I want you to clear out your things and be gone in five minutes. We're done."

Preston still did not move.

Stephen picked up the phone and punched a button. "Hello, this is Senator Stephen Wallage; could you send up a couple of Capitol Police officers? I need them to escort a terminated employee off the premises immediately. Thank you." He hung up the phone.

Preston stumbled back, horrified. "Terminated employee? I'm your Chief of Staff; I practically run this entire operation!"

"You're nothing to me anymore, I'm afraid, Preston," Stephen said coldly. He then checked his watch. "You have four minutes and twenty-five seconds."

Preston's mouth dropped open.

How had things gone south for him so fast?

Stephen's incensed stare made it impossible for Preston to remain planted in the office any longer. He spun around and scooted out, pushing Maya and Sandra aside.

Maya turned to Stephen. "You should have the Capitol cops detain him; he's a key suspect in Tess's death."

Stephen shook his head. "He didn't have a key card to the back entrance of my building. Only Suzanne, Tess, and Deborah did. I never completely trusted Preston enough to give him total access to my entire life. Turns out those instincts were right on the money apparently."

Maya paced back and forth. "But if he didn't have access to the VIP back entrance and he was never seen on the security footage out front . . ."

"What about the time lapse from the power outage?" Sandra asked.

"No, even if he entered the building during the outage, he would have had to have come back out the front when he left, which means . . ."

"He couldn't have done it," Sandra groaned.

"I am still waiting to hear back from the building to see what cards were used that night," Maya said, frustrated. "I waited for an hour on hold just to be told they had to call me back. I told them it was an emergency, but so far, crickets."

Stephen marched out from behind his desk and

headed for the door. "I'm going to go make sure he doesn't abscond with all of our files on his way out."

When he was gone, Sandra turned to Maya. "I can't believe I got it so wrong."

"What are you talking about?"

"Preston's sexual orientation," Sandra explained. "I have a gay son, Jack, and he's a football player, so I should be the last person to make any assumptions simply based on a man's immaculate manicure and expensive hair gel. I just foolishly assumed . . ."

Maya chuckled. "I wouldn't beat myself up too much. The world is changing superfast, things like that are very fluid these days; it's tough keeping up. Anyone could have made the same mistake."

Maya's phone buzzed. Her eyes lit up. "It's the security office at Stephen's building." She put the call on speaker. "This is Maya Kendrick."

"Hello, Ms. Kendrick, this is Ed Turlington."

"Yes, Mr. Turlington, nice to hear from you. Did you get the report back from the company that monitors the building access?"

"Just now. There were three entries on the night you requested with cards registered to Senator Wallage. At eight twenty-three, eight forty-six, and nine ten."

Sandra stepped closer to Maya and whispered, "Eight twenty-three was Tess, eight forty-six was Deborah, so who was the last one?"

"Tess may have left and come back, or Deborah could have returned, or—"

"Excuse me," Turlington interrupted. "It was three different cards."

Maya raised an eyebrow. "I'm sorry?"

"Each card has a unique code," he explained. "All three entries that night were from different cards."

Sandra could feel her stomach knotting.

If Tess had used her card.

And Deborah had used her card.

There was only one other card left.

And that was in the possession of Stephen's long-time loyal assistant, Suzanne.

Chapter 46

Suzanne could tell from the moment she entered the office that something was seriously wrong. All eyes were on her. Stephen. Sandra. Maya. She stopped suddenly in the doorway.

"I had a Hershey's bar on my way back from the Metro stop; did I get some on my face?"

"No," Sandra said. "You're good."

Suzanne took a tentative step past the doorway into the office. "Then what is it? I feel like I'm in some kind of trouble."

"Your VIP access card, the one to my building, do you still have it?" Stephen asked.

"Yes, I think so, why?" Suzanne plopped her bag down on her desk and fished through her stuff, finally extracting the card, waiting for an answer.

Stephen slowly walked over to her. "Suzanne, I have to ask you, did you use that card the night Tess was at my condo?"

"No, of course not, I would have said something."

Sandra studied her.

She had known Suzanne a long time.

She trusted her.

Sandra had always had a strong feeling that she was a good person, incapable of hurting anyone.

But at the same time, they were not that close.

Suzanne still worked for her husband, which made it nearly impossible for them to develop a truly deep bond.

It was entirely plausible that Sandra didn't know the real Suzanne at all. Most of their interactions had been brief and right here in the office.

"Stephen, you're scaring me; what's all this about?" Suzanne asked shakily.

"Your card was used to access the building that night. According to the security report timetable, it was the last card used. Which means, whoever did use it to get inside was the last person to see Tess alive."

"It wasn't me!" Suzanne cried. "Tess was my friend, my roommate; I was trying to help her adjust to life in DC. I never had any reason to want to harm her!"

Maya marched over and peeked inside Suzanne's bag. "Do you always keep the card in here?"

Suzanne nodded. "Yes. Always. In a little side compartment."

Maya reached in to examine the compartment. She flipped the zipper back and forth. "Looks pretty secure. And where do you keep your bag when you're here at work?"

"Underneath my desk. I like to have it close by

because I have a sweet tooth and I stash my haul of candy bars in there. Sugar relaxes me when I'm under a lot of stress, and you can imagine this job has quite a bit of stress."

Sandra joined Maya at Suzanne's desk. "Do you think someone could have taken it and put it back the next day before she noticed it was missing?"

"Maybe," Maya said, lost in thought. "Does anyone else know where you keep the card?"

"No, I never told anyone . . ." Her voice trailed off as something dawned on Suzanne.

Sandra leaned closer. "What is it?"

"I remember one time Stephen asked the staff to meet him at his condo to go over the itinerary of an overseas trip he was taking to Kiev, and Preston and I went there together, and he could have seen me take my card out of the side pocket."

"Was he here working with you that night, the night Tess was killed?" Maya asked.

Suzanne nodded. "Yes. I mean, he was back and forth between here and the Senate floor, but so was I. He could have swiped it at any time, and I would never have known because the side pocket was zippered closed. Then, the next morning he could have easily slipped it back in at any point when I wasn't paying attention." Suzanne gasped. "Oh my God, are you saying it was Preston?"

"We don't know for sure," Maya said, her eyes zeroing in on Suzanne. "But with your help, we can certainly find out."

Stephen held up a hand. "Wait, what do you mean, with her help? Just what are you suggesting?"

"This is our one chance to get Preston to confess. We set up a sting using Suzanne as bait . . ."

"Bait? Are you crazy?" Stephen wailed. "I will not allow you to put her in any danger!"

"Stephen's right, Maya; it's way too risky!" Sandra protested. "One of us should do it."

"He'll smell a rat right away if we try to convince him we know what he did. He will not suspect Suzanne. It makes sense that she would be on to him. He stole her key card."

"I don't like it," Sandra murmured.

"She won't be in any danger. We'll be there to make sure she stays safe," Maya said.

"No, absolutely not!" Stephen bellowed. "You're just going to have to come up with something else."

"But I *want* to do it," Suzanne interjected.

"I'm the boss around here, and what I say goes, and I say you're not going to do it!"

"Then I quit," Suzanne whispered.

"What?" Stephen roared. "You can't quit! I won't let you! I need you!"

"Then let me do this," Sandra countered. "I have always despised Preston. He's a sanctimonious, sleazy, slithering jerk. If he had anything to do with what happened to Tess, then I will not miss the opportunity to help bring him down! I'm sorry, Stephen, that's just how it is."

Sandra suppressed a smile.

Stephen was not used to his subordinates rebelling.

She actually enjoyed watching him flounder.

He reared back, a stunned look on his face.

He didn't know what else to say, so he remained silent.

At least for the moment.

Suzanne excitedly turned to Maya. "Okay, what do I have to do?"

Sandra was not exactly on board with this plan, but she instinctively knew that if Stephen, her boss, a powerful US Senator, couldn't stop Suzanne, what chance would she possibly have?

Maya put an arm around Suzanne and gave her a conspiratorial wink. "First thing, you make him sweat."

A devious smile crept across Suzanne's face. She scooped up her phone and tapped out a quick text; then she held up the screen for them all to see:

To: Preston Lambert
From: Suzanne Charles
I know it was you.

After nods of approval from Maya and Sandra, Suzanne excitedly pressed send.

The game was on.

Chapter 47

Suzanne sat nervously on a bench near the Nature Center and Planetarium in Rock Creek Park, an urban park authorized by Congress in 1890, filled with both paved and dirt trails for runners, hikers, and tourists on foot taking in the sights and fresh air. In a wooded area behind a thicket of trees, Maya and Sandra were hidden from view, both wearing earbuds.

"Any sign of him yet?" Maya asked.

They had a visual of Suzanne sitting on the bench as she looked around and then touched her ear with a finger and shook her head. "No, not yet."

A couple passed by with a baby in a stroller, the father trying to read a map. A park ranger drove by in a truck. But otherwise, it was unusually quiet, the area not full of many tourists. Maya could see Suzanne trying to act casual, but it was obvious she was more than a little anxious waiting for Preston to show up.

Five minutes passed.

"I'm beginning to think he's not going to show," Suzanne said through Maya's and Sandra's ear-pieces.

Maya checked her watch.

Suzanne had arranged to meet him at two o'clock. It was now twenty-four minutes past two.

Suzanne suddenly sat up erect. "Wait, I see some-one coming."

She squinted her eyes, her body tensing, but just as quickly she relaxed. "Forget it. It's just a runner."

The runner was in a Foo Fighters tank top and Nike shorts and had a fanny pack around his waist as he jogged past Suzanne. He got about twenty feet, stopped, and then turned around, walking slowly back toward her.

Suzanne leaned forward. "Wait, he's coming back . . ."

They could see Suzanne jump to her feet. "It's him."

Sandra poked her head out from behind the tree to get a better look, then turned to Maya. "I don't know why, but I expected him to show up in a Brooks Brothers suit."

"Stay calm, Suzanne; we're right here if any-thing goes haywire," Maya reassured her.

There was some rustling as he walked up to Suzanne.

"I had no idea you were a runner," Suzanne said.

"I have plenty of time to pick up old hobbies now that I've been unceremoniously fired," he cracked. "Does anyone miss me yet?"

"No, not particularly," she said coldly.

There was an awkward pause.

Preston decided to take the lead. "Okay, I'm here. What was that cryptic text you sent me about?"

"I think you know," Suzanne said.

"No, actually I don't."

"The police contacted me. My access card was used to gain entry to Stephen's building through the VIP back entrance."

Preston feigned surprise. "You were there that night?"

"Don't play games with me, Preston. I know it was you who took it from my bag."

Preston looked around at their beautiful surroundings, and then with a patronizing grin he shrugged and said, "Wasn't me."

"Don't lie to me, Preston. You knew where I kept the card. You were the only other one working with me in the office that night. It had to be you."

"I don't know what to tell you—"

Suzanne was growing frustrated. She took a step closer. "Just admit it!"

Maya frowned at Sandra and whispered, "She's pushing too hard."

Preston folded his arms, defiantly. "You could have just called me. Why arrange this secret meeting all the way out here?"

"Because I wanted to see you in person. I can always tell when you're lying just by the expression on your face, and looking at you right now, it's so obvious! Come on, Preston, tell me, why did you go there that night? What was going on between you and Tess?"

He took a step back, suddenly suspicious. "What's really going on here?" He scanned the area and then returned his dead-eyed stare back toward Suzanne. "Is this some kind of setup? Are you wired or something?"

Maya slumped over, disheartened.

He was on to them.

And way too smart to confess anything at this point.

Suzanne stammered, slowly unraveling, "N-No, why do you think—?"

He shouted in the direction of the Planetarium, "Whoever's listening, you can come out now; I know you're here! I'm not an idiot!"

Defeated, Maya and Sandra emerged from behind the tree and marched over to where Suzanne stood with Preston.

"Why, hello, Mrs. Wallage, I see you're still running around with your little side gig playing detective," he said, his words dripping with condescension. "I must say, I'm rather flattered to be the subject of one of your sting operations. I'm just sorry it didn't work out the way you had hoped."

"But it did, Preston," Sandra said. "Even though we didn't get a recorded confession, we know it was you, we know what you did, and it's only a matter of time before you will face the consequences."

He laughed derisively. "Oh, is that right? I know you are relatively new at the criminal justice game, but there's this little thing called evidence, which you don't have, so it might be a bit premature to be pointing fingers."

"We know you killed Tess," Maya growled.

"Amazing. Stephen told me you used to be a cop. If this is how you tried catching criminals, no wonder they drummed you out of the force."

Sandra instinctively shot out a hand to hold Maya back before she laid him out with a punch to the jaw.

"You want the real truth? Tess swallowed a bottle of pills because she was a deeply unhappy, unstable mess. End of story," Preston said.

"I see it differently," Maya said flatly.

Preston pursed his lips. "All right. I'll bite. Tell me. What do you think happened?"

"You knew Tess was delivering some papers to Stephen's condo while he was busy on the Senate floor, so you lifted Suzanne's key card from her bag when she was preoccupied and went over there."

Preston sneered contemptuously. "And why would I do that?"

"Because you were in love with her, obsessed with her, but she had zero interest in you because she only had eyes for her boss, Stephen," Maya said.

"Okay, yes, it's true Tess had a thing for Stephen," Preston drawled before fake pouting. "It's not like it was some big state secret. Poor thing. She was pining away for him, but it was never going to happen, not in a million years. She was so heartened by the fact that he was in the middle of breaking up with Deborah, but he was never ever going to pay any attention to her, not in any sort of romantic way."

"And why not?" Maya asked.

Preston raised an eyebrow. "Really? It's not obvious to you?"

Maya sighed, losing patience. "No, tell us."

Preston gestured toward Sandra. "Because he's still hopelessly in love with his wife."

Sandra reared back, shocked.

But she stayed quiet.

"Deborah instinctively knew his heart was somewhere else. She just assumed it was with Tess, the pretty new intern. But no, it was closer to home. Where it's always been." He paused to let Sandra take all this in, then turned to Maya, sneering. "So go on, what's next? I'm dying of curiosity!" He eagerly leaned forward. "I'm all ears."

"Tess rejected you outright, she told you in no uncertain terms that you would never stand a chance with her, and then you snapped, and thought to yourself, *If I can't have her, then nobody will.*"

Preston gasped, eyes widening. "How dramatic! I think I saw this exact same plot on one of those cheesy Lifetime movies! I think Judith Light may have played the mother."

Maya pressed on, undeterred by his infuriating sarcasm. "You let yourself in through the VIP back entrance that you knew had no cameras and when you got upstairs and she opened the door, probably expecting to see Deborah, who had just been there, you pushed your way in, and then force-fed her those pills, holding her neck and mouth, which would explain the bruising I spotted, which was what first suggested foul play. After that, you probably tossed her phone in the Potomac, since it was never found at the scene."

"Let me guess. And then, the next morning, I returned the key card to Suzanne's bag, and she never even knew it had ever been missing?"

"Exactly," Maya spit out.

"Wow, what an exciting story," Preston said, clapping his hands, applauding. "Compelling characters, fast-paced plot, but in the end, it doesn't really work due to the sad lack of hard evidence, which is why the police and the FBI are not here right now to arrest me."

"Oh, they do have the evidence," Sandra assured him. "You foolishly forgot about one thing."

"Then by all means, enlighten me," Preston said cockily.

"Stephen said you were in constant contact with him that night when he was on the Senate floor, you wanted to convince him that you were in the building with him the whole time so you sent him a flurry of texts," Sandra calmly explained. "The FBI got a warrant for your phone records and were able to pinpoint your exact location that night."

Finally, Preston's confident demeanor began to slowly melt.

"It was almost comically easy for them to place you at Stephen's condo precisely at the time of Tess's death," Sandra said. "Stephen always prattled on about how smart you are, how impressed he was with your Ivy League education, but then you go and do such a dumb rookie mistake that anyone with a high school diploma would *never* be foolish enough to make."

Preston flinched.

He was not used to being outsmarted.

Maya couldn't help but crack a smile. "Is it still too premature to point a finger?"

Feeling cornered, Preston unzipped his fanny pack and yanked out a handgun. "Who's the dumb one now?"

A disembodied voice cut through the air. "Drop the weapon!"

Preston jumped back, startled, eyes darting around, allowing Maya the opportunity to swing her leg up and deliver a roundhouse kick to Preston's wrist, knocking the gun out of his hand as he howled in pain. It clattered to the pavement next to Suzanne, who scooped it up and hurriedly handed it to Maya. She pointed it back at a bewildered Preston.

Agents Markey and Rhodes suddenly appeared out of nowhere. Rhodes pulled Preston's hands behind his back and snapped on a pair of handcuffs.

"Nice work, ladies," Rhodes said.

Markey gave a curt nod.

Rhodes rolled her eyes. "Come on, don't be obstinate."

"I'm not being obstinate."

"Then just say it."

Maya and Sandra both smirked, gleefully watching the back-and-forth exchange between the partners.

"They know; I don't have to say it," Markey insisted.

"Say it," Rhodes pressed.

"I already did, back at headquarters, when they were in our office," Markey huffed.

"They deserve to hear it again."

Markey sighed heavily. "You're never going to let this go, are you? Fine!" She turned to Maya and Sandra. "You two weren't the total disaster I thought you were."

Rhodes nudged her partner. "Oh, come on. You can do better than that."

Maya chortled, raising her hand. "No, we'll take it. Coming from her, that's like receiving the FBI Medal of Valor!"

Chapter 48

Maya had already zipped her Travelpro carry-on suitcase shut and had wheeled it to the door as Sandra tossed some dirty clothes in her twice as large Gucci Globe-Trotter that was open on top of her bed. She still had toiletries and makeup strewn all over the bathroom as well as shoes on the closet floor left to pack. Sandra could not help but marvel at Maya's frugal packing skills and impressive time management.

"How late are we?" Sandra asked, clearing some moisturizers and hand cream off the basin and into a small leather travel bag, racing back to the bed to deposit them in the suitcase.

Maya checked her watch. "We're fine. But I should order a Lyft to the airport in about five minutes so we have time to check in and make it through security in time for the flight."

Sandra scurried over to the closet, bent over, and snatched up a pair of comfortable walking shoes and some heels by their straps and hurled them across the room into the open bag on the bed. She then scanned the closet for any remaining items.

There was a knock at the door.

Maya turned to open it.

Stephen stood in the hallway. He broke into a warm smile. "Good, I caught you before you left."

Sandra crisscrossed back into the bathroom and then out again, this time wielding a hair dryer in one hand while wrapping the power cord around the base with the other. "Having been married to me for so many years, this should not come as a surprise, but I'm running behind schedule."

Stephen chuckled. "You're right. This scene right here brings back many warm memories of past family vacations."

Sandra turned to Maya. "Go ahead and request that Lyft now, Maya; I promise I will be ready by the time it gets here."

"No need to do that," Stephen said. "I have a car waiting downstairs. Parv will be happy to take you to the airport."

"What about you?" Sandra asked.

"I still have my room upstairs. I've got some calls to make. He can swing by and pick me up later after he drops you off."

"That's very nice of you," Maya said. "We appreciate it."

"It's the least I can do after all you did to clear my name. Seriously, I owe you," Stephen said to Maya, then to Sandra, "both of you."

Stephen kept his eyes trained on Sandra, who shifted slightly, uncomfortable.

There was an awkward pause as Stephen cleared his throat, like he was working up the nerve to say something. Finally, he spun back around to Maya. "I was wondering, if you wouldn't mind, um, if . . ." he fumbled.

Maya decided to help him out. "Would you like to speak to Sandra privately?"

A wave of relief washed over Stephen's face. "Yes, please."

Sandra's body tensed.

She guessed what Stephen wanted to talk about and was not sure she was ready to have this conversation.

At least not right now with her flight leaving in a little over an hour and midday DC traffic to still deal with.

Maya grabbed the handle of her Travelpro and wheeled it out the door.

Stephen called after her, "It's a black Lincoln Town Car parked outside the front entrance!"

"Okay, see you down there," Maya chirped, the door swinging shut behind her.

Sandra set about trying to close her suitcase, but the zipper kept getting stuck halfway. Stephen glided over to help her, finishing the job effortlessly.

It was her nerves that were getting to her.

He was standing so close behind her she could feel his hot breath on the nape of her neck.

"Stephen . . ." Sandra whispered.

"Just hear me out," he said. "I think us separating has been a good thing. It's allowed both of us to imagine a world where we're not together, to explore other relationships. We were in a rut, I get that, and I made a lot of mistakes, and I do mean a lot, in this marriage that I will regret until the day I die, but this time apart, it's . . . it's showed me how much I miss having you in my life, Sandra."

Sandra fought the urge to grab her suitcase and just bolt out the door, but she stood her ground because she knew in her heart what she had to do.

She spoke softly, deliberately. "I will always be in your life, Stephen. Jack and Ryan are always going to be the glue that binds us together."

Stephen puffed up with renewed determination. "I know my track record has been spotty when it's come to honesty and fidelity, the whole world pretty much knows that now, but Sandra, doesn't it mean something that I was telling you the truth all along about my relationship with Tess? I never lied to you or misled you, not once . . ."

"Yes, and I am deeply grateful for that . . ."

"I love you, Sandra. I want us to be a family again."

"I love you too, Stephen, but in the back of my mind, given our history, there are serious trust issues I am still struggling with, and I am just not sure I will ever get over them."

She could see him slowly deflating.

She reached out and took his hands and held them in front of her. "I will always be here when you need me, Stephen, as your friend, the mother of your children . . . but not your wife."

He bowed his head and nodded.

She let his hands go and took her suitcase by the handle and muttered, "I better get going."

She was halfway out the door when she heard him say, "I'm never going to stop."

She slowly turned around, curious. "Stop what?"

"I'm never going to stop trying to win back your trust," he said resolutely. "And maybe one day you'll finally see that we belong together."

"Goodbye, Stephen," she said with sad eyes before quietly rolling her luggage out the door and down the hall toward the waiting elevator.

In Sandra's mind, it was time to finally move on. And that's exactly what she planned to do.

Chapter 49

Max led Maya into the bedroom, his right hand over her eyes. "Now wait, don't peek."

Maya grinned.

"You ready?"

"Yes, I'm dying to see."

Max removed his hand and Maya opened her eyes and took it all in. When she didn't react at first, Max shifted nervously.

"You hate it."

"No, give me a minute."

Maya stared critically at the freshly painted lemon cream walls of her bedroom as Max hovered anxiously behind her.

"I decided to go with a warmer color to keep you cozy at night during our unforgiving Maine winters!" Max blurted out, eyes flicking toward Maya, trying to gauge her honest reaction.

Maya slowly circled the room, bending down to

inspect the paint job, searching meticulously for any blotches or streaks.

"I had Vanessa do a once-over when she got home from the class trip to make sure I didn't have any drips or uneven spots," Max explained.

When Maya finished scrutinizing, she turned to Max, a dead serious expression on her face, which caused him to take a tiny step back, mentally preparing for her harsh judgment. But instead, Maya surprised him, breaking out into a wide, satisfied smile. "It's flawless."

Max exhaled a huge sigh of relief. "Really?"

"Max, you did a bang-up job. I love it. I was so sure I wanted eggshell, but this lemon cream is absolutely beautiful."

"I'm so glad you like it. I have another surprise for you," he said, drawing out the suspense a bit more before continuing. "I got a job."

Maya lit up. "What? You did?"

Max nodded. "Eddie Dunlap, who retired from the force back in 2019, recently took over his family's auto repair shop and hired me to help out."

"Max, that's wonderful news."

"I worked in a garage when I was in high school. I've always been pretty good with cars."

She hugged him, happy for him.

He held her tightly for a few moments, then slowly let go. "Best news is, it's only three blocks away. I can walk to work. I'm obviously not making what I did before, but it's a paycheck. I can contribute."

"I am so proud of you."

She truly was.

Max desperately needed this boost and it could not have come at a better time. This opportunity was going to do wonders for his self-esteem. Having somewhere to go every day. Not feeling so dependent on her to take care of him all the time.

It was the first big step for him to finally get beyond those excruciatingly difficult years he spent languishing in prison.

Of course she couldn't say any of this to him out loud.

He was too macho to admit having self-esteem issues.

Instead, he refocused his attention on the newly painted walls. "Yup, lemon cream was definitely the way to go." He turned and grabbed her suitcase from the hallway, wheeling it inside the bedroom. "I'll let you unpack and get settled. Vanessa and I are making tacos for dinner."

"Sounds yummy," she said.

He was halfway back out the door when she called out, "By the way, Max?"

He turned around. "Yeah?"

"Since you worked so hard to make the bedroom this lovely and inviting, it doesn't seem fair for me to have it all to myself," she said with a seductive wink.

Max raised an eyebrow. "Seriously?"

Maya shrugged. "I don't see why we can't try it out together for one night."

He grinned. "Just one night?"

"We'll see how it goes. Baby steps."

"I'll go get my toothbrush."

He excitedly bolted out the door before she had a chance to change her mind.

Maya smiled to herself.

Maybe it *was* possible to find a new normal.

Chapter 50

As Lucas Cavill sat across from Sandra in their hardwood booth overlooking the brick and soapstone hearth with its woodburning oven, turnspit, and grill at Sandra's favorite restaurant, Fore Street in the Old Port, she finally had to admit something to herself.

Lucas Cavill had an indestructible sex appeal.

She had tried to ignore it for as long as she could.

In fact, she had made it her mission to resist his charms.

But now, on their first official date, Lucas coincidentally choosing Sandra's favorite restaurant in town, or maybe he had enlisted Maya's advice before making his final choice, she could not help but notice how handsome he was, decked out in a white open-collar shirt, dark blue sports coat, and casual Indigo Wash jeans. His tousled hair, his ocean blue eyes, his electric smile. The whole package was incredibly enticing.

She had only been back from Washington a day and a half before he called. And of course, she had turned him down again. Out of habit mostly. He explained that he had no plans to keep trying to wear her down, that he would respect her wishes and leave her alone, but before he had the chance to say goodbye and hang up she had suddenly changed her mind.

"Wait!" Sandra had blurted out.

"Yes?"

"I'm free Friday."

There was nothing but dead air for a few seconds, almost as if he could not quite believe that she had finally come around and agreed to go out with him. He quickly suggested Fore Street before she had the chance to back out, and they decided to meet at the restaurant. Sandra did not want to make a big deal out of him picking her up at the house, especially since the boys would probably both be home. Jack was up from Boston for the weekend. When she had arrived five minutes early, Lucas was already at the host station waiting. She liked that. It was a change of pace from Stephen, who was always showing up late with some "very important Senate business" excuse, as if his time was far more valuable than anyone else's.

Lucas complimented her outfit, her hair, her over-all appearance, more than once, but not so much as to make it sound creepy. When perusing the wine menu, he asked about her preferences, wanting to make sure he chose the right one. And as the waiter described the locally sourced and hand-crafted dinner specials, he kept one eye on Sandra's reaction just to make sure the selections were to her liking.

Lucas had a unique talent for making her feel special.

They settled on a marinated squid appetizer and two Turnspit Roasted Dry Rubbed Pork Loins for their entrees.

She could tell he was nervous.

He let her do most of the talking, at least until the wine came, curious to know how all the dramatic events had unfolded back in DC after he left. When the wine arrived for him to taste, he swirled it around in his glass so hard a little bit came flying out, staining his white linen napkin. Then, after a very heavy pour, he knocked over his wineglass, gesturing with his hand. Luckily, the squid hadn't arrived yet and the busboy and two waiters replaced the tablecloth and table settings with the speed of a pit crew performing repairs and replacements during a NASCAR race.

When they were left alone again, he looked down, embarrassed. "I'm usually not that clumsy."

She gave him a reassuring smile. "I'm sure you're not."

"Actually, that's not true. I am a bona fide klutz. My parents gave me a moped when I was sixteen because they couldn't afford to buy me a car and that same day I lost control and plowed into my neighbor's vegetable garden, pretty much destroying her whole summer project. She never talked to me again."

Sandra found herself laughing.

"I also broke my wrist and fractured my ankle in the same week and I wasn't even playing a sport. It's not too late to have Maya call you with some fake emergency so you can excuse yourself and call it a night."

"That's not going to happen," Sandra said, eyes twinkling.

"Really?"

"Of course not. Did you see the dessert selections on the chalkboard as we came in? You could be Charles Manson and I would still stick around so I can try them all."

"Did you just compare me to Charles Manson? I was hoping maybe Chris Pine or Ryan Gosling by the end of the night. Sounds like I still have a lot of work to do."

Cute and funny.

He took a sip of the wine left in the bottom of his glass that had not spilled out onto the table. "But I'm happy you finally said yes."

She paused, then said, "Me too. But I need to stress to you, Lucas, that I am really not ready for anything serious right now."

She instantly regretted it.

They were having fun together.

Why did she have to go and ruin it by reminding him that he should not expect this to go anywhere?

He threw his hands up in surrender. "Message received. I'm just grateful you're finally giving me a chance to wine and dine you. What is it they say? It's not the destination but the journey? Is that it?"

"Yes, I think so," she said.

"But my gut is telling me there are exciting

things ahead for us. But then again, my gut also told me I'd be an NFL draft pick and a mega famous rapper and I'm still waiting on both of those, so who knows?"

Sandra laughed again.

Maybe he was right.

Not about the NFL or rap career.

Maybe there could be exciting things ahead.

For the two of them.

Whatever they might be.

Private Investigator Poppy Harmon can see through the charms of Southern California's trickiest criminals. But when she and the Desert Flowers Detective Agency go up against a dashing dating show murderer, they may have finally met their match!

While sidekick Matt Flowers shoots a film abroad, Poppy dusts off her own acting chops to break up a Gen Z crime ring targeting seniors in Palm Springs. Tanya Cook and her gal pals have been swindling susceptible residents for all they're worth—until the gang meets Poppy undercover. Yet with the case cracked, the desert heat is on full blast as new terrors take the lead . . .

Poppy's already sweating over a menacing mystery stalker when a shocking death proves she's in serious danger. As suspicions fall once again on Tanya, finding answers may mean pulling off the most challenging performance of Poppy's career . . .

Now, with Poppy's unknown stalker rumored to be posing as one of several bachelors on a glitzy reality series, a disguised Poppy must reveal his true identity on set before he realizes hers. Does Poppy have what it takes to catch the coldblooded killer in time for the season finale . . . or should she start planning for her funeral?

Please turn the page for an exciting sneak peek of Lee Hollis's newest Poppy Harmon mystery, *Poppy Harmon and the Backstabbing Bachelor*, now on sale wherever print and e-books are sold!

Chapter 1

Poppy Harmon was having a devil of a time operating her electric wheelchair. When she pushed the joystick forward, the wheels seemed to veer right, not straight ahead, and she banged into a wall in the hallway after maneuvering out of the bedroom, trying to steer herself toward the living room.

Poppy sighed.

She was never going to get the hang of this.

She tried cranking the knob to the left but only managed to drive the wheelchair away from one wall and crash it into the opposite one. The noise alerted someone in the kitchen, and within seconds a young woman in her twenties with long straight black hair, emerald green eyes, and a bright smile that mostly disguised a somewhat hardened face suddenly appeared in front of her.

"Oh, you're up. How was your nap?"

"Fine," Poppy spit out, frowning, continuing to

push the knob forward but getting nowhere. "I hate this new wheelchair. My old one was a lot easier to operate."

"Here, allow me," the young woman said, slipping behind Poppy and manually pushing the wheelchair by the handles out to the living room and parking it in front of the large flat-screen TV hanging on the wall. "I have some tomato soup heating up on the stove for your lunch. Would you like Ritz crackers or Saltines to go with it? I have both."

"Saltines, please," Poppy answered gruffly.

"Coming right up," the woman said before snatching up the remote and turning on the TV. "Now you just relax and watch your British Bake Off show, and lunch will be ready in just a few minutes."

She bounded back to the kitchen.

Once she was gone, Poppy adjusted the itchy, stringy gray wig she was wearing, straightened her burgundy housecoat, and checked out her face in a wall mirror across from her. The retired Tony Award–winning Broadway makeup artist the Desert Flowers Detective Agency hired to transform Poppy into a ninety-two-year-old woman had done an incredibly convincing job using liquid latex, eyeliner, and face paint. Poppy looked at least thirty years older than her actual age.

And more importantly, Tanya Cook, the self-described "professional home care nurse" who answered her ad to help out with shopping, errands, meals, and to administer medications, was totally buying the disguise.

Poppy heard a thump.

It had come from down the hall, the small guest bedroom that she had set up as her office.

Poppy tried to pick up the remote off the coffee table to lower the television volume but couldn't quite reach it. She stretched her fingers as far as they would go, but the remote was still about an inch away from her grasp. Frustrated, Poppy swiveled her head around to make sure Tanya had not wandered back into the living room, and then, with lightning speed, she jumped out of the wheelchair, grabbed the remote, and quickly sat back down. She muted the TV and waited.

Sure enough, she heard another thump.

Poppy pulled back on the joystick, the wheelchair rolled in reverse, and then she buzzed back down the hall. The door to the guest room was closed. She leaned forward, turned the handle, and pushed the door open, surprised to find two more young women, both around Tanya's age, and just as pretty. One was blond and the other auburn haired. The blonde was seated at a desk meticulously going through drawers while the other one held a half-filled plastic garbage bag that she appeared to be stuffing with valuables.

"Who are you? What are you doing here?" Poppy cried.

The two girls stood frozen in place, not quite sure what to do.

Tanya appeared in a flash. She stepped in front of Poppy's wheelchair and knelt down so they were eye level, a reassuring smile on her face. "There's no cause for concern. These are my friends, Bella and Kylie; I invited them over to help tidy up the house. Don't you want your lovely home to be nice and clean for when your grandkids come to visit?"

"I suppose so," Poppy said. "How much is this going to cost me? I used to do my own house-work . . ."

"Oh no, Edna, this is included in the service. You don't have to pay anything extra. I am just here to make things easier for you."

Poppy nodded. She had momentarily forgotten her cover name was Edna Greenblatt, so she was grateful that Tanya had just reminded her. She smiled warmly at the two nervous-looking women in the office. "Thank you, girls. I may have some ginger snap cookies in the kitchen. Would you like one?"

They exchanged quick glances, and then the one with the garbage bag, Bella, shook her head and muttered, "No, we're fine."

Tanya firmly gripped the handles of the wheel-chair and rolled Poppy out of the room and back down the hall. "Come on, Edna, time to eat your soup."

"I spotted some dust bunnies underneath the desk; do you think they can sweep those up, too?" Poppy asked.

"Of course, the whole house will be spotless when they're done, I promise," Tanya said, parking Poppy back in front of the TV in the living room. "Now stay put while I finish preparing your lunch tray."

Poppy detected a slight annoyance in Tanya's tone. She was obviously getting tired of being nice to this high-maintenance old crow.

Because the fact of the matter was Tanya was no professional home care nurse. Tanya Cook and her two cohorts, Bella and Kylie, were professional criminals, allegedly running a massive financial fraud and theft scheme by infiltrating the homes of susceptible senior citizens and gaining access to their bank passwords, cash, checks, credit cards, valuables, and personal documents. Basically bleeding their victims dry right in their own homes! Tanya would scout out a vulnerable target, someone in need of in-home care, and then apply for the job with forged credentials, showing up at the door with a friendly smile and a promise to take good care of them. She would play nursemaid for about a week, gaining the trust of her charge before bringing in her two accomplices to rob the unsuspecting senior blind, even insidiously redirecting Social Security direct deposits to a dummy bank account.

Their last mark, however, a feisty widow by the name of Cecile LaCrosse, an eighty-nine-year-old battle-ax who unfortunately fell victim to the scam, was not about to let them get away with it. And so she brought in Poppy and her crew at the Desert Flowers Detective Agency to set up a sting and bring this evil coven of Gen Z witches down.

Poppy, along with her two partners, Iris Becker and Violet Hogan, took a very personal interest in this particular case because they felt a strong kinship with the victims. Although still in their sixties, they knew it was only a matter of time before they themselves might be confused, defenseless elderly victims preyed upon by opportunistic, heartless swindlers.

And so Poppy had insisted that she pose as an elderly widow, drawing on her years of acting experience from when she was a starlet in the 1980s, in order to bust up this enterprising, depraved crime ring.

And so far she had played it to perfection.

Tanya was confident enough after only three days of playing nursemaid to bring in her two sidekicks to finish the job by pillaging poor Edna Greenblatt's home until she was left with nothing but her electric wheelchair that had a mind of its own.

Tanya appeared with a wooden tray and set it down in front of Poppy. "I garnished the soup with a few garlic croutons. My own grandmother used to love the extra kick."

"It looks lovely," Poppy said, picking up the spoon with a shaky hand and scooping some up, making sure to dribble a little on her housecoat just to be convincing.

"Can I get you anything else?" Tanya asked.

"Oh, no, dear, you've done quite enough," Poppy said with a thin, knowing smile.

And she meant it.

Tanya and her friends had certainly done enough.

And they were about to discover just how "done" they actually were.

Chapter 2

Violet's loud, piercing, high-pitched voice of concern blasted through Poppy's ear. "Poppy, Poppy, what's happening in there? Are you okay?"

Poppy dropped her spoon on the tray and raised her hand to adjust the small earbud resting in the crevice of her right ear, and urgently whispered into the tiny microphone that had been pinned on the inside of her housecoat, "Violet, turn down the volume on your mic; you're going to burst my eardrum!"

"Oh, sorry," Violet said, lowering her voice. "Iris, how do you adjust the volume on this thing?"

"Here, let me do it," Iris snapped.

There was a pause.

"Hello? Hello? Is this better?" Violet bellowed, even more deafening than before.

Poppy sighed. "No, she just made you even louder."

"Hold on," Violet said.

Poppy could hear her two friends and partners bickering in the background away from the microphone that they were using to communicate with Poppy.

"Is that better?" Violet asked, almost whispering.

"Yes, much," Poppy said.

"Who are you talking to?"

The stern voice came from directly behind her. Poppy used her joystick to turn her electric wheelchair around.

Tanya stood staring at her, a plate of ginger snap cookies in her hand.

"What?" Poppy asked innocently.

"I heard you whispering to somebody," Tanya said suspiciously, eyes darting around to see if anyone else was in the house before returning her mistrustful gaze back to her charge. "Who was it?"

Her tone was unsettlingly sinister.

"Abe," Poppy said softly.

"Who's Abe?"

"My late husband. He comes to talk to me every now and then," Poppy said with a sad, drawn face. "I miss him so much. He would have loved this tomato soup." Poppy picked up her spoon to take another sip, making sure to get a garlic crouton. As she slurped and crunched, Tanya seemed to size her up, ultimately opting to believe her story, then held out the plate of ginger snaps toward her.

"Cookie?"

Poppy slowly reached out with her trembling hand and took a cookie, shoving it into her mouth, and talking with her mouth full. "Yummy."

"I'm going to see if Bella and Kylie would like one," Tanya said, turning around to head down the hall but stopping at the window. "Have you noticed that van parked across the street?"

"What van?" Poppy asked innocently.

"Desert Florists," Tanya said, staring out the window.

Poppy swallowed hard.

The van had been rented by the Desert Flowers Detective Agency. They had slapped a fake florist shop decal on the side so as not to arouse suspicion. Inside were Violet and Iris keeping a careful watch over the house. However, they had underestimated how smart and observant Tanya Cook could be.

"If they're just here to deliver flowers to a house in the neighborhood, it's taking them a really long time," Tanya said warily, checking her wristwatch. "It's been there since I arrived this morning."

"Oh, that van is parked there all the time," Poppy quickly explained. "It belongs to one of the neighbors. That's his business. He's always leaving it there and getting a ticket because he forgets to move it on street cleaning day."

Tanya peered at the van a few more seconds before deciding to buy Poppy's on the spot made-up explanation. She then continued on down the hall with her tray of cookies.

"Is everyone in place?" Poppy whispered.

There was silence.

"Violet?" Poppy asked.

Still nothing.

She had lost communication.

Either her earpiece battery had suddenly died,

or there was a problem with the transmitter in the van.

"Violet?"

"I'm here, Poppy; I accidentally hit the mute button! Sorry! Yes, we're ready; it's go time!"

"I knew I should have been in charge of the communication equipment!" Iris snorted.

Poppy braced herself just as Tanya returned from the guest bedroom/office with her empty plate. Something outside caught her eye and she raced back to the front window in time to see a uniformed police officer ducking down and circling around the house. Tanya gasped, her mouth dropping open in surprise. She quickly found her voice and started yelling, "Cops!"

Bella and Kylie came crashing out of the guest room, Kylie holding a stuffed garbage bag in her arms.

"Are you serious?" Bella asked nervously.

"Yes!" Tanya cried. "I just saw one sneaking around the side of the house! Run!"

Bella sprinted toward the kitchen, Kylie following close behind but weighed down with the bag. She finally let go of it and it dropped to the floor with a thud as she raced to catch up with Bella.

Poppy heard a man yell, "Police! Put your hands up!"

Tanya's eyes popped open in surprise and she made a mad dash for the front door. Poppy, anticipating the move, jammed the joystick of her wheelchair all the way forward, full speed, and whizzed over in front of the door, blocking her escape.

"What are you doing? Out of my way, old woman!"

Tanya screeched, furious, struggling to get around her.

Poppy sprang up to her feet and forcefully pushed Tanya back.

The miraculous sudden strength and agility of the ninety-two-year-old stymied Tanya briefly, but she was still not to be deterred. She charged forward, trying to physically shove Poppy out of the way. Poppy held her ground, knowing she was no match for the young, physically fit girl but determined to keep her from getting away. Poppy and Tanya grappled, Tanya trying to scratch Poppy's face with her nails in the hope she might release her grip, but as Tanya withdrew her nails she was stunned to find latex hanging off them, not blood.

"What the—?"

Two uniformed cops suddenly bolted into the living room from the back door off the kitchen, their guns drawn. "It's over, Tanya!"

She shuddered at the mention of her name because she knew at this moment this had all been a sting.

A con job.

And she had willfully, stupidly, walked right into it.

Tanya slowly raised her hands in the air while glaring defiantly at Poppy, who busily wiped the old-age makeup off her face with the napkin from her lunch tray.

One of the cops, a boyish, inexperienced one, struggled to unhook a pair of handcuffs from his belt loop. Finally, he glanced apprehensively over at his more seasoned partner. "Sarge?"

The older cop sighed, and assisted him in releasing the handcuffs from the officer's belt so he could snap them on Tanya's wrists.

Once her face was free of powder and latex and added wrinkles, Poppy removed her gray wig.

Tanya gaped at her, undoubtedly kicking herself for so easily buying into Poppy's now obvious disguise.

The older cop studied Poppy, then stepped forward with a big smile. "Hey, I know you . . ."

The younger cop snapped to attention and stared at Poppy, still clueless. "You do?"

"*Jack Colt, PI*!" Sarge crowed, slapping his forehead. "You're Daphne, Jack's secretary!"

The younger cop still appeared totally confused. "Who?"

"The TV show, it was on in the nineteen-eighties!" Sarge exclaimed.

"I wasn't born until 1997," the younger cop said.

Both Poppy and Sarge chose to ignore him.

Sarge was almost giddy. "Detective Jordan said he had recruited an actress to help with this operation; I just never imagined it would be *you*! This is so cool!"

Of course Poppy knew that it was she who had contacted Detective Jordan, bringing him into the case, not the other way around, but why clarify such things and potentially bruise Jordan's fragile ego?

"I am a private investigator these days," Poppy felt the need to explain.

"Wait, a *real* one? Are you joking?" Sarge asked, still beaming from ear to ear.

Poppy nodded shyly.

Sarge fumbled for his phone. "Hey, do you

mind if I get a selfie with you? My poker buddies are never going to believe this!"

Poppy did not feel this moment was appropriate for that kind of thing, but she also did not want to disappoint a fan.

Sarge basically body checked a handcuffed Tanya out of the way to get to Poppy.

"Maybe I should read this woman her rights first, Sarge," the younger cop quietly suggested.

"That can wait, kid; hold on a sec!" Sarge barked before holding his phone up and beaming while snapping a photo. He checked it and frowned. "It's a little blurry. Do you mind if I take another one?"

"No, not at all," Poppy said, keeping one eye on Tanya, who glowered at her menacingly.

Sarge tried again, this time satisfied. "Thank you, Daphne; you made my day!"

"Of course," Poppy said, grabbing the handles of the wheelchair and pushing it out of the way so the officers could escort Tanya Cook outside to their waiting squad car.

The young officer gripped Tanya by the arm to lead her out, but she refused to budge, her eyes angrily fixed on Poppy. "So you're telling me, the cops recruited some washed-up, old has-been Hollywood *star* to take us down?"

Sarge nodded. "Yeah, and unfortunately for you, it worked like a charm, didn't it?"

Tanya sneered and looked dismissively at Poppy. "Why bother with the old-lady makeup? You're already old enough to be my grandmother."

Poppy bristled on the inside but was not about to show any emotion on the surface to give this she-devil the satisfaction, calmly replying, "Yes, Tanya, you may have many more years ahead of you in life than I do, but a lot of them will no doubt be spent behind bars . . . so there's that."

Poppy opened the front door, allowing the two officers to leave with Tanya, who looked as if she wanted to smack Poppy right across the face but couldn't because her hands were handcuffed behind her back, so instead, she just raised her head high contemptuously and began to softly whistle the children's nursery rhyme "Twinkle, Twinkle, Little Star."

Poppy scoffed at Tanya's labored attempts to ridicule her Hollywood past. But given what was about to come, that unfortunately would turn out to be a very grave and dangerous mistake.